Peter Rylands, L. Gordon Rylands

Correspondence and Speeches of Mr. Peter Rylands

With a Sketch of his Career

Peter Rylands, L. Gordon Rylands

Correspondence and Speeches of Mr. Peter Rylands
With a Sketch of his Career

ISBN/EAN: 9783337062279

Printed in Europe, USA, Canada, Australia, Japan

Cover: Foto ©Raphael Reischuk / pixelio.de

More available books at **www.hansebooks.com**

CORRESPONDENCE AND SPEECHES

OF

MR. PETER RYLANDS,

M.P.

WITH A SKETCH OF HIS CAREER.

BY HIS SON,

L. GORDON RYLANDS, B.A.,

Author of "Crime: its Causes and Remedy."

———

VOL. I.
LIFE AND CORRESPONDENCE.

———

Manchester:
ABEL HEYWOOD & SON, 56 & 58, OLDHAM STREET.
London:
SIMPKIN, MARSHALL, HAMILTON, KENT & CO., LIMITED,
STATIONERS' HALL COURT.
1890.

LIFE AND CORRESPONDENCE

OF

MR. PETER RYLANDS, M.P.

R. PETER RYLANDS was born on the 18th of January, 1820. His father, Mr. John Rylands, of Bewsey House, Warrington, was the descendant of a long line of yeomen and manufacturers, who had been settled in South-West Lancashire for several generations. His mother was the daughter of the Rev. James Glazebrook, vicar of Belton, Leicestershire. He was educated at the Boteler Grammar School, at Warrington, at the time when the Rev. Thomas Vere Bayne, B.C.L., was Head Master; and while there he gave promise, by his industry and ability, of the distinction which he was in after life destined to attain.

Mr. Rylands began to take a keen interest in political matters at a very early age. In the year 1835, when he was 15 years old, a mock election was carried out by a number of the sons of electors of Warrington, the Tory candidate being a young gentleman of the name of Oliver, and the Whig candidate Master William Marson. Both sides apparently claimed the victory, which each celebrated by a dinner to their member. The dinner of the youthful reformers was held in a large room in Bridge-street, Warrington, on the 5th of February, 1835. Peter Rylands was chosen to preside, and his brother, Thomas Glazebrook, was elected one of the vice-presidents. All the proceedings were dignified and orderly, although more than two hundred young men were present. Speeches were made and toasts drunk, and Peter Rylands, in reply to the toast of his health as president, delivered a speech which would do credit to many a public speaker of mature age.

But the pursuit in which Peter Rylands was chiefly absorbed at this time and for some years after was the study of Natural History, and in company with his brother, Thomas Glazebrook, he used to make long excursions in search of specimens. The collection of insects which he then made is still in existence, and is of considerable value. But he was not content with the mere pleasure of collection ; he commenced to carry on a correspondence with other naturalists, and contributed to several magazines, among which the chief were *The Eclectic Review*, *Loudoun's Magazine of Natural History*, and *The Naturalist*. He also became a member of the Warrington Natural History Society, for which he wrote a series of papers on " The Structure of Birds considered in relation to their Habits," and another paper on the " Mimicries of Birds." Another subject in which Mr. Peter Rylands took great interest in his younger days was that of Phreno-logy, in which he was a firm believer. He became a member of the Warrington Phrenological Society, and at some of the meetings of this society, in the year 1838, he read a series of papers on the subject, entitled respectively, "On the Primitive Feeling of the Organ denominated by Phrenologists 'Cautiousness,'" "A Few General Observations on Comparative Phrenology," "Considerations respecting the Organs which do not appear to be possessed by Animals." Yet Mr. Rylands was not really of a scientific or philosophical nature, so that when the claims of public life began to clash with those of natural science, the latter had to give way, and although a love of birds and of Nature always remained, the turmoil of Municipal and Parliamentary life soon became all-absorbing.

But between the period of devotion to scientific pursuits and the period of devotion to public matters, there was to some extent a break. Up to the age of 21 Mr. Rylands had given no thought to business. He was, indeed, nominally engaged in the office of his father, who carried on business as a sail-cloth manufacturer, and had also a mill, in partnership with Mr. Greening, of Warrington, for the manufacture of iron wire; but the time he spent in the office was almost entirely occupied in reading works upon Natural History, and writing letters and articles upon the same subject. He imagined that his father was a wealthy man, that the iron-wire business was a paying concern, and that his father was in a position to leave him and his brothers comfortably off; but he was awakened to the stern realities of life by an unpleasant shock.   The sail-cloth business had entirely deserted Warrington, and the wire manufactory, which had been left for some time by the elder Mr. Rylands entirely in the hands of his partner Greening, was not in reality paying its way.   Nevertheless, Mr. John Rylands had regularly drawn an income from the concern, quite in ignorance that no profits were being made.   Mr. Peter Rylands and his brothers, having investigated matters, had their eyes opened to the fact that their father's affairs were in anything but a satisfactory condition, and they saw that, to make the wire manufacture pay, the business must be entirely re-organized and carefully developed.   In the year 1843, therefore, Mr. John Rylands and Mr. Greening were bought out, and a new firm, under the style of Rylands Bros., was established.   The development of this business required all the energies of the three brothers for some years, but, after a period of anxiety and slow progress, their efforts were crowned with complete success.   Their enterprise, their upright dealing, and their determination that they would turn out nothing that was not of excellent quality, eventually brought Rylands Bros.' wire into repute, and their firm became one of the largest of the kind in England. For some years past the firm has exported large quantities of iron and steel wire to all parts of the world.   At one time the production rose to nearly 400 tons per week, but of late years the competition of German manufacturers has made itself very severely felt, and has reduced not only the price of wire, but also the amount of orders placed in this country.   Up to 1864 the iron used by the firm was purchased from Staffordshire and Shropshire, but in that year Messrs. Rylands established works at Warrington itself for the production of puddled iron suitable for their wire mills. To the production of puddled iron was soon added the manufacture of sheets and hoops, and, in 1874, these ironworks were amalgamated with those of the Dallam Forge Company, at Warrington, and with Messrs. Pearson and Knowles' collieries at Wigan. The capital of the new company, called "The Pearson and Knowles Coal and Iron Company, Limited," amounts to nearly a million, the principal shareholders and directors being the former partners. The Pearson and Knowles Company turn out upwards of 2,000 tons of bars, plates, sheets, hoops, and wire iron weekly, while the collieries at Wigan produce about 700,000 tons of coal and cannel yearly. Mr. John Rylands, Mr. Peter Rylands' eldest brother, is now chairman of this company. The success of Mr. Peter Rylands and his coadjutors has given a great impulse to the trade of Warrington, which had for some time languished. Many other similar manufactories have been established, the town has grown greatly in size, and the value of property has largely increased. In fact, the present prosperity of Warrington is mainly due to Mr. Rylands and his brothers.

It will not be necessary for me to say that Mr. Peter Rylands was not a man whose mind could ever be entirely absorbed in money-making. So soon, therefore, as the anxiety and care required by the re-organization of the wire business were somewhat relieved, he began once more to occupy himself in literary pursuits, devoting himself specially to the considerations of religious questions. Mr. Rylands was at this time an earnest Christian, firmly believing that Christianity is the only religion fit to be held by civilized men, and that the highest obligation imposed upon the Church is that of Christianizing the whole world. This conviction naturally led to a consideration of the means by which the Church would best accomplish this great work, and in the year 1845 Mr. Rylands published a little pamphlet, setting forth the opinions at which he had arrived. This pamphlet was entitled "The Mission of the Church; or, Remarks on the relative importance of Home and Foreign Missionary Effort in the present state of the World," and was intended to prove that Home are more important than Foreign Missions. In this little pamphlet it is pointed out, in the first place, that the more highly civilized a nation is, the greater is its influence upon the world, and that it is consequently important for the Church to thoroughly Christianize England. Again, it is shown that, with the entrance of missionaries into savage lands, come also traders and adventurers, who offer the natives drink, accustom them to the vices of civilization, and do more harm than the missionaries do good; and that, therefore, until the English people are themselves truly Christian, the English Church can never do much good among the heathen. Then the total number of persons existing on groups of savage islands is compared with the number living in vice and ignorance in one of our large towns; and it is argued that the money, toil, and lives spent upon the conversion of the former few would have worked a wondrous change for the better among the multitudes of the latter. Further, the paucity of ideas in the mind of the savage is shown to put difficulties in the way of his conception of a Deity and of the Christian dogmas, whereas the intellectual activity of the civilized man will lead him to embrace erroneous doctrines, should the truth not be placed clearly before his mind. Most of the arguments in the pamphlet are sound, and it must be a matter of regret to every man who has at heart the welfare of his race, whether he be a Christian or not, that so much energy and money is wasted by the Church in comparatively futile endeavours in remote lands, while vice, crime, and ignorance flourish in our midst. All these things are bringing the Church into greater and greater discredit. It cannot fail to be observed that, while its revenues are enormous and its dignitaries wealthy, it effects practically nothing in the way of raising the moral and intellectual status of the people. As to their intellectual status, seeing that the Church has for so many centuries striven to keep the people in ignorance, it is, perhaps, too much to expect it to change its habits now; and, as to their moral status, it has always been inclined to wink at breaches of the commandments if a man will but worship regularly and repeat his Creed. The only Christian body which really gets at the people is the Salvation Army, and this the Church persecutes and hates. Therefore, although Mr. Rylands' pamphlet was written more than 50 years ago, it is as applicable to-day as it was then, and I can confidently recommend it to the careful consideration of all Churchmen.

But even more strongly can I recommend a somewhat more important work, which Mr. Rylands published in 1847; a little book of 118 pages, entitled, " The Pulpit and the People ; or, an Inquiry into the Cause of the Present Failure of Christian Agency." The object of this work was to show the superiority of individual exertion over that of a special class of paid agents. The author begins by pointing out that " Christian agency, viewed in relation to the spiritual necessities of mankind, is, at the present time, a *lamentable failure*," and contrasts the remarkable success and rapid growth of the Christian Church in its early days with its stagnation and declining influence now. The cause of this great contrast he considers to lie in the fact that the spread of Christianity in early times depended almost entirely upon individual effort. He points out that the Apostles only differed from ordinary men in their zeal and ability, that they formed no special class set apart and consecrated for the service of their God, but that any individual was at liberty to preach the Gospel and make converts, and obtain the honourable title of Apostle by common consent, by proving himself worthy of it. He proves that Paul held no rank in the Church such as is held by a Bishop now ; that, in fact, no such hierarchy as the present existed, but that in every separate town where a church had been formed, a president and other officers were chosen by the votes of the members, owing obedience only to those by whom they had been elected. There was thus no distinct order of preachers, but every man who felt that he had something profitable to say was at liberty to say it. Mr. Rylands shows how efficacious this system was, and points out how greatly the distinction between clergy and laity—which appeared first in the time of Tertullian—paralysed the energies of the Church. The evil results of this distinction he maintains to be these: That the spread of religion has ceased to be a disinterested labour of love, and has become a trade; that eloquent preachers no longer preach to those who most want preaching to, but regard their abilities as the means by which they may win honours and emoluments; that hundreds of inefficient men, having as a duty to deliver two sermons weekly, utter the most wearisome common-places upon the most trivial subjects; that sermons have, to a large extent, become a mere " routine of sacred words ; " that mere doctrinal views are elevated into a greater importance than practical godliness; that the gospel is preached to the rich, who crowd to listen to a preacher of distinction because he is " fashionable," and remain unconverted because, Pharisee-like, they believe they need no conversion; but that to the poor the gospel is not preached, because they cannot afford a suit of Sunday clothes, nor to pay the rent of a pew ; that many of the " noblest efforts, springing from the spirit of Christ's teaching, for the social and religious elevation of mankind, have had to struggle at the onset against the attacks of 'reverend' opponents, and have had to overcome the indifference of religious men whose energies were withered by sectarian frigidity and priestly domination;" that, however closely a man may conform to the precepts of Christ, yet if he refuses submission to the dogmas of "the Church," he is persecuted and anathematized as an infidel; and that, in consequence of all these things, the Church of the present day, in spite of (perhaps partly because of) its enormous revenue of more than ten millions per annum, is losing ground, whereas the primitive Church, poor though it was, advanced with gigantic strides. Well would it be for the Church if it would pay heed to such arguments and exhortations as those contained in Mr. Rylands' book; but now, at the end of 50 years, every word which Mr. Rylands wrote is still fully applicable. It is very much to be feared that all such exhortations are as words spoken to the winds. The arguments of those who utter them are based upon an assumption which is false, and that assumption is, that the Church as a body desires, alone and disinterestedly, the moral elevation of the people. It is sad to be obliged to think that this is not so. What would grieve the hearts of the Bishops and Church dignitaries far more than the bestiality of the multitude, would be the loss of prestige and influence involved in the severance of Church and State; and, though the founder of their religion was poor, and a man of the people, they would bitterly resist the proposal to employ for the common good any portion of those millions of pounds on which they wax fat and live luxuriously. The young man to whom Jesus said, "it is easier for a camel to go through the eye of a needle than for a rich man to enter into the kingdom of heaven," went away sorrowing; and quite as poignant would be the mental anguish of a modern Bishop could Jesus now address him in the same words.

But Mr. Rylands was too much a man of action to give himself up entirely to a literary career; and, having commenced at an early age to take part in political strife, and an active interest in the public institutions of his native town, he presently found that the claims of private business and a public career left no time for literary pursuits. At the age of 21 he was already well known in Warrington as a public speaker, when he joined the Reform party of the borough in the attempt to oust Mr. Blackburn, the Protectionist member. Between the years 1841 and 1848 he actively assisted the efforts of the Anti-Corn Law League by many public speeches, delivered at Warrington and other towns, in favour of free trade in corn. He was present, as one of the deputies from Warrington, at the great banquets and public meetings held during the week commencing January 30 and ending February 3, 1843, in the Free Trade Hall, Manchester, at which nearly all the leading Leaguers were present, and not long after became one of the vice-presidents of the League.

During the same time Mr. Rylands was becoming one of the leading men in Warrington. He actively assisted in procuring the incorporation of the

borough, which took place in 1848, and was elected
a town councillor in that year.   He at once began to
apply to municipal matters the sound common sense
and great business ability which were his by nature,
and which had been increased by the training under-
gone in connection with the development of the firm
of Rylands Bros.   His judgment and powers of
argument soon secured for him an ascendency in the
Town Council, by which he was, after a short time,
elected Alderman.

The subject of education was one in which Mr.
Rylands had always taken much interest; while
quite a youth he had been chiefly instrumental in
founding a British school, which is now a flourishing
institution, under the name of the People's College.
He believed that much injustice was done to Nonconformists by the system of sectarian education
which prevailed in schools, and which often prevented Nonconformists and others from sending their
children to the best school through the fear that
their religious convictions would be tampered with.
Under the influence of this feeling he eagerly united
with a number of Lancashire men, who contemplated
forming an association for the purpose of promoting
secular education.   On the 25th of August, 1847, a
meeting of these men was held at the Mechanics'
Institution, Cooper Street, Manchester, at which the
following resolutions were passed :—

On the motion of Mr. Samuel Lucas, of Manchester ; seconded by Mr. Peter Rylands, of Warrington,
    It was resolved—

" That this meeting do now constitute itself an Association, to be called 'The Lancashire Public School Association, for Promoting the Establishment of a General System of Secular Education in the County of Lancaster.' "

On the motion of Mr. Thos. Ballantyne, of Manchester ; seconded by Mr. Hugh Mason, of Ashton-under-Lyne,

It was resolved—

" That the principles enunciated in the pamphlet now laid before the meeting be adopted as those of the Association ; that the plan contained in the pamphlet be also adopted, with a view to its introduction to the House of Commons in the shape of a Bill ; and that the efforts of the Association be directed to procure an expression of public opinion in this county in its favour. A Provisional Committee was appointed, of which Mr. Rylands was a member, and on which were also nominated Mr. Jacob Bright, Mr. Jas. Heywood, M.P. (North Lancashire), Mr. Hugh Mason, afterwards M.P. for Ashton-under-Lyne, Mr. William Rathbone, Mr. John Rylands (Mr. Peter Rylands's eldest brother), and Mr. J. G. McMinnies (Mr. Peter Rylands's brother-in-law, and afterwards M.P. for Warrington).

This Association became very active. The Provisional Committee met frequently at Manchester, and public meetings were arranged in various parts of the county, as well as in Manchester, at nearly all of which meetings Mr. Rylands was one of the principal speakers. The life of the Association was a short and rather stormy one ; much opposition was met with, chiefly, of course, on the part of members of the Established Church, but to some extent even on the part of Dissenters, and, as is usual in public controversies, the designs of the Association were shamefully misrepresented. The members were declared to be opposed to all religion, and were called " Godless educationists," " advocates of a lifeless utilitarianism,"and many other hard names, employed, it is to be presumed, to conceal the weakness of the adversaries' case ; but in spite of bitter opposition in influential quarters the Association made way. In 1850 it was reconstructed on a wider basis under the title of the " National Public Schools Association," and had gained the active support of many leading men, among whom were Richard Cobden, M.P., Rt. Hon. T. Milner Gibson, M.P., Alexander Henry, M.P., President of the Association, Sir Elkanah Armitage, R. N. Philips, and Salis Schwabe. The Association did not, however, live long in its new form ; but although it failed in the sense that it did not then succeed in securing the objects for which it was formed, yet its many public meetings and the discussions to which they gave rise, must have done much to enlighten people on the subject, and prepare the way for the legislation which has since taken place in the direction advocated by the Association.

In 1851 Mr. Rylands was appointed Justice of the Peace for the Borough of Warrington, and was for many years a constant attendant on the Bench.

About the same time he was also appointed Justice of the Peace for the County Palatine of Lancaster.

In 1853 he was unanimously elected Mayor. His Mayoralty was not destined to be entirely peaceful and without incident, as, during it, two burning questions commenced to make a stir in Warrington— the Footpaths question and the Police question. The first was like a thunder-storm, furious while it lasted, but soon over, or perhaps it would be more appropriate to term it a storm in a tea-cup; while the latter remained a bone of contention for years. On the footpath question Mr. Rylands was able to plead his position as Mayor as a ground for remaining neutral, and so escaped some temporary unpopularity which would have fallen upon him had he actively taken the part of those with whom his sympathies lay. In brief, the case was this. In 1853 the railway from Stockport to Widnes was completed through Warrington, cutting certain footpaths along which the public had a right of way, and particularly a path which led from the town to Arpley Meadows, a favourite resort of the common people on Sundays and holidays. Much excitement was hereby occasioned in the town, and a Footpaths' Protection Society was formed. As the result of negotiations the Railway Company offered to make a public road along the River Mersey passing underneath the railway and leading to Arpley Meadows, and also to make a level crossing over the railway at the same spot. This simple plan would have increased the distance to be traversed in order to reach the fields by about 200 yards merely. Many leading men in the town recognising that this scheme met all reasonable objections, and being unwilling to harass the Railway Company, which was likely to be of great service to Warrington, expressed themselves satisfied. But a certain number of unpractical and unreasonable persons worked up the populace into a frenzy by declaring that popular rights were being disregarded, and insisted that a foot-bridge should be made over the line at the spot where the old path had been cut. This demand was most absurd ; the line is very broad at that point, there being many sidings for shunting goods trains, and the bridge would have to be reached by an ugly and expensive spiral staircase at each end. However, reasoning was powerless, the spark had been applied to the inflammable tinder of popular passion, and the whole town was in a ferment. The excitement was also aggravated by the importation of personal matters into the dispute, for Mr. McMinnies, who was the chief advocate for accepting the Company's offer, had incurred popular displeasure on account of action which he had recently taken in some other matters. Finally a public meeting was held on February 6th, 1854, to decide the question ; the room in which the meeting was held was crowded to suffocation, and hundreds could not gain admittance. Mr. Rylands, as Mayor, presided, and his office was no sinecure, for the meeting was an uproarious one. Mr. McMinnies and Mr. Beamont were howled at, and could with difficulty speak a few sentences between the interruptions. In the end the meeting decided almost unanimously to insist upon the building of a foot-bridge over the railway. The storm subsided as quickly as it had arisen ; the footbridge over the line was made, and proved to be inconvenient as well as unsightly, little use was made of it, a few years later it was quietly removed without a word of protest from anyone, and it is to be hoped that those men who had on such a paltry matter stirred up popular animosity against some of the greatest benefactors of the town felt heartily ashamed of themselves.

The other question which I mentioned—the Police question—was more serious, and gave rise to a more protracted struggle. In the year 1854 the police force of Warrington consisted of one chief constable, one inspector, and eight constables, which was a smaller force, in proportion to the number of inhabitants, than existed in any other important town. Constant complaints were received by the Watch Committee and by the Magistrates of assaults and robberies committed with impunity. The police force, small as it was, was often diminished by the absence of constables with prisoners at Kirkdale Gaol, and to find a policeman in the out-lying parts of the town at night was almost impossible. Some people employed a private night watchman. Mr. Rylands, as a Magistrate, had become thoroughly alive to this unsatisfactory state of affairs, and, while Mayor, in June, 1854, he succeeded in inducing the Watch Committee, of which he was a member, to propose an addition of two constables to the police force. Now, I suppose there are in all Town Councils and public bodies a certain number of

men who endeavour to gain favour with the ratepayers
by constant efforts to keep down the rates at any cost.
No matter how desirable in itself a proposed reform
may be, nor how likely eventually to augment the
wealth of the town, such men obstinately oppose it on
the ground that it will cause a temporary increase of a
penny or so to the rates. And so it was at Warrington ; and, on the question of the increase of the police
force, the short-sighted anti-reformers succeeded in
influencing the Council to such an extent that Mr.
Rylands' proposal was defeated by 12 votes to 3.   A
certain amount of heat was evidently excited by this
discussion, and the anti-reformers certainly seemed to
be adopting a very defiant attitude when, a few months
later, they proposed that the place of a constable, who
had been discharged for misconduct, should not be
filled up, and carried their proposal by 15 votes to 6.
The Warrington police force, which had been quite
inadequate before, was now still further weakened, and
consisted only of nine men, all told. However, if the
obstructionists had their own way for the time being
in this matter, in some other directions those who
wished to see Warrington progress had been successful, for a new market had been decided upon, and a
committee had been formed to superintend its construction, of which Mr. Rylands was chairman.
Proposals for a museum and library were being discussed, and in this matter again Mr. Rylands took a
leading part. Works were in progress for improving
the sewering and widening the streets of the town ;
and schemes for a cemetery were being seriously

considered. In fact, Warrington was beginning to wake up.

In November, 1854, Mr. Rylands' mayoralty came to an end. He was urgently requested to continue to hold the office for another year, but was obliged to refuse, owing to the cares of business and many demands upon his time. On this occasion he received the compliment of a public dinner, which was attended by all the principal inhabitants of the neighbourhood, and presided over by Colonel Wilson Patten, who was afterwards raised to the peerage, with the title of Lord Winmarleigh.

During the following year the question of the police force remained in an acute stage. Mr. Rylands resigned his seat on the Watch Committee, as he would not be responsible for the orderly government of the town while the force was so small; whereupon the Committee, it would almost seem out of spite, reduced the force still further to seven men. Long discussions on the subject took place at almost every meeting of the Town Council, and Mr. Rylands at length succeeded in getting the number fixed at the former amount, namely, 10 men in all.

In 1855, for the first time since the incorporation of the borough, the election of Mayor was not unanimous. This circumstance was probably owing partly to personal and partly to political feeling. There was gradually growing up in the Town Council at this time a party of narrow-minded men, who were jealous of the great influence which Mr. Rylands had obtained in the Council. They could not see that it was both natural and even advisable that a man who not only possessed sound common sense and great business ability, but also the power of expressing himself clearly and convincingly, should be a leader in the Council. They refused to recognise the abilities by which Mr. Rylands had won for himself so influential a position. They only saw that while his opinion always carried great weight, theirs was often disregarded in a way that much wounded their self-esteem. They, therefore, declared that Alderman Peter Rylands had got the Town Council under his thumb, and that it was necessary the Council should be emancipated. The election of Mayor seemed to give them their opportunity, and, actuated by a petty jealousy, they determined to strike at Mr. Rylands through his friend, Dr. Hardy, who had been proposed as a candidate. Political feeling also had some force, and Tory Councillors were requested to support Mr. Joseph Chrimes, because he was a Tory. Again, hitherto no shopkeeper had been elected as Mayor, and the proposers of Mr. Chrimes excited class prejudices in his favour by saying that there was a conspiracy among the upper classes in the town to keep municipal honours in their own hands, and calling upon shopkeepers in the Council to vindicate the rights of their class by supporting Mr. Chrimes. The result of all this was, that Mr. Chrimes was elected by 18 votes to 15. This was a most unfortunate election. Hitherto the deliberations of the Town Council had been on the whole harmonious, and the elections of Mayor unanimous. Had the supporters of Mr. Chrimes been willing to make a compromise, that gentleman might have been unanimously elected the following year ; but nothing could induce them to forego the miserable pleasure of annoying Mr. Rylands, and showing him that "he was not to have things all his own way." From this time there were in the Warrington Town Council two bitterly hostile parties ; acrimonious discussions were frequent, sarcastic letters to the *Warrington Guardian* were numerous, and personalities were frequently indulged in.

The epistolary warfare in the columns of the *Warrington Guardian* produced much polemical writing of considerable ability, but the letters which attracted the greatest amount of attention were those which appeared over the signature of " Oliver West," and soon became generally known as " the ' Oliver West ' letters." These letters appeared at frequent intervals throughout the year 1856, commenting freely upon municipal matters, and vigorously satirizing any Warrington public man who seemed to be impelled by jealousy, personal feeling, ambition, love of notoriety, or party spite, rather than by a desire to promote the best interests of the town. Personalities were carefully avoided, but many prominent men who had been guilty of mean or spiteful conduct in public matters had their actions held up to public scorn in a way that made them writhe. Nearly every one in Warrington was asking who could be the author of these letters. Some of those attacked pretended not to mind ; others went about vowing vengeance, and inquiring for the author. The excitement became

very great ; several names were mentioned, and one
or two leading men were publicly charged with the
authorship ; but the secret was known to very few,
and was perfectly well kept. The Editor of the
Guardian, even though an action for libel was insti-
tuted against him by one man who had been most
unmercifully ridiculed, yet refused to disclose the
name of the author ; and, however near the truth
men's guesses and suspicions may have been, the
secret is as much a secret at this day as it was 40
years ago. As the writers are now dead, there is no
indiscretion in saying that these letters were the work
of more than one man, and that Mr. Peter Rylands,
Mr. J. G. McMinnies, and the Rev. Ralph Allen
Mould were the joint authors. Mr. Rylands was
suspected at the time of having a hand in the production of the letters, but it was impossible for such
suspicions to be confirmed.

On the 15th of October, 1856, the new market was
opened. Before this time the Warrington Market-
place had been simply an open square ; now this
square was covered over with a shed, and a new and
convenient Market Hall built adjoining it. For some
years the question of a market had been discussed in
Warrington. In 1852 a scheme had been proposed
which met with much opposition, and had to be aban-
doned. In the following year, however, Mr. Rylands
again took the question up. and succeeded in getting
a Warrington Improvement and Market Act passed
by Parliament. A committee of the Town Council
was then formed, of which Mr. Rylands was elected

chairman; but then arose questions of cost, site, size, form, &c. Some men kept raising discussions on side issues to disguise their hostility to the whole scheme; some obstinately insisted upon their own pet plan, and would hear of no other; and some, by advocating a niggardly and cheese-paring policy, would have spoilt the new market altogether. However, by the employment of much tact, and with the assistance of other public-spirited men, Mr. Rylands brought the matter to a triumphant conclusion. The foundation-stone was laid in October, 1855, and the market was opened amid universal acclamation a year later.

In this year a Police Bill was passed by Parliament appointing Inspectors to report upon the Municipal Police Forces, and providing that every town whose force was up to a certain fixed strength should receive a Government grant in aid. Colonel Woodford, the Inspector under whose supervision the Warrington Police Force came, sent a letter to the Watch Committee representing to them that the town was much under-policed, and recommending that the number of the force should be increased from 11, at which it then stood, to 24. Mr. Rylands raised a discussion in the Town Council on this letter, but the Watch Committee refused to take any action. In May, 1857, Mr. Rylands again returned to the charge with a motion that Colonel Woodford's suggestion be acted upon, and supported his proposal in a long and closely-argued speech; but after a discussion, which lasted two days, the motion was lost by 21 votes to 5. Mr. Rylands kept raising this question at intervals, and his arguments, backed up by constant complaints of unchecked depredations, began to produce some effect, so that when in January, 1863, Colonel Woodford again drew attention to the inadequacy of the Police Force, it was clear that a good many of the old opponents of an increase were beginning to waver. In December of that year the Watch Committee themselves came forward with a recommendation for the appointment of one more inspector and two constables, which was endorsed by the Council. The force now amounted to 15, which was, however, still far too few for a large and rapidly increasing town like Warrington ; but public opinion was growing, new members were being elected to the Council, and in March, 1864, Mr. Rylands had the satisfaction of carrying a motion of no-confidence in the Watch Committee by 18 votes to 2. A new Committee was appointed which at once recommended an increase of the police force to 29 men in all ; this proposal was adopted by the Council, and thus Mr. Rylands won the battle which he had been fighting for nearly 12 years, and to his exertions Warrington at length owed the advantage of an efficient body of police.

Meanwhile the town had been in many ways improved ; a Cemetery had been opened, a Public Hall had been built, the Museum and Free Library had been completed, and other public works of greater or less utility had been carried out, in all which improvements Mr. Rylands took an active part.

In 1859 he had been unanimously invited by the Liberal party in Warrington to stand as the Liberal candidate in opposition to Mr. Greenall, who had represented the borough since 1847; but was obliged to decline owing to the pressure of business engagements. From that time, however, he continued to take an active part in the discussion of public questions, addressing meetings on various political subjects both in Warrington and elsewhere, and in 1868, when he was again asked to stand, he found himself in a position to consent to do so.

Mr. Greenall had then held unchallenged possession of the seat for 21 years, and the candidature of Mr. Rylands excited much bitterness of feeling among the Tory party in the borough. As the contest proceeded and the Tories began to perceive that Mr. Rylands would be a very dangerous opponent, their bitterness greatly increased, and in the speeches at their meetings very strong expressions began to be made use of which provoked retaliation on the part of their opponents, and thus as the election day drew near party strife in Warrington grew more intense and more envenomed than ever before or since. As the conviction was more and more borne in upon the minds of the leaders of the Tory party that there was a very strong probability of their losing the election, they became like men striking out at random, and so long as they could only succeed in hitting their adversaries they were not particular as to the fairness of their blows. Perhaps the most discreditable of their tactics was the publication in the *Warrington*

Guardian of a series of letters as advertisements, filled with coarse abuse of Mr. Rylands and his leading supporters. The two great questions on which the election was fought were the Disestablishment of the Irish Church, and the Ballot. These miserable letters, which were signed " Benjamin Darby," made no attempt whatever to argue out these great questions or others with regard to which the Liberal and Tory parties were at variance. There was no discussion of principles in them. They attacked not measures but men.

The fact that Mr. Rylands had ceased to be a Dissenter, and become a Churchman, was turned to his discredit ; the amount of money he had subscribed to local charities, etc., was ferreted out and compared with that subscribed by the wealthiest men in the town in order to make him appear mean. In every possible way, previous actions of his were mis-represented and placed in an odious light. It is, however, pleasant to think that such contemptible tactics failed to effect their purpose.

On the nomination day and the day of election the excitement in the streets of Warrington was intense, and order was with difficulty maintained. Matters came to a crisis about a quarter of an hour before the close of the poll, when a rumour was rapidly circulated among the Liberals that a number of working men belonging to their party had been made drunk and shut up in a yard by the opposite party. A body of Liberals went to the place indicated, but were stopped at the gate by a band of rough men armed with bludgeons, who succeeded in preventing an entrance being made, and seriously injured three of those who attempted to enter.

The poll closed at four o'clock, when, according to the Conservative figures, Mr. Greenall had a majority of 78, and according to the Liberal figures, a majority of seven. It was scarcely possible for anyone to doubt that Mr. Greenall was really elected, and the night was spent by the Tories in frantic demonstrations of joy. The morning, however, brought them an unpleasant shock, for the Mayor announced that, according to his official polling book, Mr. Rylands had received 1,984 votes and Mr. Greenall 1,957, giving Mr. Rylands a majority of 27.

This result, so unexpected, since the close of the poll, by both parties, was due to the fact that in the midst of confusion caused by a great pressure of voters, some seventy or eighty of Mr. Greenall's supporters gave in their voting cards, not to the poll-clerk, but to one of the check-clerks acting in Mr. Greenall's behalf. The men then left the booth under the impression that they had voted. The check-clerk entered the votes in the check-book, but in the hurry and confusion prevailing at the time omitted to see that they were properly entered in the poll-book. The result was that Mr. Rylands had a majority of recorded votes. The leading Conservatives demanded that under these circumstances the election should be declared null and void. The Mayor, however, considered that he had only to do with the official poll-book, and held it to be his duty to return Mr. Rylands as member, maintaining, also, that Mr. Rylands could not legally refuse his election, even if he wished.

The Tories were very angry at this decision. They accused the Mayor of partiality, and called upon him to resign. But the Mayor, Mr. Neild, acted extremely well all through the difficult circumstances in which he was placed—he disregarded abuse, and did his duty without flinching.

When Mr. Greenall's friends found they could produce no impression upon the Mayor, they decided to lodge a petition against Mr. Rylands' return. This they did, and Mr. Baron Martin was appointed to try the case. The question was really a very simple one, and after hearing all the evidence the judge gave his decision to the effect that if there had been any omission to record in the poll-book votes which were "legally tendered," it would be his duty to order those votes to be added to the list, and to give the candidate in whose behalf they were tendered the benefit of them ; that the legal tender of a vote consisted in the voter giving his name to the poll-clerk, and telling that functionary for whom he polled ; that in the case considered it had been proved that the votes in dispute had not been tendered to the poll-clerk at all ; that the giving in of the cards to somebody who happened to be sitting at the table was not the legal tender of votes ; that, consequently, the votes in question were not lost, for they were never recorded ; that they were not recorded because they were not tendered ; and that, in fine, to say the election ought, on that account, to be declared void, was "an absurd and ridiculous proposition."

This election was certainly a remarkable one. Possibly no case precisely similar has ever been recorded ; nevertheless a similar result might conceivably occur under our present system of ballot voting ; for, suppose the majority of the elected candidate were very small, say 5, and suppose there were 30 spoiled votes ; now, it is quite possible that 20 of these spoiled votes might be intended for the beaten candidate and 10 for the victorious one, in which case the successful candidate would represent a minority of voters. But no one would dream of demanding that an election should be declared void because a number of votes were "spoiled," that is, not "legally tendered," or that an attempt should be made to discover which candidate each spoiled vote was intended for, in order that the candidates might be credited with them. Therefore the taunt which was on one or two occasions subsequently directed against Mr. Rylands by the Tory Press, and once by a Tory member of Parliament, that he was the member for the minority of Warrington, was utterly without point. Mr. Rylands himself had no scruples about taking the seat he had thus won, because he felt convinced that about 200 of his supporters had been tampered with, and prevented from voting, and that, if the election had been fairly fought, he would have had a considerable majority. He, therefore, considered himself no less morally than legally the member for Warrington.

I do not intend to dwell at length upon the various incidents of Mr. Rylands' Parliamentary career, because these may be learnt from the perusal of the correspondence to which this sketch is an introduction, and of Mr. Rylands' speeches, which are published in a separate volume. I shall merely refer briefly to some of the more important questions with which he was concerned.

Mr. Rylands was extremely well fitted, both by natural ability and by long training, to take at once a leading position in the House of Commons. The experience which he had been gaining for so many years in the miniature parliament of the Warrington Town Council, had made him a ready debater and practised in dealing with public questions; while his natural business ability, and his close acquaintance with business matters, not only caused him to look at all public questions from a thoroughly common-sense point of view, but especially qualified him to form an opinion upon financial and economical affairs. He, therefore, saw with great disgust the extravagance which characterised (as it still does) the great spending departments of the State, more especially the naval and military departments, and the Diplomatic Service; and, as he never hesitated to condemn wasteful expenditure, irrespective of the party responsible for it, he soon obtained a reputation for sturdy independence. He also identified himself with the cause of Social Progress, particularly with regard to the liquor traffic, on which subject he not only moved several resolutions, but was one of the promoters of a

Bill in the sessions of 1870 and 1871 to prohibit the sale of liquors on Sunday. He also became a vice-president of the License Amendment League, the chairman of the Warrington branch of the National Education League, a member of the committee of the London Chamber of Commerce, a member of the Cobden Club, a member of the committee of the Land Reform Association, and a vice-president of the National Union for the Suppression of Intemperance ; and in many other ways showed his sympathy with the cause of social and economical reform.

His activity during the years 1869-74 was very great, and the subjects to which he devoted himself very numerous ; indeed, so intensely had he applied himself to his public duties that his health was much impaired, but he had the satisfaction of feeling that he had won for himself a considerable reputation and a leading position among the advanced section of Radicals.

No doubt he expected that the Warrington electors —especially now that they had the protection of the ballot—would reward his labours by returning him again to Parliament by a large majority ; but, as every one knows, a wave of Tory re-action swept over England in 1874, and, in company with a large number of other Liberals, Mr. Rylands was overthrown by it. His total poll on this occasion was 2,201, while Mr. Greenall's was 2,381, the latter being, therefore, elected by a majority of 180.

Mr. Rylands thereupon accepted an invitation to contest South-East Lancashire—a forlorn hope. The two Liberal candidates spared no pains, but were defeated by a considerable majority.

Although Mr. Rylands was disappointed at being thus excluded from the new Parliament, it was really by no means a disadvantage to him, for he stood sadly in need of rest, and was enabled, in 1876, to return with renewed vigour to the House of Commons as member for Burnley, a far more satisfactory constituency to him than Warrington had been.

The Conservatives being now in office, Mr. Rylands felt more free than he had previously been to criticise wasteful expenditure, and to denounce jobs and abuses of all kinds. He also turned his attention to foreign questions, and often spoke, both in Parliament and in the country, in opposition to the foreign policy of Lord Beaconsfield, whom he distrusted profoundly, and whose methods he considered most dangerous. All through this Parliament again his energy was remarkable, and the range of subjects of which he made himself master very wide; but his labours undoubtedly told still further upon his health.

In 1880 Mr. Rylands was again elected member for Burnley by an increased majority. He looked with pleasurable anticipation to the future, for the Liberal party was again in power, and Mr. Gladstone's Midlothian speeches gave promise of much prosperity to the country from prudent administration and wise and progressive legislation. But the event was very different, and as time went on Mr. Rylands began to find Parliamentary life distasteful, and began gradually to lose confidence in the leader whom he had

hitherto enthusiastically admired. He entirely disapproved of much of the foreign policy of the Government, and was particularly disgusted with their
discreditable mismanagement of Egyptian affairs; but
the measure of his annoyance was filled up by their
vacillation in regard to Ireland. He welcomed the
Land Bill, and believed that, if it had a fair chance,
it would go very far towards pacifying Irish discontent ; and he could scarcely find words to express his
contempt for the weakness of the Government in not
making up their minds boldly to try the effect of a
generous policy of conciliation in Ireland. In private
he denounced the Coercion Bill in strong terms,
affirming his belief that the whole effect of the Land
Bill would be neutralised by it, and of Mr. W. E.
Forster he never could speak without irritation. He
attempted in the House of Commons to give practical
effect to the opinions he entertained on this subject,
but was immediately so inundated with remonstrances
from his constituents in Burnley, who implored him
not to embarrass Mr. Gladstone, that he sank his
independence, and, by his votes, supported a measure
which he detested. This was a very bitter experience
for a man of such strong convictions and such independence of character as Mr. Rylands. He writhed
under the compulsion to which he yielded, and the
whole volume of his pent-up wrath was directed
against Mr. Gladstone. It was Mr. Gladstone who,
as head of the Government, was responsible for this
mistaken policy, and it was the remarkable influence
of Mr. Gladstone upon men that led his constituents

to insist upon their member's loyalty to his leader. It was Mr. Gladstone, therefore, whom Mr. Rylands made responsible for the humiliation he felt in voting one way while his convictions pointed in another.

It will be said that Mr. Rylands was not compelled thus to sacrifice his principles, that a member of Parliament is not a delegate, and that it was his duty to act according to his convictions whether his constituents liked it or not. This is quite true, and I have not one word to say in defence of the course Mr. Rylands then took, but I may plead certain things in extenuation. Mr. Rylands was getting on in years, and to be obliged to find and work up a new constituency would have been very irksome to him, more especially as failing health, the result largely of over-work, rendered him disinclined for much exertion ; under these circumstances the loss of his seat at Burnley would have been practically equivalent to the termination of his public career. Burnley suited him, he liked the Burnley people and they liked him. What wonder then if he hesitated to take a step which might alienate the good will of his strongest supporters in that borough ? Besides, if the Government had been turned out he did not believe that any other could have been formed in which he could have confidence. I might also plead that it is of almost daily occurrence for members of Parliament to sacrifice their principles for party or personal ends, but if a man has done wrong it would be no excuse for him could he say that everyone else has done wrong too, though it might be to some extent a palliation of his conduct.

In the very case of which we are speaking other Liberal members acted in the same way, some of them even members of the Government. Mr. Chamberlain repeatedly expressed to Mr. Rylands his disapproval of the Coercion Bill, telling him that Mr. John Bright was equally opposed to it, and urged him to vote against the Bill. Mr. Rylands replied, "No; if I, and other Radicals oppose this Bill, our constituents will say to us that if Bright and Chamberlain, whose Liberalism is beyond question, can support Mr. Gladstone on this question, surely they may expect us to do so. No! we won't sacrifice ourselves, but if you and Bright will resign we will not hesitate to support you." However, Mr. Chamberlain would not resign, for though he would have been pleased enough to see Mr. Gladstone's Government overthrown by the votes of others, he was not the man to burn his fingers in pulling the chestnuts out of the fire for himself.

Another measure of the Government which Mr. Rylands regarded with intense dislike was the adoption of the Clôture, and in this case again he refrained from opposing the Government, in conformity with the wishes of his constituents.

The conduct of the Irish members also made Parliamentary life less pleasant than it had previously been, the all-night sittings and the occasional strong language indulged in by some members of the Irish party, together with their general obstructive tactics, gradually rendered that party distasteful to him, and having once become prejudiced against them he began to credit the many current reports as to their complicity with crime in Ireland. This dislike was much intensified by the action of the Irish party with regard to the elections in 1885, and he was extremely annoyed that Mr. Parnell should request the Irish voters in Burnley to oppose him, as he considered that he was entitled to the gratitude of the Irish people, quite forgetting that in their estimation all obligations had been cancelled by the Coercion Act.

In the year 1885, therefore, Mr. Rylands was dominated by two powerful feelings: a feeling of distrust and dislike of Mr. Gladstone, which had grown, little by little, since 1880, until it amounted almost to a monomania ; and a feeling of disgust at the Irish party. Half-a-dozen years previous to this he would never have allowed his judgment to be warped by prejudices such as these, but overwork during the sessions 1868-74, 1874-80 had worn out his constitution. His health was now very seriously impaired—far more so than he himself or any of his friends ever suspected, and in consequence of this failing of bodily vigour, there was bound to be a failing of intellectual vigour ; his mind was no longer as active and as keen as it had formerly been ; he could no longer view a question under all its different aspects, and take the same broad view of acts and events ; a feeling of weariness and disinclination for change had come over him. I myself heard him remark about this time that "really, there is very little difference now between Liberals and Conservatives; so much has been done in the last fifty years, such rapid progress has been made, that there is scarcely anything which urgently calls for reform."

It will now be easy for anyone to understand the attitude which Mr. Rylands adopted in relation to Mr. Gladstone's Home Rule Bill. In fact, there was nothing at all surprising about it. Supposing that any one beforehand had been asked to consider this hypothetical case : on the one hand, a man who intensely disliked and distrusted Mr. Gladstone, who was extremely annoyed with the conduct of the Irish members, and who even believed them capable of countenancing crime, and who had begun to long for intellectual rest, and view with disquietude any political change ; on the other hand, a measure proposed by Mr. Gladstone to satisfy the demands of those Irish members, and supported by them, and embodying a political change of such magnitude as to be almost revolutionary. Now put the question, what will be the attitude of that man towards that measure ? There is but one answer possible,—he will certainly oppose it.

Mr. Rylands' opposition to Home Rule probably caused more astonishment, especially among Liberals, than the opposition of any other man. The majority of the dissentients were Whigs. Everyone knew that they were only waiting for such an opportunity of seceding to the Conservative party. In the case of other Radicals it was not difficult to suspect interested motives. But Mr. Rylands was regarded as an advanced Radical, and he was known to be a man whose honesty was beyond question. The news of his defection, therefore, came upon Burnley Liberals, and, indeed, Liberals all over the country, as a great shock. They did not know that failing health and increasing age had made him more a Conservative than a Radical in his sympathies; and they did not know that, owing to the decay of mental vigour, he had allowed two powerful prejudices so to obscure his judgment as to prevent him forming an impartial opinion on any matter upon which they were able to operate. Had he been ten years younger he would have taken a different course; and his numerous admirers, who viewed with grief a line of action so opposed to his earlier convictions, and so different from his former actions, understanding how he came to follow such a line, would banish from their minds all desire to blame, even if they entertained any, which they do not; for it is certain that those thousands of men who have been fired by his earnest words, and who have admired his integrity and honesty of purpose, remember only the great measures of progress which he helped to pass, and the many years of self-sacrificing toil which he devoted to the public service, a toil in which he wore himself away.

It may be that if Mr. Rylands had retired from public life in 1885 his health might have been restored. It is impossible to say, but certainly he was quite unfit to go through such a trying ordeal as the election of 1886. To find the bulk of his former supporters in opposition to him; to see that many of those who were formerly his most ardent admirers condemned him ; to be accused, in the heat of a bitter controversy, of having been actuated by unworthy motives ; to be obliged to fight for victory as, perhaps, he had never fought since the first Warrington election, if even then—such physical and mental trials as these might have broken down the health of a strong man, how much more, then, that of one whose constitution was already seriously undermined ? It is not too much to say that this election hastened his death. He gained a narrow victory, hardly earned, but was not allowed to enjoy it, for very serious symptoms shortly after appeared, and, in spite of all that doctors could do, he slowly but steadily sank, and eventually expired, unconscious and free from pain, early in the morning of Tuesday, February the 4th, 1887. His death was a loss to politics, for public men of his stamp are not too common. He was a thoroughly able, conscientious, and hard-working man. He honestly strove to do his duty, and at the close of his life could have truly declared that his exertions had assisted in making the world a little better when he left it than it was when he entered it. Well would it be if every man could say the same.

CORRESPONDENCE.

———

No. I.

Col. J. WILSON PATTEN.

Bank Hall,
Warrington,
Jany. 1, 1869.

Dear Sir,—

On my arrival here I have heard that the inquiry into the Warrington Election Petition is fixed for the 1st of February, and that Baron Martin is the Judge entrusted with it. It has occurred to me that there may be some little difficulty in making proper arrangements for the latter, and that I might be able to obviate it by placing Bank Hall, with a proper equipage, at his disposal during the inquiry.

It is obvious, however, that, under the circumstances, it would be improper for me to do so, unless with your entire concurrence and that of your Election Committee, or, indeed, without some grounds for believing that the political party in the borough with which you are connected could be induced to view the matter in the same light with myself, namely, as an act of public duty to the Mayor and the Borough, without the slightest political object.

With such concurrence, but not otherwise, I would invite Baron Martin to Bank Hall, and offer him every accommodation in my power ; and in that case you would, perhaps, oblige me by such a reply as I could forward to him with my invitation ; but pray do not hesitate to express any opinion on the subject entertained by yourself or your political friends. I should quite understand that yours and their decision, even if opposed to the above suggestion, was founded on reasonable grounds, and should, of course, be entirely guided by it.

Believe me,

Yours faithfully,

J. WILSON PATTEN.

No. II.

Colonel WILSON PATTEN.

Bank Hall,
Warrington,
Jany. 4, 1869.

Dear Sir,—

Having heard, through Mr. White and the Mayor, that you were likely to coincide in the suggestion which I made to you, that I should invite Mr. Baron Martin to Bank Hall for the time of the inquiry into the Warrington Election Petition, I sounded the latter on the subject, and I learn from his reply to me that he thinks it better not to accept any private hospitality during the circuit which he is about to make. Under these circumstances I have informed the Mayor.

Accept my thanks for the expression of your confidence,

And believe me,
Yours truly,
J. Wilson Patten.

No. III.

Right Hon. W. E. GLADSTONE, M.P.

Hagley,

Dec. 31, 1868.

My Dear Sir,—

Before complying with your request as to Mr. John Crosfield, I write to make sure that his works are in Lancashire, and that he is so much on that side the border as not to be open to objection in the character of a non-resident? Satisfied on this point, I will cheerfully comply.

I am rejoiced at the announcement with which you close, and I remain,

Very faithfully yours,

W. E. Gladstone.

———

[This was in reference to a request that Mr. Gladstone would use his influence to have Mr. John Crosfield placed upon the Commission of the Peace for the County of Lancashire.]

No. IV.

Mr. GEORGE HADFIELD, M.P.

Conyngham Road,
Victoria Park,
Manchester,
Jany. 30, 1869.

My Dear Sir,—

I earnestly hope you will keep your seat. So useful and welcome a colleague will be very acceptable.

The statement in the *Times* I read with satisfaction. There is, as usual, a little of the Americanism in it, but it is in the right direction, and bespeaks a willingness on their part. We have no news yet from the Envoy, but we expect it daily. Mr. Bazley is in Manchester. We can proceed no further until we hear from America, and the Session is fast approaching, and I hope we shall all be in our places in the House.

It is an important measure, and may have a *world-wide influence*.

Excuse haste.

Yours truly,
Geo. Hadfield.

[This letter refers to the Convention which had just been signed, appointing four Commissioners to whom the " Alabama " dispute should be referred ; which was, however, rejected by the American Senate.]

No. V.

Mr. GEO. HADFIELD, M.P.

Conyngham Road,
Victoria Park,
Manchester,
Feb. 5, 1869.

My Dear Sir,—

Accept my hearty congratulations on your successful maintenance of your seat in the House of Commons yesterday. You have done a public service, and I hope your life and health may be long to enjoy your well earned honour. I must not call on the loved and honoured ones now in heaven, but I could relish the thought of your Father, my old friend, and the Rev. J. Turner and others, participating in the pleasure occasioned by your achievement.

Command me in the House of Commons whenever I can be useful to you, in matters of practice and otherwise.

Let me walk with you over the offices, etc., when convenient.

I remain,
Yours very truly,
Geo. Hadfield.

No. VI.

Mr. ALFRED ILLINGWORTH, M.P.

> Daisy Bank,
> Bradford,
> Feb. 5, 1869.

My Dear Rylands,—

Let me congratulate you on the result of your petitions, a report of which I have seen in this morning's *Examiner and Times.*

We shall, I trust, meet " all well " and ready for active service in 10 days. You would see that we get thro' triumphantly, saving Forster, and doing justice to Ripley. What next we scarcely know; if we are *honest* the seat will go to its rightful owner, Miall.

> I am,
> Yours faithfully,
> Alfred Illingworth.

[Mr. Ripley was soon after unseated on petition, and Mr. Miall obtained the seat.]

No. VII.

Mr. T. B. POTTER, M.P.

> Buile Hill,
> Manchester,
> Feb. 6, 1869.

Dear Mr. Rylands,

Let me offer my congratulations; I am thankful you have come off with flying colours. What an excellent article in the *Examiner and Times* to-day.

Greenall is scarified.

> Yours truly,
> Thomas B. Potter.

No. VIII.

LORD DUFFERIN.

> 8, Grosvenor Square,
> March 26, 1869.

My Dear Mr. Rylands,—

I shall be very happy to place Mr. Smith's name and Mr. Rigby's name in the Commission of the Peace for the County Palatine, but I am so overwhelmed with similar applications from different parts of the Duchy that with the consent and approval of several members of Parliament who met me for the purpose of discussing the point, it was arranged that for the present I should make a batch consisting of only the more prominent names on the lists furnished to me. Even in this restricted form the addition I am contemplating is enormous, and could only be justified by the necessity for redressing the disproportion created by the late Government.

In giving you three I have gone beyond what was recommended, and I am in hopes, therefore, you will not press for the two others, though, of course, at a future time, or, indeed, at any time, I shall be always anxious to pay great attention to any suggestion you may make.

Yours sincerely,

DUFFERIN.

P.S.—Of course, if you find the Chancellor more malleable, that circumstance would alter the case.

No. IX.

Miss BECKER.

Manchester National Society for Women's Suffrage,
28, Jackson's Row,
Albert Square,
May 9, 1869.

DEAR SIR,—

Mr. Jacob Bright's amendment to give the municipal franchise to women-ratepayers will come on for discussion in committee on Mr. Hibbert's Bill *to-morrow*, Monday, May 10.

I earnestly hope that you will give your support in his generous efforts to obtain for women-taxpayers some measure of justice.

In *non-corporate* districts *all* persons rated for the relief of the poor have votes in local affairs under the Health of Towns Act. Women in Manchester have expressed great surprise and dissatisfaction at finding that women in the country could vote while they were excluded. Should Mr. Bright's amendment be carried this anomaly would be removed.

I have for so many years associated your name with such eloquent and powerful advocacy of liberal principles that I am most anxious we should obtain your help in the cause of justice to women.

Believe me to be,
Yours sincerely,
LYDIA E. BECKER.

No. X.

Mr. EDWARD MEDLEY.

3, Penley Grove Street,

York,

June 16, 1869.

Sir,—

I beg to thank you for opposing the passing of Mr. Hughes' inconsistent and unjust Sunday Trading Bill. Since the year 1847 Bills of a similar character have been brought before the House from time to time. Those Bills were opposed by Mr. Joseph Hume, Mr. Thos. Duncombe, and others since departed, and we now seem to be in need of someone to check the progress of Bills of such a mischievous and vexatious character. I was in the Lobby on the Wednesday afternoon after you had talked it out, and would have spoken to you, but there was not then time. Having lived from 1831 to 1868 in the parish of St. Luke's, London, in a poor neighbourhood, as a small shopkeeper, I know something of the wants and necessities of the poorer classes, thousands of whom have but one room to sleep and live in. If food was bought on Saturday in summer time it would be unfit to eat on Sunday. I am certain that if this Bill becomes law that there will be many tons of meat and fish spoiled and unfit for food, which, otherwise, would be purchased by the poor, cheap and wholesome for themselves and families. I gave evidence before the Committee in 1847, contending that if the 29th of Charles II. was put in force against poor people it was very onerous, and that we do not require a more stringent law. If it were not for trespassing too much upon your time, I could give you many cases of hardship. I will just mention some of my own. The first was for selling a two-pound loaf to a man at half-past five in the afternoon who had to work all night in the gas-works close by. I pleaded that bread was an article of necessity in this case, nevertheless I was convicted in 5/- penalty and costs. Believing I was convicted wrongly I declined to pay. A short time afterwards when I came home to dinner, I found a broker had been put in, and two table-cloths and a hearth-rug had been seized, which my wife had just bought. Fined afterwards for a halfpenny biscuit; next for a pound of flour; again for a pennyworth of oatmeal, at half-past eight in the evening, for a woman that was ill; and on one other occasion—five times in all. Not one of them in church time. To protect ourselves and the poorer people we formed associations in different parts of London, and at last I think the Magistrates got sick of these cases; very few of them would convict if they could help it. In 1848 and 1849 Bills were brought into the Commons and defeated, but in 1850 the promoters adopted a different mode of tactics. They introduced their Bill early in the session in the Lords, and it was referred to a committee. I was the first witness called. Upwards of 200 questions were put to me. Ultimately the Lords passed the Bill. When sent to the Commons they would not proceed until they had the evidence printed which had been given before the Lords, and, when printed, it was referred to a committee. Ultimately, after a good deal of discussion, the Commons rejected the Bill. Since that time the same party has introduced a similar Bill about every other year. Since 1847 I have taken a leading part in opposing those Bills; and I hope, sir, with your assistance we shall be successful now. The Bill, if passed, would bring discredit on the Legislature, and in thousands of cases prevent the poor from obtaining the common necessaries of life. Compared with this Bill, the Act of Charles II. is a good law, for under it we can sometimes turn the tables upon our oppressors. Some of our committee watched whose carriage came to Jolington Church on Sunday. They found one to be the Vicar's, who happened to be an advocate for prosecuting us. We took a summons out against his coachman for exercising his worldly calling upon the Lord's Day. The Vicar pleaded in justification that his wife had been confined, and he had brought her to be churched. The Magistrate accepted the plea, and after that the small shopkeepers were not molested. I will just beg, sir, to call your attention to the evidence of a gentleman who, from his position in early life and afterwards was, perhaps, more competent to give an opinion upon this question than any other man. I mean the late Mr. Charles Pearson, the city solicitor, who gave evidence in 1847. After stating that in enforcing the Act of Charles II. there were riots— complete riots—he is asked if he is prepared to recommend anything. He says, " I am not prepared to recommend anything. It is a question full of difficulties, and great responsibility would rest upon anybody with any reputation who would recommend to Parliament a measure with reference to a matter of 'this kind." The cumulative penalties which Mr. Hughes now seeks to obtain by his Bill was tried to be obtained under the Act of Charles II. I think about 80 years ago a man sold, not one only, but, at different times, several loaves of bread. The Magistrate convicted him not upon one offence only, but on more. The man brought his case before the Superior Court, and Lord Mansfield said that the Legislature never contemplated more than one offence in one day. If they had, then a tailor would be liable for every stitch he took in making a garment, a shoemaker a shoe, and so on ; and the conviction was quashed. I am compelled to be here, but hope to be in London before the Bill again comes on in committee. I beg to apologise for this trespass upon your time.

I am, sir,

Your obedient servant,

EDWD. MEDLEY.

No. XI.

Central Association for Stopping the Sale of Intoxicating Liquors on Sunday,

> 43, Market Street,
> Manchester,
> June 30, 1869.

DEAR SIR,—

Our Executive Committee, feeling very grateful for
your courageous and able advocacy in the House of
Commons of a measure which would nearly abolish
Sunday intemperance, unanimously adopted, at its
meeting on Monday last, the accompanying resolution
of thanks, which we have the greatest pleasure in for-
warding you.   Trusting that the energetic labours in
which you take so responsible and prominent a part
may soon prove successful in preventing the evils
inseparable from the Sunday liquor traffic,

> We are, dear sir,
> Yours very truly,
> R. WHITWORTH,
> T. A. STOWELL, M.A.,
> Honorary Secretaries.

The following is the resolution referred to:—
" That this committee tender their sincere thanks
to Peter Rylands, Esq., for his able exposition in
Parliament of the justice and necessity of including
the stopping of the Sunday sale of intoxicating liquors
in the general measure projected by the Government,
and they rejoice to learn that Mr. Bruce, M.P., the

Home Secretary, in reference to the motion made on the 22nd of June, promised that the subject should have the best consideration of the Government ; and further, this committee regard the resolution and speech of Mr. Rylands as appropriate expressions of the desire of the working classes, and anticipate that they will inspire with new courage all who are labouring to secure the stopping of the sale of intoxicating liquors on Sunday.'

No. XII.

Mr. RYLANDS' REPLY.

1, Gloucester Place,
Hyde Park,
London,
July 1, 1869.

Dear Sir,—

I am much gratified by the kind manner in which your committee have recognised my effort in the House of Commons to secure attention to the question of Sunday closing. I should have been glad if the motion could have been brought on at an earlier hour, as it would not only have rendered my task much more agreeable to myself, but would have enabled several members, including Mr. Jacob Bright, Mr. Baines, Mr. M'Laren, and Sir Wilfrid Lawson to have supported me by their speeches. However, the best was done under the circumstances, and I sincerely hope may not be without good effect. Again thanking you for the kind terms of your letter, and your committee for the resolution which they have adopted,

Believe me, dear sir, yours sincerely,

PETER RYLANDS.

No. XIII.

Rev. EDWARD MATHEWS, M.A.

(Travelling Secretary to the Central Association for Stopping the Sale of Intoxicating Liquors on Sunday.)

43, Market Street,
Manchester,
July 13, 1869.

DEAR SIR,—

I beg to send you a reprint of your speech on the Sunday Closing question. Our committee have decided to ask the Town Councils, Boards of Guardians, and Boards of Health to pass a resolution similar to the one you moved in the House of Commons. I send a copy of our appeal to the Town Councillors, and enclose the note of our Hon. Secs. This will be rather expensive, but Mr. King, of Rochdale, and Mr. Baines, of this city, have each given us £100, so that we feel cheered. I shall be writing in a day or two to your firm in Warrington. I anticipate they will encourage our efforts by a liberal subscription. Last week I attended the annual meeting of the British Temperance League, and arranged with Mr. Bradley, the Temperance Agent, to distribute our publications in Warrington. I have sent him a large bundle for this purpose.

I wrote to Mr. Haughton, of Dublin, and asked him kindly to reply to Mr. Newdegate. He sent me a letter which I had copied and sent to each London daily newspaper. I have only seen it in the *Daily News* and *Standard.* There has been a number of letters in the *Morning Star* on the subject.

Mr. Thompson, of Pin Mill, will move your resolution in the next meeting of our Town Council. Mr. Birch, jun., will second it. To-morrow the working men's Sunday Closing League meet to arrange for an open-air meeting on a large scale.

We are still keeping in view a good deputation to the Premier before the close of the session of Parliament.

Yours obediently,
EDWARD MATHEWS.

No. XIV.

Mr. W. D. CHRISTIE.

32, Dorset Sq.,
July 30, 1869.

My Dear Sir,—

Permit me to congratulate you on the effect of your motion and speech. You have at any rate secured a Committee for next year. Those with whom I spoke last year thought it then hopeless to try for a Committee. You will, I think, not require to be cautioned as to the selection of members, and against schemes which will be prepared between this and then for getting members and witnesses agreeable to the Foreign Office.

On the subject of " Extraordinary Expenses " I may be able, perhaps, to give you some useful information of detail. So far as my experience extends (but I know nothing of Constantinople), I think that you will not find much really objectionable in them, and that Ministers have to complain of the Foreign Office in several matters in connection with them.

If Otway has been correctly reported, in his answer to Mr. Shaw about the Consul at Buenos Ayres, he has misrepresented matters much. Mr. Parish had a very small appointment in China. He was transferred to a small appointment at Buenos Ayres, Vice-Consul. Luckily he was Acting Consul-General for some years; but that was a piece of luck and favour. Nothing that Otway said, even if it were all true, could explain the increase of £100 of last year.

Believe me, yours very truly,

W. D. CHRISTIE.

No. XV.

MR. W. D. CHRISTIE.

32, Dorset Sq.,
Aug. 12, 1869.

MY DEAR SIR,—

I am sorry Mr. H. Bulwer has given notice of his amendment. He told me the day before the House was up he was thinking of it, and I immediately expressed a hope that he would let the House of Commons Committee sit first. A Royal Commission will virtually be a soft cushion for the Foreign Office. There will be a safe chairman, and Government will select the members. The evidence is all taken quietly and privately, and, when ultimately published in mass, not read : whereas you can get the newspapers to give daily reports of a House of Commons Committee. I will try and see Bulwer to-morrow, before I leave town.

I hope Otway's pledge to give you a Committee is so distinct that you can keep him to it. Arrangements with Bulwer, if you could make them, about the composition of the Committee, might lead to his acting with you more cordially; and, if you have Gladstone and Bright with you in feeling, you might, perhaps, agree with them on some chairman who would be entirely satisfactory to them.

Also, it would be a great aid for united action if you could come to some compromise with Bulwer and those whose opinions on the subject he would greatly influence, about salaries for the greatest places; and I do not despair of putting this matter before you between this and next session in a manner which may, perhaps, have some effect on your mind. I go very heartily with you for reductions in many ways, and principally through changing *management*, and stopping jobbery and nepotism, great sources of prodigality.

Yours very truly,

W. D. CHRISTIE.

I think it may be fairly said against Bulwer's proposal that the Diplomatic Service is not a large enough field for a Royal Commission; if it were the whole Civil Service it would be different.

No. XVI.

Mr. W. D. CHRISTIE.

32, Dorset Sq.,

Aug. 16, 1869.

My Dear Sir,—

I am detained in town, but I have thought it better, on further consideration, not to go near Sir H. Bulwer about his commission.

I am very much annoyed at his proposal. You will remember my telling you the first day I had the pleasure of seeing you, that it was difficult to say what line he would take. He has now put himself in a position as between you and the Government, which may enable him to do what will be agreeable to Lord Clarendon and the Foreign Office connexion, and they will now be glad to make use of him for reducing the next year's investigation to a minimum of efficiency with a maximum of softness.

I think from the terms of his motion he has sought to profit by your and Mr. Shaw's* separate notices ; and, as you are going to combine, that may help to thwart him, and it will be still better if you could get Lord Sandon to act with you and Mr. Shaw.

If you can get Gladstone and the earnest retrenchers and reformers of the Government to keep to Otway's promise to you of a Committee, and if Lord Sandon would bring the Tories to your aid, you would, I

* Member for Burnley.

should hope, easily beat Bulwer, whom Lord Clarendon and Otway will certainly wish to aid.

I shall myself be very much disappointed if Bulwer gets the Government to parry your attack by appointing a Commission, Bulwer has got hold of the *Pall Mall Gazette*, and I have a suspicion that that article about your motion came from him. The *Star* is all right on your side, and will, I hope, when the time comes, help effectually against Bulwer's motion.

You will see in Bulwer's letter in one of the *Pall Mall Gazettes*, in reply to a very unjustifiable allusion to him by Lord Russell, that he mentions that he asked for a peerage. He (Bulwer) has for a long time been at daggers drawn with the Foreign Office; and there is a fact against him of having sold an island, which he had bought cheap, dear to the Sultan, when he was ambassador at Constantinople. He ought not, of course, to have had pecuniary dealings with the Sultan.

Yours very truly.

W. D. CHRISTIE.

No. XVII.

SIR HENRY LYTTON BULWER.

53, Upper Brook Street,
11th August, 1869.

My dear Sir,—

You will see a motion of mine as to a Royal Commission. But I will concert with you on the matter before anything comes off, and do nothing that can clash with a proper enquiry into the subject concerned, nor with the credit you deserve for the attention you have paid to it.

Very truly yours,
H. L. Bulwer.

No. XVIII.

Mr. CHARLES WELLS.

(Author of " Mehemet the Kurd," etc.)

11, Southampton Street, Strand,
August 10th, 1869.

Dear Sir,—

Permit me to thank you for your courteous reply of the 5th inst. It is a great satisfaction to find that a man of ability and courage has, at last, determined to probe the sores in our diplomatic and consular system. I take the liberty of enclosing a letter on this subject in the *Morning Post*, which explains facts which possibly you may not know, and which, certainly, would appear incredible to the ordinary public, but which are, nevertheless, indisputable. The Government has, moreover, never attempted to deny what I said. Many Turks I have met in London, who have held high position in the Government, have often lamented to me the vast injury done to England and Turkey by the interpreters, and expressed their surprise at the English Government not giving any encouragement or reward to those who devoted themselves to the study of Oriental languages. At present, they tell me, the interpreters are the real Ambassadors and Consuls, and not being either Englishmen or Turks, they have naturally neither the interest of England or Turkey at heart. The character of those men is, moreover, notorious in the East.

It would appear, however, that the English Government is not desirous of remedying this evil, judging from my experience. On my completing my study of Oriental languages at King's College, London, and receiving a Special Prize for " Proficiency in Turkish," the Principal wrote to the Foreign Office, recommending me, but in vain. Subsequently I myself applied to Earl Russell and others in similar positions, but to no purpose ; and quite lately the Earl of Denbigh kindly offered to speak to the Earl of Clarendon about me. He submitted to him testimonials as to my proficiency in Turkish, Arabic and other languages, from the Turkish Ambassador, the Turkish Consul General, and others, " the advisability of employing a man with my qualifications in the East." Lord Clarendon's reply, strangely enough, I think, makes the recent Debate in the House of Commons the plea for not acceding, stating that, owing to the consequent reduction of consulates, "there will at present be but little prospect " of his meeting Lord Denbigh's views in my favour. I have written to Lord Denbigh saying that Lord Clarendon appears to forget that your arguments were directed against the dragoman system, and that you urged the advantage of obtaining economy, and superior efficiency by employing English officials knowing Turkish instead of gentlemen who require interpreters with exorbitant salaries. I believe I took a correct view of the objects of your speech, and that it was a strange distortion to make the reduction of consulates consequent on it a plea for not accepting the services of a man who could have dispensed with interpreters.

With apologies for troubling you, I have the honour to remain,

Yours faithfully,

CHARLES WELLS.

No. XIX.

Mr. ROBERT RISLEY.

Aug. 12, 1869.

Dear Sir,—

I was gratified by your note. 'Tis true I am the next in rotation for the Mayoralty, but the Lawrences are moving heaven and earth for a second go in for the present Lord Mayor. Nothing can be in worse taste than this, for William Lawrence holds his seat for London by a very slight thread, and for the *family* to make opponents of the junior aldermen below the chair, seems a want of that cunning they have always had a reputation for. Besides, I fought hard for William's seat in the late contest, and this is my reward.

Whether Lord Mayor or not, I shall be glad to see you.

I remain,

Yours sincerely,
Rob. Risley.

No. XX.

Rt. Hon. JOHN BRIGHT, M.P.

Rochdale,
August 28, 1869.

My Dear Sir,—

I think you may get all you want from Mr. Moran, Secretary of Legation of the United States in London, if you can call upon him some day when you are in town.   I do not wish just now to trouble Mr. Sumner with letters not absolutely necessary to be written.

I can explain this more fully when I see you.

If you write to Mr. Moran you may say that I recommended you to write to him.   His address is

Benjamin Moran, Esq.,

U.S. Legation,

London.

I suppose you will have a terrible attack ready for us in February.

Yours sincerely,

John Bright.

No. XXI.

Mr. J. H. RAPER.

Parliamentary Agent of the United Kingdom
Alliance.

41, John Dalton St.,
Manchester,
Sept. 15, 1869.

DEAR SIR,—

Our Executive Council have a great desire to have
your presence at their annual meeting in the Free
Trade Hall, on the 19th October. You will have a
glowing welcome, and you know the Hall well. As
there will be a goodly band of all shades, you will not
have a great responsibility resting upon your mind
for speaking purposes, and all information necessary
will be forthcoming. Say "Yes," if you can, to the
invitation duly sent by our secretary some days ago.

Apologising for being a party to press a good and
willing horse,

I remain,
Yours very respectfully,
J. H. RAPER.

No. XXII.

Mr. WILLIAM STOKES.

> 71, Robert Street,
> Manchester,
> October 1, 1869.

My Dear Sir,—

I have not succeeded as I had hoped to do. The *greater* wars, cost, etc., are on the enclosed paper, but the smaller ones, such as Persia, China, Burmah, etc.. etc., I cannot specify.

The forces of Europe are from 5,500,000 to 6,000,000 of armed men ; and, as nearly as I can calculate, their cost to the European States (including Great Britain) will be :—

Actual cost per annum	£130,000,000
Loss of labour, etc. ,, ...	120,000,000
Total	£250,000,000

> Yours very truly,
> WILLIAM STOKES.

———

(PAPER ENCLOSED IN THE ABOVE LETTER.)

Total cost of French War for 22 years, from 1793 to close of 1815 (the Peace of Amiens, of course, omitted)..................	£1,210.047,986
Average annual cost of ditto for 22 years	£55,002,181
The Crimean War lasted from 2 to 3 years.	
Total cost of war, about	£110,000,000
Average annual cost.............	£38,011,972
The Abyssinian War lasted 8 months.	
Total cost	£8,773,000

No. XXIII.

Mr. RICHARD SHAW, M.P.

Holm Lodge,
Oct. 6, 1869.

My Dear Sir,—

I was very sorry to miss saying " Good night " to you and Mrs. Rylands on Monday evening. I thought you were following me into the cloak-room. The crowd was so great I could not get back.

I have just been reading your speech last night in Manchester ; it is very good.

I think reciprocity* is once more done for. I have just been talking with a rank Tory, who denounces the whole thing as a piece of d——d rot ; and Lord Stanley gave them their quietus at Liverpool.

I want you to come to me on Monday, and remain over Tuesday. I am entertaining some of my political friends on those evenings, and I should like to introduce you to them. We dine at 7 both evenings.

With kind regards,

Yours very truly,

Rich. Shaw.

* One of the many aliases of Protection.

No. XXIV.

Mr. EDWARD MATHEWS.

(Central Association for Stopping the Sale of
Intoxicating Liquors on Sunday.)
43, Market Street, Manchester,
October 12th, 1869.

Dear Sir,—

We are looking forward to the pleasure of hearing
you and other members of Parliament at the Free
Trade Hall, at our Public Meeting on the 2nd of
November. If the Premier would receive a deputation on the subject in November it would be of great
value, as the Government is preparing its measure.
By the desire of an influential member of our Committee I write to ask if you would kindly communicate
with the Premier, and ascertain if he would consent
to receive a deputation in November, at such part of
the month as would best suit his convenience. We
should be glad to have a good notice, so as to secure
a very influential deputation. By the enclosed you
will see that some religious Bodies have already
appointed deputations to accompany ours.

Awaiting your reply,
Yours obediently,
Edward Mathews.

No. XXV.

Mr. EDWARD MATHEWS.

43, Market Street,
                    October 23rd, 1869.

Dear Sir,—

Your note was read to our committee yesterday; it was felt to be all-important that the deputation to the Premier should be very influential, even if it involved a delay till Parliament meets. If by an earlier deputation we can secure a recognition of the Sunday Closing Question in the Queen's Speech it would be of great value. I beg to send you the resolutions which will be proposed. Sir Thos. Bazley will not be with us till the middle of the proceedings, hence we have arranged for him to speak to the 3rd resolution.

Can you kindly be with us at the preliminary meeting at the Trevelyan ?

Yours very truly,
Edward Mathews.

No. XXVI.

Miss BECKER.

Manchester National Society for Women's Suffrage.

28, Jackson's Row,
Albert Sq.,
Oct. 18, 1869.

Dear Sir,—

I am desired by the Executive Committee to invite you to take part in the annual general meeting of members and friends of the above society, to be held in the Mayor's Parlour, Town Hall, Manchester, towards the end of November. The precise time is not yet fixed, but if, as I hope, you will be willing to attend the meeting, I will take care to inform you directly the arrangements are completed.

I desire to express our earnest thanks for the support you gave to Mr. Jacob Bright on the Municipal Franchise Bill, and the hope that the same may be continued in behalf of the Bill which he has pledged himself to introduce for removing the electoral disabilities of women as to the Parliamentary Franchise. The urgent need of this measure is exemplified in the fate of the Married Women's Property Bill. One year's delay in passing this measure involves the confiscation of sums which, at the lowest computation, must be set down at twenty million pounds sterling. This one year of the Married Women's Property Bill deals with much larger pecuniary interests than the whole question in perpetuity of the Irish Church Bill.

It must be obvious to every one that interests so great in extent would not have received such careless and indifferent treatment at the hands of the Legislature had they concerned a class which had a right to representation in Parliament.

Believe me to be,

Yours very truly,

Lydia E. Becker,

Secretary.

———

No. XXVII.

Mr. EDWARD MATHEWS.

Central Association

for

Stopping the Sale of Intoxicating Liquors on Sunday.

82, Norfolk St.,

Sheffield,

Nov. 13.

Dear Sir,—

We are to have a demonstration here on the 29th in favour of your Bill. If you can be with us kindly apprise me by return post.

We will have one in Warrington. When can you attend? Kindly fix the day. I will come and work up the meeting. I am working the press. See enclosed.

Yours very truly,
E. MATHEWS.

No. XXVIII.

MR. J. H. RAPER.

United Kingdom Alliance,
41, John Dalton St.,
Manchester,
Nov. 18, 1869.

DEAR MR. RYLANDS,—

I wrote you last week asking the favour of completing your half promise if Sir Wilfrid Lawson came to Liverpool you would stand by him. We have been compelled to go to press for Monday, the 29th, with the announcements, and have ventured to announce you. I hope you will be at liberty to attend. It will not impose much responsibility, as we have one of the most able of America's sons (Samuel F. Cary, ex-member of Congress), to aid us on that night. He is a noble freetrader into the bargain. You will not regret hearing him.

Yours very respectfully,
J. H. RAPER.

No. XXIX.

Sir WILFRID LAWSON, M.P., Bart.

Hutton Hall,

Nov. 19, 1869.

Dear Mr. Rylands,—

Many thanks for your kind invitation to Warrington. I am sorry to say that I cannot accept of it, as I have an engagement on Thursday afternoon at home, which I could not meet were I to be at Warrington on Wednesday evening. I should have really liked not only paying you a visit, but also seeing the wonderful town which, with a "public" in every street, yet returns an M.P. who votes for the Permissive Bill!

I hope that I shall see you on the platform at Liverpool, and hear you make as good a speech as you did at Manchester. You call yourself a weak brother, but nobody else will call you so.

I am pleased that you did me the honour of reading the Carlisle speech. I hadn't time to give your Diplomatic motion a word of praise, as it took me all the time to sort those Bishops and Peers. Let us form a solemn league and covenant to abolish all Bishops and Lords, and have this country governed solely by Baronets and radical M.P.'s!!

Hoping to see you at Liverpool,

I am,

Yours truly,

Wilfrid Lawson.

No. XXX.

Mr. A. H. BROWN, M.P. (Wenlock).

Richmond Hill,
Liverpool,
Nov. 19, 1869.

Dear Mr. Rylands,—

I am very glad to hear you addressed the Madeley people during your visit there; it will do a deal of good; and I am much obliged to you for the kind manner in which you mention me. I hope, when we meet in London, I may have the pleasure of thanking you personally.

The memorial of the Town Council of Wenlock, requesting the appointment of Messrs. Antus and Davis, was referred to me. I informed the Lord Chancellor of the politics of those gentlemen and their position, and also said that it was thought no more Conservatives should be appointed to the office of J.P., as they already predominated in the proportion of 8 to 1. Further, I sent up the names of Mr. G. Norris and Mr. G. Man for the appointments. These gentlemen will be, I understand from a letter received to-day from the Lord Chancellor's Office, made magistrates; but the only point in the mind of the Secretary to Lord Hatherley is whether the other two should be made also. I have written back to them, repeating the reasons I stated before. I think the matter is in good train now, and I do not see any reason to apply to Glynn. The two names you submit are most eligible for appointment, and, if there is any chance, I will try what I can do.

Believe me,
Yours truly,
A. H. Brown.

No. XXXI.

Mr. RICHARD SHAW, M.P.

Holme Lodge,
Burnley,
Nov. 23, 1869.

Dear Sir,—

We are going to celebrate the return of our friend Shuttleworth, for Hastings, by a public meeting on Saturday evening next, and I want you to come and join us. Sir James and Ughtred are most anxious that you should; and I promised them that I would write and ask you to come and stop with me. Sir James wishes us to dine with him on Saturday, and go from thence to the meeting. *I will have no excuse*, and if you can stop over Sunday so much the better.

Yours very truly,
Rich. Shaw.

You will be expected to say a few words.

No. XXXII.

Mr. ROBERT RAWLINSON.

8, Richmond Terrace,
Whitehall,
London, S.W.,
Nov. 3, 1869.

Dear Sir,—

I have just seen a report of a speech, made by you in Warrington, in the *Examiner* of 26th ult. You directly accuse me of writing an " unjustifiable " report on the Warrington smoke nuisance, and you say that you will so represent to the Government. You will be, of course, at liberty to do so ; and if I should be called upon to defend my report, I hope to justify every sentence in it, and to very materially increase the strength of any remarks as to the nuisance unnecessarily caused in Warrington by smoke. Your remarks as to my visit to Mr. Beamont, an old friend, I cannot consent to notice further than to say you have evidently a very bad opinion of poor human nature. I shall not shrink, however, from justifying that portion of my conduct also. Pray, for your own sake, dismiss prejudice as much as possible, and allow me to say that it ever has been, and is, my earnest endeavour to do my duty, publicly and privately, as becomes an honest man ; subject, of course, to the infirmities of poor human nature. My report, I say, is a tame abstract of the evidence as given in public, and as published in the local papers.

Mr. Beamont in no degree influenced me; and, as a
man of recognised honour among honest men, he
never attempted to do so.

> I have the honour to be,
>
> Your most obedient servant,
>
> ROBERT RAWLINSON.

No. XXXIII.

Mr. ROBERT RAWLINSON.

> 8, Richmond Terrace,
> Whitehall,
> London, S.W.,
> 26th Nov., 1866.

DEAR SIR,—

I duly received your letter of the 22nd inst. I think
you have both spoken of me and have written to me
under wrong impressions. I was, until I read your
letter, profoundly ignorant of party politics in Warrington. The memorial to the Home Office asking
for enquiry, contained (I think) above one thousand
signatures. I made enquiry honestly, to the best of
my ability, and if I exhibited partiality it was uncon-
sciously. My dining with Mr. Beamont was as an old
friend of more than twenty years' standing, but, until

you informed me, I never knew his politics. (I think you and I are on the same side, if this can have anything to do with the question.) Of Mr. Davies I knew absolutely nothing but through the enquiry.

The Home Secretary has not been partially informed by me, as, appended to my report, were verbatim copies of the evidence as printed in the Warrington Newspapers, and even the Editorial comments.

You say I failed in my duty at Warrington. I, of course, cannot be the judge. I think that you have publicly attacked me wrongfully ; but, if you press your accusations at the Home Office, and I should be called upon to defend myself, I will do so to the best of my ability.

In the public servant I have never sunk the private friend, but private friendship will not bend me from the course of truth and duty.

The Sanitary Act, 1866, has been passed by Parliament, and is in force. A duty has been imposed upon the Home Secretary; and if I, as an instrument under the Act, at his orders, have a very disagreeable duty to perform in conducting smoke nuisance enquiries, I shall do the best I can, utterly regardless of such censure as yours or the contingent consequences.

I have the honour to be, dear Sir,
Yours obediently,
ROBERT RAWLINSON.

No. XXXIV.

Miss BECKER.

Manchester National Society for Women's Suffrage,
28, Jackson's Row,
Albert Sq.,
Dec. 9, 1869.

My Dear Sir,—

Enclosed is copy of the Resolution which we ask you to move at our meeting, also of the Bill we propose to recommend for adoption. We count ourselves very fortunate in receiving your support to our cause, for principles, however just, need to be clearly and ably set forth if they are to make way.

Believe me to be,
Yours sincerely,
Lydia E. Becker.

No. XXXV.

Mr. C. E. MACQUEEN.

Financial Reform Association,
13, Eldon Chambers,
20, South John St.,
Liverpool,
Nov. 26, 1869.

My Dear Sir,—

Mr. Michael Daly, a thorough Custom House reformer—to the extent of reforming it off the face of the earth altogether—is particularly anxious to see you on the subject ; and he thinks, rightly or wrongly, that a word or two from me might improve his chances of an interview.

He has been connected with the Custom House between 20 and 30 years, has had a great deal to do with such reforms as have been effected, and was the right-hand man of Mr. F. B. Horsfall in his attempts to obtain a consolidation of the Customs and Excise Departments. He was lately transferred to the Board of Trade, but was sent back to the Customs because, to the horror and amazement of some of the *subs*, he not only rooted into abuses involving shameful and utterly useless waste of the public money, touching statistical returns relating to Trade, but was resolutely bent on exposing and doing away with them.

I have read two reports of his, which some of the *honest* officials, including Sir L. Mallet, were for having printed by order of the House of Commons; but others seem, and no wonder, to have considered them too damaging for official publication.

The revelations are absolutely astounding ; and Mr. Daly got his *congé* from the Board for presuming to make them, headed though the Board be by so thorough a reformer as John Bright was in his un-official days. *Entre nous* Mr. Daly had an interview with Mr. Bright, who then called the Custom House " an Augean stable," but who has since permitted his subordinates to burke the attempt made to cleanse it.

The task is one to make name and fame for any M.P., even if he were previously unknown ; and I know of none more likely than yourself to undertake it. So I told Mr. Daly, who expects to be in Lanca-shire about ten days hence, and will do himself the honour of calling upon you — *i.e.*, with your permission.

Yours truly,

C. E. MACQUEEN.

No. XXXVI.

Mr. MICHAEL DALY.

11, South Crescent,
Bedford Sq., W.C.,
Dec. 16, 1869.

My Dear Sir,—

I have sent you the reports containing the evidence, etc., brought out by the select committee 1862/3, on the proposed consolidation and reform of the Revenue Departments.

I have also sent you a return, ordered by the House in 1861, of the number of people employed, cost, etc., which may be of interest. There has been no such return made since.

Enclosed is an article from *The Produce Markets Review* of last Saturday, touching the part of the question which we were discussing at your house the same day—the heavy indirect tax which the present system imposes on the public.

There can be no doubt that public opinion is now ripe for this matter ; and I feel assured that you will have little or no difficulty in disposing of it. The time has come for a settlement of the question, so that in the next move made towards that object the final blow, if well directed, will be given to the present very discreditable system.

Believe me,
My dear Sir,
Very faithfully yours,
M. DALY.

P.S.—I have just had to-day's *Daily News* sent me, and forward it by this post. I have marked something relative to this question, which you will see.

———————

No. XXXVII.

Mr. MICHAEL DALY.

11, South Crescent,
Bedford Square,
W.C.,
Dec. 17, 1869.

My Dear Sir,—

I forgot to tell you, in my note of yesterday, that the vacancy at the Board of Customs has been filled up by the appointment of Sir F. Doyle, Bart., who was, as you are aware, the Receiver General of Customs.

It is said (I do not know with what truth) that Sir F. Doyle's place is not to be filled up ; but the same thing was said as to the vacancy at the Board.

I proposed the abolition of the Receiver General's departments in both the Customs and Inland Revenue, as you may see by my evidence : in neither case are they of more use than the fifth wheel of a coach.

But this, after all, is only a mere detail of the whole scheme of Reform, which should be dealt with broadly and comprehensively.

Mr. H. Caulier, whose letter appears in the *Daily News*, is one of those men who defend the present system vigorously, and by whose advice the Board have been induced to add largely to the public expenditure, under the guise of improvement. I know of no branch which calls more for a thorough reform than Caulier's.

Very faithfully yours,
M. DALY.

No. XXXVIII.

Mr. MICHAEL DALY.

11, South Crescent,
Bedford Square,
W.C.,
Dec. 25, 1869.

My Dear Sir,—

I had some conversation with Sir Louis Mallet on the day before yesterday, respecting your diplomatic movement. I told him that as from his great experience in connection with the Foreign Office and the Board of Trade, both at home and at Foreign Courts, great value would attach to his evidence, my impression was that you would be glad of his aid in the event of a select committee being appointed. He wished me to tell you that, if you will call on him when you get to town, he will be very happy to see you, and talk the matter over, as he will be glad to render what assistance he can.

I told him you thought of having an introduction to him through Mr. Bright, but he wished me to say that there is no necessity of that. He will be just as well pleased if you will go direct and introduce yourself.

I think you may rely on him as a thorough and an honest reformer; but, of course, in his position he can only express an opinion and offer advice, not at all times a grateful task. But it is one of the great scandals of the public service of this country, that those very men who are most willing, and at the same time most able, to reform that service, are never afforded the opportunity, or permitted to attain the position which would enable them to do so.

Very faithfully yours,

M. DALY.

No. XXXIX.

Sir SYDNEY WATERLOWE.

Carpenters' Hall,
68, London Wall,
Jan. 11, 1870.

My Dear Sir,—

Southwark Election.

The friends of the Liberal Party are of opinion that Sir Francis Lycett and I ought to refer our relative claims upon the Electors to the Arbitration of five Liberal Members of Parliament, two to be named by each Candidate, and an umpire chosen by the four. If we agree upon the conditions of reference, which we shall probably do to-morrow, I should feel very much obliged if you would act as one of the Arbitrators on my side. Could you meet the others on Thursday or Friday? Please telegraph " Yes." I shall understand what you mean.

Yours faithfully,
SYDNEY H. WATERLOWE.

———

[Sir F. Lycett retired in favour of Sir Sydney Waterlowe, but the party was no better off, as another Liberal candidate, Mr. G. Ogden, came into the field, splitting the party, and allowing the Conservative, Lt.-Col. M. Beresford, to be elected. The same insane course was taken in 1874, three Liberals standing for the two seats

against one Conservative, with the same result.
Thus in Southwark a seat was presented by
the Liberal Party to the Conservatives for 10
years, from 1870 to 1880.]

--- ----

No. XL.

Mr. W. D. CHRISTIE.

32, Dorset Square,
Dec. 29, 1869.

My Dear Sir,—

You will see what has happened about the re-
appointment of Messrs. Fenwick and Schneider to
the Magistracy, and the subsequent cancelling of their
new commissions, Lord Dufferin, it is said, not having
been aware of the circumstances under which they
were removed by Lord Devon from the commission
of the peace. Now, my opinion is, that Messrs.
Schneider and Fenwick have great reason to complain that they are singled out for punishment.
Disraeli allowed all the others similarly reported at
the same time guilty of bribery to escape, and he even
gave Sir Edmond Lacon and Mr. Goodson, two of his
supporters, general praise.

My object in writing to you about this is to tell you
that Mr. Monson (Lord Monson's brother), appointed

during the last twelve months Consul at Foyat (a very pleasant Consulate), was reported by the Reigate Commission guilty of bribery. He had been a candidate there, and he was scheduled by the Commission as a briber. Reigate was disfranchised. The Revising Barrister this year has struck off the list of county voters all who were scheduled for bribery at Reigate. Mr. Monson, the candidate, and a source of corrupt practices, is rewarded with one of the First Consulates which Lord Clarendon has had to give away. It will be said, doubtless, that *he* did not know the circumstances. They must have been known in the office.

This may interest you *apropos* of Foreign Office management.

Hoping that you persevere in your intention of moving early for a Committee to inquire into the management of the Diplomatic and Consular Service, with a view to economy and efficiency, I propose now, if it is agreeable to you, to send you between this and the meeting of Parliament, observations on different points of management which, if you do not turn them otherwise to account, will give you a notion of what I should say as a witness in answer to questions.

I hear that the Foreign Office is busy at economies. You will have seen that they reduced Venezuela. Up to the time of your motion they had been systematically increasing and *improving* those appointments; and in the Diplomatic Services Act of last session (which passed unnoticed) they increased the pensions of the Chargé d'Affaireships, such as Venezuela, from £700 to £900.

Believe me, yours very truly,
W. D. CHRISTIE.

No. XLI.

MR. EDWIN BARTON.

Central Association
for
Stopping the Sale of Intoxicating Liquors on Sunday.

43, Market St.,
Manchester,
Jany. 13.

DEAR SIR,—

I send you a note just received from our Welsh Agent (Mr. Jones), containing abstract from a letter received from G. O. Morgan, Esq., M.P. for Denbighshire. It seems our friends in Wales are anxious to have upon the back of your Bill the name of a Welsh Member, and they prefer Mr. Morgan, and have pressed him. I may say that our Committee fully agree if it meets with your approval, and, if so, perhaps you will kindly write Mr. Morgan.

Yours respectfully,
EDWIN BARTON.

No. XLII.

Mr. G. OSBORNE MORGAN, M.P.

> 20, Bolton Street,
> Jany. 27, 1870.

My Dear Sir,—

I am obliged to you for your note of the 25th.

In default of your finding any better or weightier name (which I should think would not be difficult), I shall be glad to have my name on the back of your Sunday Closing Bill.

> Yours truly,
> G. Osborne Morgan.

No. XLIII.

Miss BECKER.

Manchester National Society for
Women's Suffrage.

> 28, Jackson's Row,
> Albert Sq.,
> Feb. 8, 1870.

My Dear Mr. Rylands,—

Thank you very much for your kindness in sending me the Warrington paper, and for the support you gave to the good cause. We begin the session with good prospects, and we outsiders will do all that lies in us to support our Parliamentary champions, who are working so generously in our behalf.

We are having a public meeting this evening at Crewe in support of the Bill.

With kind regards to Mrs. Rylands and yourself,

I am, yours truly,

LYDIA E. BECKER.

No. XLIV.

MR. W. D. CHRISTIE.

32, Dorset Square,

Jan. 27, 1870.

MY DEAR SIR,—

I send you by book-post two parliamentary papers of the last session of last Parliament, relating to Foreign Office, and a privately-circulated pamphlet of mine of 1863 relating to my Brazilian Mission.

You will find in the last some matters bearing on " management " of the service : for example, Lord Malmesbury's strange proceedings as to filling up the Naples mission ; and something about secretaries and attachés towards the end.

I am wishing and hoping, of course, that my case may be brought out as an illustration of the patronage and aristocratic nature of the system. I am the youngest of the Diplomatic pensioners, put on a pension against my will when I was 47, and under circumstances of great injustice. Lord Russell, in fact, wanted to quiet the clamour about the reprisals he ordered, and so gave out at once that I was not to go back to Brazil. I was just ripe for a pension, so he made use of the pension for the purpose, and saddled the public with £900 a year. But I will give you a brief resumé of my case before your motion comes on.

I also enclose a pamphlet published last year by a young attaché, who argues in his own interest, and states the discontent of all the young ones who want promotion. He is, of course, for a close service, will be angry at Layard's* appointment, and would growl also if I or any other pensioner were re-employed. I object altogether to this close service system ; but it is as well always to know what is said on the other side, and this pamphlet is very absurd and open to ridicule in parts.

It would be well on the meeting of Parliament to get from the government the continuation of correspondence with the Foreign Office about the agency system. That system is a very important bad feature

---

* Layard had previously been retired on a pension. His re-entry. therefore, into active service, and appointment to an important mission to Madrid would, of course, have the effect of checking promotion in the lower ranks of the Diplomatic service.

of Foreign Office " management." Bulwer is, I believe, much opposed to it.

Believe me,

Yours very truly,

W. D. CHRISTIE.

No. XLV.

MR. W. D. CHRISTIE.

32, Dorset Square,

Jan. 31, 1870.

MY DEAR SIR,—

I am obliged and gratified by your letter. I have no interest now in defending Lord Russell, who sacrificed me in the most deliberate and meanest manner; but he was right in his dealing with the Brazilian Government through me. That, however, it does not concern me now to press. He deliberately sacrificed me, and has inflicted on me immense injury.

I may tell you that I was on very friendly terms with Cobden to the last, and that he expressed to me his regret at having given so much heed to Mr. Bramley Moore. I saw Bright on my return from Brazil, and he blamed me for having made no endeavour, before I called on the Admiral to make reprisals, to make the Brazilian Government privately informed of my instructions. This was the *gravamen*, as he called it, of Lord Malmesbury's charge. Now, the fact is, that I did make such an endeavour privately, but my mouth was closed. I endeavoured with the French minister, but what passed between me and him was confidential. Lord Russell knew of it, of course. He made no defence of me against Lord Malmesbury's specific charge. I was even forbidden by the Foreign Office to allude to that endeavour in the pamphlet you have read, and a sentence so alluding, which I had printed, was struck out. I told Bright in 1868 how it was.

Yours very truly,
W. D. CHRISTIE.

No. XLVI.

SIR HENRY L. BULWER.

Hotel du Parc,
Hyères,
Feb. 6, 1870.

MY DEAR SIR,—

I had a motion for a Royal Commission, you for one in favour of a Committee with reference to the Diplomatic service.

Had the question merely related to expense, yours would, I think, have been the most appropriate, but

H

as the whole system to be adopted with reference to
an important branch of the public service with which
members of the House of Commons are not, as a
general rule, practically acquainted, has more or less
to be decided, I am of opinion that my proposition
was most suitable to the case.

The Government, however, is, I hear, more disposed
to agree to a Committee than to a Commission.   I
merely write, therefore, to say I shall cordially concur
(though, you know, I don't hope very much from Committees) with you on the course you propose taking,
and, if I happen to be on the Committee, give you my
best assistance.

I confess that I think a proper diplomacy can do so
much good, and prevent so much mischief, that I do
not grudge it any beneficial expenditure, but my present opinion is that this service might be made more
useful and less costly, and hence my reason for
thinking that the subject well deserves enquiry.

I am, Dear Sir,
Yours very truly,
H. L. Bulwer.

No. XLVII.

Mr. W. D. CHRISTIE.

32, Dorset Square,
Feb. 9, 1870.

My Dear Sir,—

I send you by book post some general remarks on the Diplomatic and Consular Services and Foreign Office.

I see that Otway has taken the initiative. I hope you are satisfied with him. But I hope you will not allow him to prevent you from making a statement before the Committee is agreed to.

I may caution you that Otway is very intimate and in frequent consultation on this subject with Sir H. Drummond Wolff, a former clerk in Foreign Office, who is a very keen Tory and a notorious follower and worshipper of Lord Malmesbury. It is as well you should know this. I hear that Otway is very much opposed to Hammond in the Foreign Office. I do not like the words of his motion ; the construction, indeed, is ungrammatical. I hope you will be able to get words inserted so as to secure inquiry into the management as well as the constitution of the services.

Yours very truly,
W. D. Christie.

No. XLVIII.

Mr. W. D. CHRISTIE.

32, Dorset Square,
Feb. 13, 1870.

My Dear Sir,—

Mrs. Christie informed me as we came home that news had come to Mrs. Rylands of your having a domestic loss, on which I beg suitably to condole with you, and which is likely to embarrass you in your dealings with Mr. Otway.

I am so strongly persuaded that there is mischief in Otway's movements that I write to express my strong hope that you will be able to insist on his postponing the motion till you can attend the House. It is due to you. His being in a hurry for the estimates is probably humbug. Though Otway is, as I believe, opposed to much of the Foreign Office management, Hammond is more powerful than he in the Office, and with Lord Clarendon ; and I distrust Otway's friends and associates very much. It is not only Wolff; Borthwick, the editor of the *Morning Post* and *Owl*, is a friend of his, and the pamphlet I sent you has been much puffed in the *Owl*, and it probably represents Wolff's and Otway's views of Diplomatic Service Reform.

Bouverie has gone out of town, leaving word that he will probably not be back till next week. I have no doubt whatever as to the superiority of Bouverie for chairman over Brand, who knows nothing at all about the Diplomatic Services, and has been whipper-in under Lord Russell—a very bad training.

I have heard to-day something which makes me think that the Government wish for Brand, and not Bouverie. Pray have Bouverie if you can decide it. There is no one else of the same rank and position.

I heard also that Arthur Russell and Cartwright, the member for Oxfordshire, and son of Sir Thomas Cartwright, a former diplomatic Minister, were likely to be named on the Committee by the Government. One of these two, who are great friends, would be enough; and get rid if you can of Arthur Russell, who is Lord Russell's nephew, but himself a good man. Cartwright is, I believe, a very able man. He is a new member.

I cannot say how much I hope you will make Otway wait for you, and that you will make a debate on the appointment of the Committee. Bouverie's being out of town may be another reason for waiting. I hope to get him to say something in a debate.

As to witnesses, I hope you will make Otway understand that you mean to call witnesses from among the Diplomatic servants who are in this country on Pension, and name Sir Henry Bulwer and myself. You will also do well—indeed, it is very important—to ascertain, when the Committee is appointed, who are the diplomatists and consuls at present at home on leave of absence, or expected home shortly on leave. The Foreign Office can, of course, furnish a list. They are quite likely to bring home men suited for their purpose, and send back to their posts others whose evidence they would not like.

Believe me,
Yours very truly,
W. D. CHRISTIE.

— — — —

No. XLIX.

Mr. RICHARD SHAW, M.P.

Reform Club,
Feb. 19, 1870.

My Dear Sir,—

I fear you will not get Whitwell on the Committee. Glyn showed me the list last night. Lefevre, Cartwright, and Campbell are on, and, if Whitwell is to be on, it must be in lieu of Campbell. On the other side there are Sclater-Booth, Lord Stanley, Lord Sandon, not Graves. I asked Glyn not to nominate until after he had seen you, and he agreed.

Holmes spoke well, but did not carry the House with him.

We go to No. 13 to-day, and I shall be glad to see you to-morrow, and Mrs. Shaw will enjoy a chat with Mrs. Rylands.

Yours very truly,
RICHARD SHAW.

L.

Mr. W. D. CHRISTIE.

32, Dorset Square,
Feb. 20, 1870.

My Dear Sir,—

I cannot tell you how much I wish that you could get Grant Duff substituted for George Lefevre. He would be very much better than Gladstone, Junr., if you could get him. I am not in a condition to say that Grant Duff will act, for his work at the India House may prevent it. But I am sure that he would wish very much to be on the Committee if it were possible, and would be disposed to make some sacrifice in order to sit on it. He was the originator of the enquiry which took place in 1861, but it was then taken out of his hands, very much as it has now been taken out of yours. And Grant Duff's aspirations have been much more for the Foreign Office than the India Office, where he is placed.

The Government would, I should think, be glad to have him rather than Lefevre.

Yours very truly,
W. D. Christie.

LI.

Mr. W. D. CHRISTIE.

32, Dorset Square,
Feb. 23, 1870.

My Dear Sir,—

The Foreign Office deserves a whipping for the return they have made to Mr. Shaw's motion. I enclose a memo. on the subject.

You will see in the list Mr. L., Consul at B., receiving for himself fees amounting to more than £1,600 a year. This appointment of Mr. L. has been always a scandal. He was a man living in foreign capitals— Paris chiefly—by the prostitution of his wife, a very pretty woman, who fascinated many great people. Lord Clarendon appointed Mr. L. to this lucrative consulship without any consular antecedents or known fitness. It has always been supposed that Mrs. L. had claims upon Lord Clarendon. The Queen's Messenger last year used to bring up L.'s appointment constantly against Lord Clarendon.

If he goes before the Committee he might be judiciously and rather closely questioned on what proofs there are of Mr. L.'s fitness, why he was selected, who recommended him, etc.

Yours very truly,
W. D. Christie.

No. LII.

Mr. MICHAEL DALY.

11, South Crescent,
Bedford Square,
W. C.,
Feb. 19, 1870.

My Dear Sir,—

I went down to the House of Commons, where I had an appointment with Mr. Macfie, yesterday evening, and I entertained the hope of having the pleasure of meeting you there, but I was not fortunate enough to fall in with you.

Mr. Macfie has been called upon by the Edinburgh Chamber of Commerce to present a memorial to the Treasury praying for a reform of the present system in the Customs, and he has been anxious to discuss the matter with me. I promised to call upon him at 10 a.m. on Monday next, and talk the thing over. But I should like to have some conversation with yourself on the broad question of Consolidation and Reform, and which must necessarily embrace all those details at which so many people, official and non-official, are now nibbling or driving. If I thought I should be likely to find you at home on Monday at 12 o'clock, and it would not be inconvenient to you, I would take the liberty of calling on you.

I should have thanked you before for the paper containing your speech, every word of which I read with great interest. It was excellent, one of the best practical addresses made to any constituency during the whole recess.

Very faithfully yours,

M. DALY.

No. LIII.

MR. SAMUEL PLIMSOLL, M.P.

Agar Town Coal Depot,

London, N.W.,

Feb. 21, 1870.

MY DEAR SIR,—

Mr. Shaw and I thought you would like, or, at least, have no objection, to have your name on the back of my Bill, and therefore ventured to put it on. As I cannot be at the House to-day, I thought it better to write, so that if you object, I may remove it before the bill is printed.

I am,

My dear sir,

Yours very truly,

SAMUEL PLIMSOLL.

No. LIV.

REV. G. S. REANEY.

Warrington,
March 3, 1870.

DEAR MR. RYLANDS,—

We are very indignant with Forster; he looks to me something like a humbug. The Bill, as it is, will not meet with our approval (Nonconformist). If the Government will force it through by the help of the Tory party, we can only bide our time, and when the next fight comes leave Gladstone to our Tory friends. I think the measure is a compromise all on one side. I am utterly surprised that the Cabinet ever imagined that the Nonconformist party would accept such a pro-Church measure. If this is the Liberalism of the men for whom the Dissenters fought tooth and nail, I think we made a terrible blunder. I don't hesitate to say, from the information I have, that the passing of this Bill in anything like the form it now has, will end in the break-up of the Liberal party and the return of Dizzy with Derby to power. Anyhow, the effect produced upon us by the conduct of Forster is that we shall never trust him or the Premier again with full confidence. Oh, that Bright were well! I understand all that Bright said both in public and private about Forster and his Bill. I hope you are all well. Please remember me to your sister and Mrs. Rylands.

Yours faithfully,

G. S. REANEY.

No. LV.

Mr. W. D. CHRISTIE.

32, Dorset Square,
March 16, 1870.

My Dear Sir,—

I like your questioning of Hammond very much. It reads very well. I return the evidence with my marginal notes, and to-morrow I will take from you the other copy.

I wish you would look at the circulars describing the mode of employing secretaries. They are in the appendix to the Diplomatic Committee's report.

I think you have not brought out the most important point as regards the reports of Secretaries of Legation. They ought to be reports made by the Minister, revising his Secretaries'. See my note in margin on questions 374 and 375.

I feel sure that if you go through your details as to the Diplomatic Services with Hammond, you will find Otway and others more and more with you. The general impression has been that your only wish was to reduce expenditure.

Yours very truly,
W. D. Christie.

No. LVI.

Mr. W. D. CHRISTIE.

32, Dorset Square,
March 18, 1870.

My Dear Sir,—

Thanks for your note.

Hammond was very excited after the room was cleared, in the lobby. He will have a dreadful fit of the gout after all this is over.

If you feel disposed to go straight at Lord Malmesbury's jobbery, I can prime you with minute details. I have the Foreign Office lists of the time, so that it will be very easy to make out the cases.

If you look at Mr. Earle's evidence before the Diplomatic Committee of 1861, you will see that he went out of his way to say that Lord Clarendon favoured his friends and Lord Malmesbury did not (!). Mr. Earle was lately Tory M.P. for Maldon, and was at one time Disraeli's private secretary. A reference to this piece of evidence and some examination of Lord Malmesbury, to show the injustice of the comparison, might be so managed as rather to please Lord Clarendon.

Till to-morrow,

Yours very truly,
W. D. Christie.

No. LVII.

Mr. HUGH M. MATHESON.

Heathlands,
Hampstead, N.W.,
March 30, 1870.

Sir,—

I am quite sure that when you referred to Consul Gibson in your speech last night, you must have spoken in ignorance of the fact of that gentleman's death, as I cannot believe that you would willingly have harrowed the feelings of his relatives had you known that he could no longer defend his own character and reputation.

But I am no less certain that if you will quietly and dispassionately refer again to the Parliamentary Papers, China No. 3, 1869, you will regret having condemned in such unmeasured terms the conduct of Mr. Gibson in a position of extreme difficulty, whatever may be your general view in regard to the attitude that ought to be assumed by the Diplomatic servants of the Crown in foreign and semi-civilised countries.

According to the report of your speech in the *Times* your description of Mr. Gibson's proceedings is extremely unfair, as you will, I feel sure, admit, on carefully reading the narrative of the whole events at pages 26 to 30, and Sir R. Alcock's despatch to Lord Stanley at pages 35 and 38, to which I very particularly direct your attention.

Mr. Gibson's conduct was most hastily condemned at the Foreign Office before any despatches were received, and he himself was degraded to the rank of an Interpreter. But it is due to his memory to say that his firm, temperate, and consistent conduct secured for him the singularly cordial esteem of the Chinese community, for on his leaving the Island he was presented with an earnest address signed by 84 merchants and shopkeepers of Taiwanfou, mourning his departure " on account of his upright and straight-forward conduct in office." In addition to this, the Heptai, or Military Governor of Amping, the very town which had been occupied under his instructions, loaded him with unprecedented honours, and emphatically declared before a number of Chinese and Europeans, " There goes a just and honourable foreigner ! "

That Mr. Gibson's condemnation was cruel and unjust in the extreme I felt very deeply at the time, and have taken the liberty of sending you a copy of a letter which I addressed to the newspapers on the subject.

The result of Mr. Gibson's measures has justified their wisdom in the most marvellous and complete manner, peace and harmony having reigned among all classes to an extent before unknown. But it is unhappily true that, from the effects of grief and mortification at the cruelly unjust treatment he received from the Home Government, poor Mr, Gibson died at Amoy shortly after his return to the mainland.

It would be satisfactory if, on reflexion and a re-examination of the subject, you could see your way to repair the injury which your severe remarks have caused to the reputation, dear to survivors, of an excellent man and an able and conscientious public servant.

I am, Sir,
Your obedient servant,
H. M. MATHESON.

————

No. LVIII.

Mr. HUGH M. MATHESON.

3, Lombard St.,
London, E.C.,
April 2, 1870.

Sir,—
I thank you for your note, though I cannot but regret that you have still failed to see the facts in their natural light. If it were true, as you stated to the House, that because of undue delay in delivering a quantity of camphor, and satisfaction not being obtained, Mr. Gibson had proceeded to bombard Amping to bring the authorities to reason, all reasonable men should have joined you in condemning the proceeding. But the reason why I drew your atten-

tion to the Papers was that the story was in reality widely different. I shall not argue it further beyond saying that when the Viceroy of Foochow at last sent over a high authority to settle the matters, and it was found that he had not brought sufficient authority to dismiss the wicked mandarins, and coolly announced his intention to return without doing anything, a crisis had arrived which called for a display of firmness on the part of Mr. Gibson if life and property were to be in any degree secure to British subjects from that day forward. Mr. Gibson accordingly determined to occupy Amping as a material guarantee, while the Tantai should return to the mainland for fresh instructions. This was effected without a shot being fired, and Mr. Gibson returned to Takao to find that all his just demands were immediately acceded to, and in due time, on the return of the Tantai with proper powers, redress was obtained, and one red-handed murderer was executed.

I do not think it is fair to make Mr. Gibson responsible for what took place at Amping after he had left, and without instructions from him, and which had no effect whatever in procuring the settlement. He was indirectly, but, it is fair to say, very remotely responsible. The naval officer having incautiously withdrawn his men on board ship, a band of Braves from Taiwanfoo came down and occupied the place. He conceived it to be his duty to drive them out, and succeeded in doing so, some lives being sacrificed in the affray. Had he not held possession of the ground I presume he would have been blamed by his superiors.

In judging of the action of men in the position of Mr. Gibson at that time, I think forbearance and consideration should be shown by those who are entirely unacquainted with the character of the official classes in China. And with regard to your reflection upon the missionaries, I am not careful to defend them, as you have utterly mistaken their character. These are men of whom Great Britain has reason to be proud. They are doing a noble work in China, and if they cannot take the view of events around them which you take at this distance, I fear I must, without meaning offence, prefer their opinion to yours.

I remain, Sir,

Your faithful servant,
H. M. MATHESON.

No. LIX.

Mr. AUGUSTUS F. LINDLEY.

Author of " Ti-Ping Tien-Kwoh," etc.

10, Myddleton Square,
E.C.,
March 31, 1870.

Sir,—

Allow me to congratulate you upon your able reference to Chinese matters the other evening in the House. I entirely agree with all you said. It was the truest (and, therefore, most unpalatable) as well as ablest exposition on the subject since the late Mr. Cobden's famous opening of the China debate in May, 1864.

I have attentively studied Chinese matters and our policy towards that country for many years ; and have written much on the subject, besides having lived there for more than five years, during which time I travelled extensively. If it were not that I am now so busily engaged in literary matters, I should certainly have taken up the cudgels in support of your speech in the *Times* and *Standard* ; if, however, you do so, and notice Commander Gurdon's letter in yesterday's *Times*, I shall be willing to place at your disposal any quantity of published evidence proving and corroborating your case. By forcing opium upon the Chinese we caused all the wars, and our

officials have invariably acted with lawless aggression.
The thing is notorious, and I have exhaustive documentary and other proof of it.

Truly yours,

AUGUSTUS F. LINDLEY.

———

No. LX.

MR. W. D. CHRISTIE.

32, Dorset Square,

April 5, 1870.

MY DEAR SIR,—

I am glad to have the evidence, and will send to-
morrow, hoping to get yesterday's then ; and I will
try to call on you Thursday morning.

I do not know if they are misprints, but if not, it is
very curious and important that Forbes' outfit money
was repaid only on Feb. 16, 1868 (he received it in
1859), and that he only repaid £800. What has
become of the other £300 ? He would have been
entitled to £1,100 as well as Lowther and myself.
This is worth inquiring into if the printing is correct.

I suspect that Lowther tried to avoid repayment
(this would explain what he said to you about his
furniture), and that on their making Lowther repay

they were obliged to go back upon Forbes and make him repay, too. He repays six days after Lowther. They both had the same agents—Bidwell and Alston.

I am glad to see that Lowther mentioned my pension, and I hope he will ask me about it.

I have heard from Spring Rice that he is to be examined after Easter.

Yours very truly,
W. D. CHRISTIE.

No. LXI.

Mr. W. D. CHRISTIE.

32, Dorset Square,
April 9, 1870.

My Dear Sir,—

1. I see that Alston denies stoutly that Conyngham's accounts were confused. I am surprised. I strongly suspect it is an *official* denial, but how to get inside I cannot tell you.

2. I hope you will pursue with further questions, which I enclose, the law expenses of the Foreign Office.

3. Mr. Bingham's was a dreadful career. Lord Malmesbury forced him out of the Secretaryship of Naples in 1852 to make way for your friend Lowther,

and was afterwards *obliged* to make him Chargé d'Affaires at Venezuela. You should get Bingham before the Committee. It would be fine fun. He is a very clever, amusing fellow, but a dreadful scapegrace.

4. Alston has got into a sad mess about the Consular pensions. See my questions enclosed.

5. There is still some mistake about Forbes' outfit —the sum; but it is of no public consequence. He ought to have received £1,100, as I did, which is not the full outfit for Rio. He was second from a second-class mission (Dresden), and I from a second-class mission (Buenos Ayres). My case and his are parallel.

6. I have been trying, without success, to find my copy of Mr. James Murray's circular. Alston has given you a favourable version of it, and told you a very clear story. He ought to produce a copy of the circular, which his friend Murray could, of course, furnish him with. Also, he ignores T. Bidwell, the present man, son of his old partner, and his partner now and at the time when Murray advised his clients to go over. And Bidwell was Private Secretary to Lord Malmesbury, who gave Murray the appointment. Also C. Spring Rice, when he became Superintendent of Consular Service, gave up his agencies; and the Superintendent of Consular Service was of lower rank than Chief Clerk.

Yours very truly,
W. D. CHRISTIE.

No. LXII.

Mr. ANDREW REID.

Land Tenure Reform Association.
>9, Buckingham St.,
>Strand,
>>May 2, 1870.

Dear Sir,—

Will you not allow me to retain your name upon the General Committee, or, at least, upon the list of our members, until after the meeting in July? The programme will not be regularly adopted until then, and by that time it may be that you will see your way clear to go still with us. It would be a matter of grief that one so advanced in his views, and such a valuable ally, should be lost to us. Pray keep with us if you can.

>>Yours very truly,
>>>Andrew Reid.

No. LXIII.

Mr. HENRY LABOUCHERE.

May 5, 1870,
2, Bolton St.

Dear Mr. Rylands,—

I enclose you some questions which I think would, if asked, enable me to give the Committee some details respecting the inner life of an Embassy and Legations. I am going to Paris, but if you would send me a line next week to the "Grand Hotel," letting me know when you wish me to be examined, I would come over to London.

Yours faithfully,

H. Labouchere.

No. LXIV.

Mr. HENRY RICHARD.

Peace Society,
19, New Broad Street,
London, E.C.,
May 14, 1870.

Dear Mr. Rylands,—

I enclose the resolution to which we shall ask you to speak on Tuesday evening. It will be, I think, just in your line.   We need not tax you to make a very long speech, but I don't want to fetter you at all.

With many thanks for your kind promise to be present,

I remain,
Yours very truly,
HENRY RICHARD.

No. LXV.

MR. JOSEPH HARRISON.

County Court Office,
Warrington,
May 12, 1870.

DEAR MR. RYLANDS,—

Enoch Morgan called upon me yesterday for the half-year's rent of the house and land at Thelwall, due the 1st inst.

To save him the trouble of communicating with you I paid him the amount.

I saw a very elegant silver trowel and polished wood mallet this morning, which were to be used to-day in laying the foundation stone of your brother's house at Thelwall, and I suppose the " member for Warrington " will soon follow suit.

The elevation of Charles Holmes and Peter Smith to the Borough Bench, through your instrumentality, appears to give great satisfaction to the inhabitants generally, but, really, the latter gentleman is an " enigma."   I was, the other day, congratulating him upon his newly-acquired honour, when he was ungracious enough to say, " he did not seek it," " he did not want it," and " he thought it no honour." However, whether he appreciates it or not, you have the satisfaction of knowing that you have faithfully redeemed your promise, and considering the state of political feeling in Warrington, and the very prominent part he took in the Council on the " vote of thanks question " (which, I confess, was a great mistake), I think he has been treated with great consideration, which, I regret to say, he does not seem to value.

Hoping you are quite well,

I remain,
Yours very respectfully,
JOSEPH HARRISON.

No. LXVI.

Miss BECKER.

Manchester National Society for Women's Suffrage,
28, Jackson's Row,
Albert Square,
May 19, 1870.

My dear Mr. Rylands,—

I beg to thank you for your votes in favour of the Women's Disabilities Bill.   The result shows that we have a hard battle to fight, in which I trust we may rely on your continued support.

Yours sincerely,

Lydia E. Becker.

No. LXVII.

Mr. W. D. CHRISTIE.

32, Dorset Square,
May 27, 1870.

My Dear Sir,—

I heard your examination of Lord Clarendon yesterday.   I think you will know now that he is skilful, plausible, and humbugging.   If I might give you a little advice, I would not ask him any more questions to which you know that he will give you answers adverse to your views. On the subject of open competitive examination into the Diplomatic Service he was sure to be against you, and his answers will have more authority with the public than the innuendo of your question.

If you will let me have his evidence as soon as you can by book post, I will suggest a few questions on his yesterday's evidence ; and, if it is agreeable to you, I will call on you on Monday morning, before you go to the Committee, at eleven if that is not too early. Lord Clarendon has not been a Minister abroad since 1839, that is, 30 years ago. Great changes since in the service.

I have heard that the whole of my letter has been read except the paragraph about Eastwick. But I think, and I wrote to Bouverie, that my letter ought to be printed if Otway's question remains on the minutes.

Yours very truly,
W. D. CHRISTIE.

No. LXVIII.

Mr. J. K. ASTON.

Bounty Office,
Dean's Yard,
Westminster,
June 6, 1870.

Sir,—

If your amendment to the Bounty Superannuation Bill cannot be entered upon on the 9th inst., for want of time, I must appeal to you to withdraw it.

It is very essential for the Bounty Office to be able to pension Mr. Hodgson, and that this Bill, which stood over from last year, should not be further delayed this Session.

Of course, a Department is always most unwilling to ask any Honourable Member to forego his proposed course of action; but as the rules of the House, in going into Committee of Supply, etc., give you other opportunities of stating your views on the subject of superannuations in general, and as this Bill is intended to remove doubts as to the past practice of the Bounty Board, and to reduce the amount to be in future granted for superannuation, I do appeal to you, as a matter of business and kind gentlemanly feeling, to allow this little Bill to now pass without opposition, taking to yourself a more fitting opportunity of enforcing your wide views upon the House and country.

Mr. Hodgson is 86, and yet likely to live 4 or 5 years. It will be cruel and unwise, by delaying the

Bill, to keep him, with his impaired faculties, at the head of a large Monetary Office.

Asking the favour of a reply,

I am, Sir,

Your faithful servant,

J. K. ASTON.

No. LXIX.

MR. JOHN GRITTON.

Lord's Day Observance Society,
20, John St., Adelphi, W.C.,
June 15, 1870.

MY DEAR SIR,—

We have been endeavouring to promote petitions in favour of your Sunday Closing Bill, but have not met with much success.

The committee are now arranging a circular to members on the subject, to be put in their hands on the 28th, but, before settling the form of it, may I beg to know whether it is your intention to push for a division on the 29th, or whether, in face of Mr. Bruce's engagement to bring in his Bill next session, you will be content simply to provoke discussion ?

I rather fear that an adverse Division would cause the Government to make their Bill less strict than

they are now prepared to do.   Of course, a favourable
Division would tend in the opposite direction.

I am,

My dear Sir,

Very faithfully yours,

JOHN GRITTON.

No. LXX.

Mr. ROBERT WHITWORTH, Hon. Secy.

Central Association
for
Stopping the Sale of Intoxicating Liquors on Sunday.

43, Market St.,

Manchester,

June 21, 1870.

DEAR SIR,—

As desired by you, we have written Messrs. Birley,
Candlish, Morgan, Allen, and Jacob Bright, requesting them to take part in the Debate expected on the
29th, and would be glad if you will also press them to
be prepared for the occasion, as I have not all their
private addresses.

We expect upwards of 10,000 signatures to our
Manchester petition, which shall be sent up shortly.

The working men are holding a meeting in the open air here on the 27th, in Ancoats district, when I hope to take the chair for them. I need hardly say any details you may require shall be at once sent you, or Mr. Mathews will wait on you if preferred.

Again thanking you for the good you have done this noble cause by your advocacy,

I remain,

Yours faithfully,

ROBERT WHITWORTH,

Hon. Secy.

No. LXXI.

MR. W. D. CHRISTIE.

June 29, 1870.

MY DEAR SIR,—

Those who wish for reforms in the Foreign Office as you do should make known in such ways as you can to Gladstone that if Lord Granville succeeds Lord Clarendon, Hammond's rule will practically continue, while Lord Kimberley's appointment would be the knell of Hammond's power. I do not think Hammond could stay with Lord Kimberley. They were long under-secretaries together. Lord Kimberley knows him and the Office, and is a vigorous, determined man. Lord Granville will fall into Hammond's hands.

There is a very good letter of Lord Kimberley (then Lord Woodhouse) in the Appendix to the Report of the Consular Committee of 1858.

Yours very truly,
W. D. Christie.

No. LXXII.

Mr. HENRY LABOUCHERE.

Grand Hotel,
Paris,
June 30, 1870.

Dear Mr. Rylands,—

I will be before the Diplomatic Committee on June 30 ; if not, I shall have caught the small-pox, which is very bad here. The hour is, I think, two o'clock. It is a mystery to me why clerks in the Foreign Office are not to be appointed by competitive examination. In the Diplomatic Service it may be urged that if they are expected to go into society, you must have persons accustomed to society; but clerks in the Foreign Office have to copy, and not to attend balls. If they are expected to be able to keep secrets, I do not see how the Secretary of the Foreign Office is able to test

K

their capacity to do so. The fact is that the Foreign Office is a close Corporation. Clerks only are admitted who belong to a certain number of families who seem to have established a hereditary right to do nothing there, and who are cousins and social hangers-on of the Minister. As long as Parliament listens to the *ex parte* evidence of Ministers and Under-Secretaries this will continue. Beyond mere assertion, Clarendon cannot say one word for keeping up the present system of direct appointment.

Yours truly,
HENRY LABOUCHERE.

No. LXXIII.

MR. HENRY LABOUCHERE.

Union Club,
July 4, 1870.

DEAR MR. RYLANDS,—

Before I forget it and go to Paris, I want to call your attention to an observation of Otway's.

He said that the number of despatches written did not bear out my assertions respecting the amount of work done at an Embassy.

Now, unless explained, nothing is more deceptive than the number of despatches as a criterion respect-

ing the work, for, by the rules of the Foreign Office,
each subject has its despatch ; thus, one despatch
will be the acknowledgment of the receipt of another,
another acknowledging the receipt of a letter from
the Queen (and she sends her correspondence to her
numerous cousins through the Foreign Office) to a
relative, another stating that a former letter has been
received by a courier. I have written half a dozen of
these despatches in half an hour, and, of course, they
swell the number written in a year. I think that you
might elicit this fact from a witness by a few adroit
questions.

The best way, however, would be to ask for the
despatches written to the Foreign Office whilst I was
at Dresden ; or, if this is declined, the précis of
these despatches. There is at the Foreign Office a
Précis writer, who enters, or ought to enter, all the
despatches.

Yours truly,
H. LABOUCHERE.

A Minister at a place like Munich will, of course,
occasionally write a political despatch. The question,
however, is, is this despatch worth the money it
costs ?

No. LXXIV.

Mr. J. C. McCOAN.

Levant Herald,
> Constantinople,
> June 24, 1870.

Sir,—

As you have, I see, given notice of a motion on the subject of the recent burning of the Pera Embassy, I take leave to send you some *matériel* on the subject in 4 copies of the *Levant Herald*, forwarded by this mail. In doing so I need merely add that I have absolutely no animus or motive whatever but the public interest in view, as I venture to say will be vouched for by my old and honoured friend Sir Henry Bulwer, should you have occasion to speak with him on the subject.

I was myself an eye-witness of the disaster. I *saw* the engines lying idle at the very crisis of the fire; I was told by one of the only two men near them that they would not work, and afterwards by Mr. Gribble (the Embassy chaplain) that their hose was completely worthless, and that he himself had stuck his fingers and thumbs into the holes in them. All this is now denied by Sir H. Elliot and Mr. Vice-Consul Suaracino (the "keeper" of the Embassy and other public buildings here, appointed on Sir H. Elliot's recommendation), but all the evidence I have been able to gather supports the version given in the *Herald.*

In any case, the copies sent may, perhaps, be useful, and if so, my object in sending them will be served.

I am, Sir,

Your very faithful servant,

J. C. McCoan,

Ed. *Levant Herald.*

————

No. LXXV.

Mr. C. E. MACQUEEN,

Financial Reform Association,

Lord Street,

Liverpool,

July 11, 1870.

My Dear Sir,—

I thank you heartily on behalf of Council and Treasurer for your two influential recruits, and considering what a fanatic, self sacrificing, I am in this matter, I think I may venture to add, on my own account also.

Oh! that other members would follow your most excellent example. If they did we should be enabled to send lecturers all over the kingdom, instead of being engaged in a constant struggle to keep our heads above water.

Papers and almanacks have been sent to Messrs. Mellor and Bentall, and during the session the paper will be forwarded to them in London, as well as to their private addresses in the country. The same plan will be adopted with regard to other subscribing M.P.'s.

Again thanking you or your kind exertions on our behalf,

I am, my dear sir,
Yours truly,
C. E. MACQUEEN.

No. LXXVI.

SIR HENRY L. BULWER.

Clarendon Hotel,
169, New Bond Street,
London,
July 17, 1870.

MY DEAR SIR,—

I did not mean to say anything witty or comical the other day in answer to the question you put, and was so far confused by finding people imagine I did that I stopped in the explanations I had meant to give you, and which I will give you now, though I beg you to consider what I say private.

I look upon our position as to Greece as exceptional :—

1st. There is her conduct in the special instance we have under consideration.

2nd. There is her general conduct under our so-called protection.

The course we are taking as to the first seems to me small and shuffling for a nation that is straightforward and great. The parties against whom we have a grievance, and with whom alone we have to do, are the Greek Government. Their conduct is clear from the correspondence long since before us. Do we mean to do anything upon it or do we not? All the material that can possibly be required for an opinion is before us. If we do, let us do it ; if we don't, let us say we don't. But to invent an *excuse* for doing *nothing*, and to *pretend* to be doing *something*, is mean and paltry.

We talk of inquiry ; inquiry about what, or whom ? The Government and the Government officials we know enough of, and they are not likely to teach us more. The brigands ? We know that those who were poor have been caught and killed, and that those who were rich have escaped. The outsiders ? Supposing we discover that gentlemen in the opposition party visited the brigands : well, everybody visited them—priests, peasants, gens-d'armes, Government officials ; they seem to have been the best possible company ! What then ?

Thus we are keeping the matter open on a flimsy, unworthy pretext, *pretending to look for* culprits, and turning our eyes from the culprits who are just in front of us.   I can't bear this conduct in England.

So much for the brigand case.   Now for the protection one.   If I take a lad out of an orphan asylum and bring him up, and feed him and clothe him, and I at last find that when he becomes a man he does everything he ought not to do, and nothing that he ought to do, I withdraw my protection from him.

This is just our position with Greece.   There is no fault that a State can commit that she has not committed, no virtue that a State ought to possess that she has displayed.   People say this is the fault of the form of Government.   I don't know the cause. I see the result, but it is more likely the result will be the same if the form of Government be the same.

At all events, if things are to go on as they have gone on, I don't want England to be mixed up with them.   Thus, you see, my views are very simple. My resolution would be framed so as to give me the best means of explaining them, if I bring on the matter, which, possibly, my recent complication may prevent.   In that case you shall be the first to hear.

Yours very sincerely,
HENRY BULWER.

No. LXXVII.

Mr. W. D. CHRISTIE.

32, Dorset Square,
July 21, 1870.

My Dear Sir,—

Your motion about secret service money has not yet come on.

Lord Clarendon answered you that he thought your questioning him at all about his expenditure of secret service money was an unpleasant imputation. It implied that you thought him capable of spending the money wrongly.

Now, in 1849, Lord Clarendon spent £1,700 of secret service money in Ireland on a newspaper, and he was ultimately advised by the present Lord Halifax, whom he consulted, and who was then Chancellor of the Exchequer, that he had made an improper use of secret service money, and he refunded the £1,700. You will see all about this in Hansard, February 19, 1852.

Another thing I wish to say to you about secret service money. Hammond and Lord Clarendon answered you as if everything as to secret service money was done on the responsibility of the Secretary of State for the time being. But if there are continuous payments, as no doubt there are, Lord Clarendon or any other Secretary of State carries on what his predecessor has determined—a pension say : Do you believe that Lord Clardendon would go into

the merits of every pension granted by a predecessor ?
Then it comes again to there being a permanent
officer in the office who knows more about it than the
Secretary of State for the time being.

Yours very truly,
W. D. CHRISTIE.

———

No. LXXVIII.

MR. HENRY LABOUCHERE.

2, Bolton St.,
Piccadilly,
July, 1870.

DEAR MR. RYLANDS,—

You will see in a letter signed by a Parisian
Resident, in to-day's *Daily News*, the following
statement :—" Mr. Layard had been aware of this
candidature and had spoken to M. Mercier on the
subject, although unfortunately he did not inform his
own government of either fact until after the protests
of the French Government."

I am the Parisian correspondent, and I happen to
know that this statement is correct. Would you mind
asking the following question :—Mr. Rylands—to ask
Mr. Otway whether there is any foundation for a
statement which appears to-day in a Parisian

correspondence of the *Daily News* that Mr. Layard was aware of the candidature of Prince Leopold of Hohenzollern, and spoke to M. Mercier on the subject before the action of the French Government in the matter, but did not communicate this important information to the Foreign Office until it had learnt it from other quarters.

They may try to twist out of it, or they may even deny it ; but you have only got to repeat the question with the usual peroration ; so I understand my hon. friend to assert that there is absolutely no sort of foundation for this report, and the Foreign Office has no reason to believe that Mr. Layard had heard of this candidature before, etc.

This will, I think, show the public that as far as information is concerned, we pay too highly for getting nothing, by keeping up the parade of a large legation.

Yours truly,

H. Labouchere.

No. LXXIX.

Mr. P. F. CAMPBELL JOHNSON.

The Athenæum,
July 31, 1870.

My Dear Mr. Rylands,—

This evening it is proposed to take the second reading of a Bill to add £7,000 a year to the expenses of the Judicial Establishment of this country.

This Bill is called " The Judicial Committee Bill," and this morning there is an admirable leading article of one column in the *Times* newspaper, throwing the greatest ridicule on the *inefficiency* of the measure, well worth your perusing and digesting.

The fact is, the *whole* Appellate Jurisdiction, whether with reference to this country, the Colonies, or India, requires a *remodelling*, and it is necessary to take it up next session. You will, therefore, no doubt urge the postponement of this ridiculous Bill till next session, so as to enable the whole question to be gone into ; and not at the complete end of the session to add, without enquiry, £7,000 a year to the expenses of this country.

Yours,
P . F . CAMPBELL JOHNSTON.

No. LXXX.

Mr. GEORGE POTTER.

Bee Hive Office,
10, Bolt Court,
Fleet Street,
July 30, 1870.

Dear Sir,—

On the other side you will find a list of names of gentlemen who are supporters of or subscribers to the *Bee Hive*, which is established to instruct and guide working men upon the great political and social questions, the settlement of which will greatly affect the future of this country. Another speciality of the *Bee Hive* is to inform public men of the opinions and movements of the working classes.

My object in addressing you is to respectfully solicit you to become a subscriber of one guinea per annum, in return for which a free copy of the paper will be sent to you weekly. Although that sum is more than the cost of the paper, the conductors will use the difference to extend its circulation and usefulness.

Yours obediently,
George Potter.

No. LXXXI.

GEORGE POTTER.

Bee Hive Office,
10, Bolt Court,
Fleet Street,
Aug. 12, 1870.

DEAR SIR,—

I beg to acknowledge the receipt of your letter containing cheque for £1 1s. 0d., being subscription to *Bee Hive*. Enclosed is receipt for same, which I forward with my best thanks.

Yours obediently,
GEORGE POTTER.

No. LXXXII.

MR. J. D. LEWIS, M.P. (Devonport.

Westbury House,
Petersfield,
Hants,
Aug. 4, 1870.

DEAR RYLANDS,—

You will, I am sure, not forget to take charge of Clerical Disabilities Bill, putting it on for to-morrow, if it comes to us to-day, and then (*i.e.*, to-morrow) moving that we agree to Lords' amendments; or, if it comes to us to-morrow, putting it on for Monday and leaving it to me.

I send you the enclosed, which Hibbert has forwarded to me from Mr. Beresford Hope. It might be as well if you see him in the House, to say that we propose to accept the Lords' amendments, else we shall lose the Bill. If Collins, or any opponent, attempts to divide the House, of course you must divide. All that the Lords have done is to strike out the clause permitting an ex-clergyman to *return* to the clerical profession. This clause was not put into the Bill till the last minute, and it may be fairly said that the Bishops who threw it out are the best judges on the point. I have written to Bruce, stating our intentions, also to Glyn.

You know your plan is to take the 11.30 train from Waterloo to Petersfield on Saturday, with a return ticket. You arrive at Petersfield at 1.17, and will be met there.

Yours very truly,
J. D. Lewis.

No. LXXXIII.

Mr. J. D. LEWIS, M.P.

Westbury House,
Petersfield,
Hants,
Aug. 5, 1870.

Dear Rylands,—

I have just received the enclosed, which I think so important that I send up a special messenger. After clause 6 (as the Bill now stands) the Lords seem to have omitted the accompanying clause, which was clause 8 in the original Bill. I think it must have been done through inadvertence. It is desirable that this clause as altered should be re-inserted, but if so doing would risk the Bill, it would be better to leave it alone. Perhaps you would show it to Bruce. I am in hopes the Bill has not come down to us till to-day, in which case you would be rid of all trouble, as I shall be up on Monday.

Yours truly,
J. D. Lewis.

No. LXXXIV.

MR. JOHN GRITTON.

Lord's Day Obervance Society,
20, John St., Adelphi, W.C.,
Aug. 5, 1870.

My Dear Sir,—

Will you permit me, in the name of this Committee, to thank you for the efforts you have made during this session to promote Sunday Closing of Public Houses by Legislative enactment.

This Committee trusts that sufficient pressure may be brought to bear on Mr. Bruce to secure from him in the Session of 1871 a measure which, although it may not go as far as we could wish, may at least considerably reduce the time during which intoxicating liquors may be sold on the Lord's Day.

We have a long and severe fight before us, but may hope that earnest efforts of right-minded men may overcome even the tremendous obstacles which lie in our way.

I am,
My dear Sir,
Your faithful servant,
John Gritton.

No. LXXXV.

Mrs. JOSEPHINE E. BUTLER.

Ladies' National Association
for the
Repeal of the Contagious Diseases Acts.

280, South Hill, Park Road,
Liverpool,

Oct. 20, 1870.

My Dear Sir,—

I forget whether I have told you that our Free
Trade Hall meeting is fixed for the 16th of November.
We are reckoning greatly on your presence.   Indeed,
Mr. Bright and Mr. Fowler make it almost a condition
of their taking part that you shall be present on the
platform, so as to have a pretty strong platform (with
a few others) to advertise.   I earnestly trust, and so
do 1,400 ladies of our association, that nothing will
prevent you being present.

I remain, Dear Sir,
Yours faithfully,
JOSEPHINE E. BUTLER.

P.S.—I do not mean to say that these ladies will be
present at the meeting.

No. LXXXVI.

Mrs. JACOB BRIGHT.

Alderley Edge,
Nov. 9, 1870.

Dear Mr. Rylands,—

I hear you have refused to come to our meeting on the 16th against the Contagious Diseases Acts, and that you have given as your reason that you are intending to serve on the Royal Commission. I trust you will reconsider this decision, as it is already well known that you are against the Acts. If Mr. Dalrymple can speak in public in favour of the Acts, I cannot see why you should not speak against them. The Government does not pretend to have chosen men for the Commission whose opinions are not already fixed, otherwise Mr. Fowler and Mr. Bright would not have been asked to sit upon it. I hope you will come. This is a critical time in the agitation of our cause, and we must try to make a strong impression before Parliament meets. The Colchester election has done much, and some Liberals are grumbling at having lost the seat; but the Government is beginning to understand by that defeat that we are implacable. We are doing our utmost to secure a good meeting. There will be many ladies present. Will Mrs. Rylands come, and bring any friends with her she can? You do not need to *speak* if you would rather not, and in any case, a few minutes' speech, just to show your sympathy, is all

that would be desired.   We have plenty of speakers
who can expose the Acts ; what we want are names
that command influence.   Mr. Millar writes us he
will be prevented from coming.   Mr. Potter is
doubtful ; but if you and my husband and Mr. Fowler
are present, that is enough to make the meeting an
important one, for you are all men who can command
a hearing on the floor of the House.

Excuse this pressure, and believe me, with kind
regards to your wife,

Very sincerely yours,

Ursula M. Bright.

No. LXXXVII.

Right Hon. Sir GEORGE O. TREVELYAN.

31, Park St.,
Grosvenor Sq.,
Oct. 24, 1870.

Dear Mr. Rylands, –

I am much gratified by the article which you have
sent, and by your assurances of approval and future
support.   It is of vital importance to take occasion of
the present crisis to direct our interest in any reform
into a Radical channel.   I am not without hope that

even before Parliament sits we may have an opportunity for a demonstration.

Would it be impertinence in me to urge you to master the subject as you have mastered others? Army Reform has hitherto failed in Parliament from the paucity of Army Reformers. We must attack *en échelon*.

I remain,
Yours very truly,
G. O. TREVELYAN.

No. LXXXVIII.

MR. DUNCAN MACLAREN, M.P. (EDINBURGH).

Matlock Bank,
Near Derby,
Nov. 27, 1870.

MY DEAR RYLANDS,—

I duly received your letter in Edinburgh, for which accept my thanks.

I was glad to learn yesterday, from London, that you were to be one of the Contagious Diseases Acts Commissioners of Enquiry. Before Parliament broke up, Mr. Jacob Bright, who had been spoken to by Mr. Bruce on the subject, asked my opinion as to who would be well qualified men, and I at once named you ; and he agreed with me, but doubted whether you would accept. I am very glad to hear that you have accepted.

In your letter you refer to the article in the *Saturday Review*. I read it carefully. The writer (supposed to be Dr. Lyon Playfair), it is plain, had not seen the second edition of my pamphlet, where his main argument is met by anticipation in a supplementary note (not in the first edition), p. 17.

There are just two points in the *Review*. The one is that the 7,766 women originally in the towns (p. 229, 2nd edition)—and there were now only 3,016—were never pretended to have existed *all at the same time*, but were avowedly the total accumulations of the five years. This my speech, of course, made clear. You say you have not the Parliamentary Paper with you, but the " Report " on which I comment is printed verbatim, at full length, as appendix III (2nd edition pp. 21, 22, 23). Read top of p. 22, where the statement commented on by me is made. Nobody can doubt that the Report is *intended* to lead the public to believe that the number of women in these districts is *now* much reduced compared with what it was in former years, whereas I have shown that there has been a steady increase in the number of women, during each of the last four years. This is proved to have been the intention of the Report (to mislead), by the fact that it has always been so used in arguments, in both Houses of Parliament, and in speeches and papers read in public meetings outside, and Mr. Bruce (Home Secretary), in a conversation I had with him before the return was published, said distinctly, giving these figures, that the number of women had been *reduced* in that proportion, more than a half.

The first line of the succeeding passage, p. 22, about men, also shows that this was the intention (to mislead) about the number of women, for it says, " The Return ALSO shows a decrease by one-half of the number of men," etc.

If it was honest to take all the women registered during the five years as a total, and contrast them with the existing number, why not take the number for ten years, or fifty years, and contrast them in the same way ?   It is a most dishonest way of misleading the public, by merely *inferentially insinuating* the false statement, without plainly telling a direct falsehood. Suppose the number of women *had been*, at first—

<pre>
            1st year...................... ..1,000
            2nd year 2,000
            3rd year 3,000
            4th year......... 4,000
            5th year......................5,000
                                          ——————
                    Total............15,000
</pre>

With this growing steady increase in the number, what would have been thought of you or myself if either of us had used the words of this report, and merely said that of this 15,000 there had been removed, from the causes stated, 10,000, leaving only 5,000. Everyone would have cried shame on us, for concealing the fact that, under the operation of the Act, the number of women had been five times greater during the last year than during the first.   Yet this is what is done in the Report.

The second point which the Reviewer lays hold of is the alleged number of 1,770 women in Devonport district at the commencement of the Act. This matter I have dealt with so fully at page 17, that I need not trouble you with any additional remarks.

I have had a correspondence with Captain Vivian, M.P., of the War Office, on the subject, and he says the framer of the report, Harris, is to go before the commissioners to be examined on the charges contained in my pamphlet, and to vindicate the accuracy of his report. This is all right, that he should do so; but it is equally right that commissioners who, like yourself, have strong views on the subject, should carefully examine for yourselves, beforehand, what the charges are, and on what evidence they are supported, so as to be able to unravel any sophistical statements which may be made by putting the proper questions to him.

I don't ask you to believe my statements to be accurate on my authority, but I ask you to examine them by the light of the documents on which they are founded, and in particular I ask you to read carefully *all the notes* in the second edition, because they embody many important facts not included in my speech.

What an excellent meeting at Manchester! My wife unites in kind regards to Mrs. Rylands and yourself.

Ever yours,

D. McLAREN.

No. LXXXIX.

Mr. JACOB BRIGHT, M.P.

Alderley Edge,
Manchester,
Dec. 9, 1870.

My Dear Rylands,—

Is the inquiry of the Royal Commission (C. D. A.) going to be a hole-and-corner affair in harmony with all past proceedings on this subject? I am told the Commission sits on Wednesday next at Plymouth, that everything is to be private, only that the associations for and against the Acts are each to have a representative there. Please tell me if I am well informed, and do me the favour to keep me informed of the way you proceed. I trust to you more than to any other man on the Commission to give fair play to the opponents of the Acts. At Plymouth there is a surgeon of the name of Wolferstan who has great information. Be sure you get everything out of him if he is a witness. I understand Massey is to be chairman. He would be the tool of any Government, as he was of Lord Palmerston's. I take for granted the Commission has been appointed to report in favour of the Acts. An early reply will oblige. You appear to have had a great meeting! send me your paper.

Very truly,

J. Bright.

No. XC.

Mr. JACOB BRIGHT, M.P.

Alderley Edge,
Manchester,
Jan. 8, 1871.

My Dear Rylands,—

I have a note from Dr. Charles Bell Taylor, of Nottingham, on the subject of the Royal Commission (C. D. A.) He wishes to be called as a witness, and hopes that you may be able to manage it for him. In that case, it would be necessary for him to have some communication with you beforehand, so that you might not fail to draw from him all the information he wishes to give. Dr. Taylor knows, perhaps, more on this subject than any other man; therefore, if the Commission desire information his evidence ought to be fully taken.

Waiting your reply,

Very truly,
J. Bright.

No. XCI.

Mr. W. D. CHRISTIE.

32, Dorset Sq.,
Jan. 1, 1871.

My Dear Sir,—

I begin, as in duty bound, by wishing you and Mrs. Rylands a happy New Year.

I begin the new year with a resolution to write, if possible, more legibly.

I have been often thinking of writing to you. In a month your labours will begin again. I can find no one yet who can tell me why Otway has left the Foreign Office. Some say there has been a row; others that it is in consequence of general dissatisfaction with him, and that all last year they complained of his idleness, as well as his modes of proceeding in and about the Committee; others, again, think that he has been opposed to some of Lord Granville's policy as between France and Prussia. The thing is kept so secret that Grant Duff told me only yesterday he could learn nothing.

I hear that Shaw has given up to Holmes the management of the Consular inquiry. Is this so? I hope that Holmes will be willing to call me, and enable me to complete my information about consular reductions, etc.

I propose as soon as the Committee is reappointed, to write to the Chairman and ask for an opportunity of revising my memorandum on the Foreign Office, and then send it in again, making it clear that I understood I was asked by the Chairman to send in a written statement ; but whether it was the Chairman or you, it really makes no difference, for the Committee ratified the request.

I shall wish to give in to the Committee in writing, or in a new examination, a precise statement for my plan for the Diplomatic Service of Private Secretaries and Clerks, showing in each case, with the Consular absorptions and reductions, the difference of expense.

I observe that the Foreign Office did not furnish the list of absences on leave you asked for. It has also come to me since I had the pleasure of seeing you, that the saving of £8,000 mentioned by Otway at the end of the session, is the pretended saving of the return given by the Foreign Office before the Committee was appointed, which I showed you was fallacious, and you expounded it all clearly in the speech you made in the House before the Committee was appointed.

Yours very truly,
W. D. CHRISTIE.

No. XCII.

MRS. F. PENNINGTON.

17, Hyde Park Terrace, W.,
Jan. 24, 1871.

DEAR MR. RYLANDS,—

Our Secretary, Mr. Banks, who worked under Dr. Bell Taylor above a year at Nottingham, warned me very seriously this morning that we must not let him see the evidence before the Royal Commission ; he says that he will publish anything he hears or sees directly, without the least scruple ; so I told him, or rather he proposed to write at once to Mr. Kingsford and warn him. I thought it better to warn you too, as Dr. Taylor said at our committee meeting last night, he had been smoking a cigar with you the previous night, and had " strengthened you considerably." (This called forth a general shout from the committee that you did not require strengthening.) I thought, however, you might perhaps have told him things you would not care to have published as coming from you, and might like to warn him. He writes no end of letters and articles for the papers, but owns with his usual candour and good nature, that not one in fifty is ever inserted. We have had to reject several for *The Shield*, because the language was so violent, but he never seems to resent it. I suppose he thinks it is a law of Nature now. In haste.

Yours very truly,

M. PENNINGTON.

No. XCIII.

Mr. W. D. CHRISTIE.

32, Dorset Square,

Feb. 27, 1871.

My Dear Mr. Rylands,—

I have been an invalid more or less ever since I was unable to see you one evening in this house, and I am still weak and not able to get about much.

I have just written a note addressed to the Chairman of the Diplomatic Committee, asking to be allowed to revise my memo. on the Foreign Office.

I now have, *confidentially*, supplied to me by Griffith, the printed correspondence between him and the Foreign Office and the Treasury. I could let you see it *confidentially*, if you wish it. You could not ostensibly make use of it, but it gives a wonderful insight into Foreign Office ways. Hammond and James Murray are both convicted of mis-statements, which, of course, they will not apologise for or acknowledge. In the end the Treasury supports Griffith against the Foreign Office and enables him to beat Hammond and Murray. Would you like to see it?

Have you ascertained yet whether Shaw gives up the management of the Consular question to Holmes or not?

Yours very truly,

W. D. Christie.

No. XCIV.

Mr. C. E. MACQUEEN.

Financial Reform Association,
Lord St.,
Liverpool,
March 4, 1871.

My Dear Sir,--

Thanks for your notification and intention *in re* Petition.

Can you extract from any military friend in the House or out of it, the exact terms of the declaration said to be required from, and made by, every purchaser of a commission, to the effect that he has paid no more than the regulation prices for it.

I wrote to a Major General, who is one of our subscribers, about it, and he sent me most stringent extracts from the Queen's Regulations against over regulation prices, but not the declaration ; so I wrote to him again, and in his reply, received this morning, he says :—" On receiving your note of the 28th ult., I wrote to a gentleman in London, well-informed upon military matters, and in his reply he informs me that he has not seen anything of the form referred to, nor has he any knowledge of such a declaration being in existence. My own impression is that there is no separate formal declaration, the regulations being so explicit upon the subject of purchase."

As a statement to the contrary has often been publicly made and not contradicted, so far as I am aware, I think that the " impression " must be erroneous. Can you ferret out the fact, if so it be ? I want it to shot a protest against paying one penny more than regulation prices.

Yours truly,
C. E. MACQUEEN.

No. XCV.

Mr. EDWIN BARTON.

(Secretary to the Central Association for Stopping the Sale of Intoxicating Liquors on Sunday.)

43, Market Street,
Manchester,
March 10, 1871.

Dear Sir,—

I shall be glad if you will kindly send me half a dozen copies of your Bill, also, if convenient, to furnish us from time to time with Petition reports.

May I trouble you also to give me some idea of the date of second reading ? I have the enquiry from all parts, and as our committee meet on Monday, shall be glad if you may have time to write prior.

We are thinking of a great city meeting at the Guildhall under the presidency of the Lord Mayor.

Would it be advisable? Our magistrates' memorial is progressing in grand style—about 1,000 signatures already. I send you by book-post two or three documents. Petitions are being sent out wholesale. We shall have a grand petition movement this year. I wrote to Mr. Bruce the other day, giving him some idea of what he may expect.

Respectfully,
Edwin Barton.

No. XCVI.

MAJOR-GENERAL WHITTINGHAM.

35, Queensborough Terrace,
Kensington Gardens, W.,
March 10, 1871.

Sir,—

I may tell you *in confidence*, as a householder of small means, most interested against needless increase of taxes, that I never was more astonished in my life than when I heard a Liberal Government proposing— whilst abolishing purchase in the army—a bill to compensate the officers, not only for the regulation prices of their commissions, but actually, also, for those private and illegal extra-regulation prices, for which the officers have not a shadow of a claim, either

M

morally, or legally, or equitably. I have served regimentally more than thirty years, and commanded a regiment for seven years, and was all the time well aware that extra prices were illegal and made at the risk of the officers concerned. The Horse Guards constantly issued circulars to the same effect, and though the practice may be said to have been *winked at* (and *privately known*) by the highest authorities, I yet do not think any just claim for extra prices can be rationally maintained by uninterested persons.

I, at all events, who have rather lost, on the whole, than gained by such practices (little as I had to do with them, as it happened), shall grudge, very much, paying now a tax on that account.

I cannot consent to be publicly quoted *by name*, but (in the interest both of truth and of my own pocket) I should be glad to see this extraordinary and indefensible assault on the public purse frustrated.

I am, Sir,
Your obedient servant,
A RETIRED GENERAL.

P.S.—I enclose my card for yourself alone.—F. W.

No. XCVII.

JUDGE HARDEN.

Warrington,
March 9, 1871.

The Judge of the County Court presents his compliments to the honourable M.P. for Warrington, and would respectfully beg of him to hand the enclosure to Mr. Ayrton, and to back it with all the earnestness he knows full well the subject requires, and it is, indeed, no trifling matter. The Judge hopes that it is not figuratively, though it assuredly is literally, true, that at Warrington the County Court "stinks in the nostrils of the public."

———

No. XCVIII.

Mrs. F. PENNINGTON.

17, Hyde Park Terrace, W.,
March 2, 1871.

Dear Mr. Rylands,—

There is a very strong feeling in our committee (C.D.A.) that some of the subjected women should be examined ; we shall not consider the case complete unless they are. Can you do anything to further this ? I was asked to see you and ascertain, but I am doing *two* hours' work in every *one* as it is, and cannot get over to see you. I know you will be grateful too for escaping the loss of time it would cause you ! We are also very much pressed by friends in all parts about Mrs. Butler giving evidence. I know you have this in hand too, and hope you may manage it. I had a letter from her yesterday in which she says that her committee (which means Miss Becker, Mrs. Bright and Miss Wolstenholme) are strongly against her giving evidence unless she is " dragged up." But she is evidently quite willing to come herself, and I think even dragging her up would be better than not having her. I don't think she would do us harm by her evidence, and her appearance in the flesh would remove some prejudices from the minds of commissioners. They no doubt expect her to be a large, rawboned, strong featured individual about ten feet high, and I doubt whether they will believe she is the real " Simon Pure " when they see her. Mrs. Milleson and I indulged in a little fling at the Commission in the *Shield*, which comes out this week. You must forgive us, for our friends in all parts of the country are threatening to slacken work, under the impression that the Commission is going to seal the fate of the Acts by an adverse verdict. I did so long to be able to say that we knew they would not, but you need not be frightened, I said nothing of the kind. Mr. McLaren is to try and see you and other friendly M.P.'s to-day about Parliamentary action. Mr. Pennington called to see you last night but found you out. Jacob Bright and others are for delaying Fowler's motion, but I can't help thinking this a mistake. They say so many M.P.'s will shelter themselves behind the Royal Commission, and abstain from voting, but these will be mainly our opponents and *very shaky* friends. Those who are heartily with us will give their votes irrespective of any expected report of the Royal Commission, and we shall at least know upon whom we may rely. Our position must be made worse by the adverse report of the Commission, and if we wait for that we may lose all chance of bringing on the question effectively this year. I am so sorry for all your time and labour spent on this wretched business. I hope the size of the testimonial is not to be proportioned to the time spent in earning it, or you will have to find another house large enough to hold it !

I meant to write a few lines, and this is the result.

Yours very truly,

M. PENNINGTON.

No. XCIX.

Mrs. JOSEPHINE E. BUTLER.

Ladies' National Association
for the
Repeal of the Contagious Diseases Acts.

280, South Hill, Park Road,
Liverpool,
March 13, 1871.

My Dear Mr. Rylands,—

I have written to the Secretary of the Royal Commission to tell him that the only portion of the subject on which he has called me to give evidence, on which I can consent to give evidence, is public opinion in the North on the subject of the C. D. Acts, and especially with reference to the views of working men, with whom I have had a good deal of intercourse.

The Commission, I am told, deals only with *facts*, but as the persons to whom I refer are for the most part electors, it seems to me that their opinions on this subject may be regarded as facts which may in future elections practically influence the whole question, more than the opinions of medical men, etc.

I have, however, said to the Secretary that this is the *sole* point on which I am willing to give evidence, and asked him, if it should be thought not worth while for me to give such evidence, to let me know whether I am released from appearing at all.

This would be a great relief to me ; not that I fear in the least standing before the Commission, nor that

I shall have any difficulty in giving briefly and clearly the information I have to give, but it seems some of our friends are so much averse to my giving evidence at all, that I shall be glad, by not doing so, to avoid incurring their displeasure. As it is, I only consented to give this evidence as a private individual, and not as Secretary to the Association of Women, who do not recognise any authority in the Royal Commission, and who are indifferent to its verdict, even as I am myself, as far as the great moral question is concerned.

If I have to come up, I shall be glad to put in your hands a sketch of what I have to say. I suppose I shall not be judged to be guilty of " contempt of court " if I absolutely decline to answer questions on any other part of the subject.

I remain,
Yours very truly,
JOSEPHINE E. BUTLER.

No. C.

Mr. EDWARD CROSSLEY.

Park Road,
Halifax,
March 11, 1871.

Dear Sir,—

I am very much obliged to you for writing to me on behalf of the re-election of Mr. Stansfield. Any other course I should have most strenuously opposed.

Our Committee decided simply to wait upon Mr. Stansfield with a resolution maintaining their hostility to the C. D. Acts, expressing the hope that when the time came for decision Mr. Stansfield would vote unhesitatingly against the Acts, and also congratulating him upon receiving a seat in the Cabinet. Some of our extreme members talked of opposition more, I believe, as a show of fight than anything else.

Mr. Stansfield has given us a very candid and courteous interview, and has said as much as he was at liberty to do without committing Government.

I am glad to have your assurance along with Mr. Mundella's that Mr. Stansfield is with us. We have expressed ourselves hopefully to him, and if we have used severe means in the past, it has been with the object of thoroughly rousing the attention of Government to the subject. I sincerely trust the Royal Commission will do its utmost to report as early as possible, so that the matter may be decided this Session.

Mr. Stansfield has stated that this will very likely
be accomplished.

I remain, Dear Sir,

Yours sincerely,

Edward Crossley.

No. CI.

Mr. JOHN GORDON M'MINNIES.

Farington,

April 27, 1871.

My Dear Peter,—

You have had a busy week, and we are all satisfied
with the result, so far as we know it.   I suppose Lowe
will carry his new proposals, whatever they are, and
that the gentlemen below the gangway will not support
Disraeli in any vote that amounts to one of want of
confidence.

I can give you no idea of the despair and dishearten-
ment which the recent conduct of the ministry has
occasioned to its best and most useful supporters in
this part of the country.   The feeling is that all the
efforts made by the party in 1868 have been made
useless, and we are all very greatly discouraged.
Gladstone has put us in a false position by these
proposed taxes and this excessive expenditure.   There
has been some talk of a private remonstrance with

him, coming from the various towns in the country, on the way in which he is leading the party. Forster has thoroughly estranged the most active dissenters, and now this unpardonable retrogressive financial policy has made what was bad enough before still worse. Gladstone must use his majority to carry his measures and beat the Tories, and not accept their help to beat his best friends. John Crosfield has been in correspondence with him about this feeling on the part of the Liberals in the country, and Gladstone, in his reply, seems to blame the House for driving him into extravagant estimates. He mentions particularly some " ultra Liberal " who boasted to his constituents that he had forced him into the additional estimates of last session for the defence of Belgium. He says that this " ultra Liberal " spoke against the Budget on Monday night, and I suppose he must have meant Fawcett. I do not think Gladstone, in his long defence of himself in reply to John Crosfield, is successful. He says he was forced, but he ought not to have allowed himself to be forced. Bright would not have done so. He seems to trace everything to the additional vote for £2,000,000 and 20,000 men last session, but he should have kept cool and waited. His majority, or most of them, would have supported him, and time and events would have justified him. I hope this will be a lesson to them all.

With kind regards to Carrie,

I remain,

Yours affectionately,

J. G. M'MINNIES.

No. CII.

Mr. JOHN CROSFIELD.

Llandudno,
April 29, 1871.

My Dear Peter,—

I received your letter yesterday and told Hadfield he must be sure to give your speech verbatim as written by you. I also ordered him to print 250 copies in pamphlet form.

We shall come to you on Tuesday, the 9th, as arranged, if, in the meantime, Parliament is not dissolved and you are all sent back to your constituents!

Much as I disapprove of the increased expenditure, I do not wish to see a majority against the Government on Monday night, and I hope you below the gangway will support Mr. Gladstone when the division takes place on the 2d Income Tax.

I wrote to Gladstone last Sunday, telling him how disappointed the Liberals in Lancashire were that he had not resisted this great expenditure, and how it damaged us as a party. I got a long and courteous reply by *return of post*, which I will show you. I was delighted with your speech. We consider it the best you have made, and will raise you to a high position in the House and the country. Mackie,* as usual, showed his love for you by quoting every bit he could find in the Tory papers against you. You will see a letter in the *Examiner* signed, " A Liberal."

<hr>

*Editor of the *Warrington Guardian*

I trust you will carry the Budget on Monday night; it would be a great loss to us if the Government went out of office now.

Yours very truly,
JOHN CROSFIELD.

No. CIII.

MR. C. E. MACQUEEN.

Financial Reform Association,
Lord Street,
Liverpool,
May 3, 1871.

MY DEAR SIR,—

I send you half a dozen of the Almanacs for distribution if you will take the trouble, and shall be glad to forward more for the same purpose, as we are overstocked, and the thing is likely to be more serviceable abroad than lying on our shelves.

Mr. Gladstone has, no doubt, said and done good and great things in his time, but I don't see that past performances afford any palliation whatever for present backslidings, and to tell you the plain truth my faith in him has long been of a very flickering description.

Are we to expect genuine Freedom of Trade as well as Household Suffrage from the Right Hon. Ben. ? It seems quite on the cards.

Yours truly,
C. E. Macqueen.

No. CIV.

Mr. J. GORDON M'MINNIES.

Farington,
5 June, 1871.

My Dear Peter,—

Politics are in a very unsatisfactory state. Government are greatly to blame. There never was a party worse led. I suppose nobody expected the Liberal party to keep together, and for Gladstone to keep the majority more than some five years ; but we did not expect to see the party macadamised in the third session. The beginning of the evil was that stupid increase of the estimates last July, and of course Lowe's Budget made everything worse. People who knew Lowe at Sydney, say that he is a traitor, a traitor by nature, that he cannot help betraying anybody with whom he is connected. " Lowe's dodges " became quite a phrase in the House there, and the gentleman who has this opinion of Lowe and who knew him well in Australia, told our friend Smith Robinson that some day or other he would ruin this Government, intentionally, and not by accident or blunder.

At the same time I think the Government have reason to complain of their friends, and especially of those below the gangway. Our advanced friends have not been loyal to the party and their leaders, and they have played into the hands of the Tory party by their everlasting motions and speeches. Take White's motion the other night—no good object was served by it, and no good object could be served by it; it was simply a waste of time. The result of all is a session lost. I am afraid the Army Bill and the Ballot Bill will both be lost. I do not care for the Ballot, but the Liberal party in the country are wild for it. The Army Bill I shall regret, for I think it the best measure introduced to Parliament for years. I quite agree with you as to the injustice of paying for over-regulation prices, but the three millions unjustly paid is well earned by the abolition of the purchase system, and so would ten times three millions. Besides, these reforms in England are always compromises, and mostly compromises at the expense of the taxpayers. The gift of 20 millions to the slave-owners could not be justified, and it was opposed by many good and earnest politicians. A duty on corn was levied for three years after the Country and Parliament had come to the conviction that duties on corn were unjust and impolitic, and so on in other instances which I do not remember now.

I hope Government will be supported by votes and silence, for nothing could be worse than a change of government and a dissolution just now. The Liberal party would go like chaff before the wind. I do not know precisely how we stand in Warrington. I am told that Todd thinks we have no chance of winning, but we cannot get him to mark a list. He is incorrigibly lazy and inefficient. Every year will tell in our favour, but I fear that upon the last Register we should be beaten hollow. If there is a chance of an early dissolution we must meet together (which we have not done for some time) and consult as to our action.

I have not seen George Crosfield for some time, but I gather from a conversation with Mrs. George, that he is thoroughly disgusted with Gladstone's conduct and the course of politics generally. In fact we are all very much down on our luck, and the Tories are correspondingly jubilant. They had a dinner party of the captains, etc., at the Lion, the other day, which appears to have been no great affair, but it no doubt keeps them together and ready. I have not read the speeches.

I am glad you have enjoyed your holiday. I was not in Warrington during Whitsun week, until the end of it, for my house was not quite habitable, and my people were moving.

I am,

My dear Peter,

Yours affectionately,

J. G. M'MINNIES.

No. CV.

Mr. F. PENNINGTON.

Broome Hall,
Surrey,
June 3, 1871.

Dear Mr. Rylands,—

Mrs. Pennington has read to me the letter from your Secretary [Mrs. Rylands], which gives a short and clear account of the most important part of the draft of Report of Royal Commission. (I congratulate you on the possession of such a secretary). Mrs. Pennington goes to town on Monday morning next, and purposes to call at your house to look at the Draft Report, if you have no objection. If you have, please drop a line, that she may not trouble you. We hear that several Commissioners are disposed to recommend the adoption of the Act of 1864, which enforces the examination of any woman, who any one swears they have reason to believe has infected them. I think you will agree with me that this is a retention of the most odious part of the present Acts, and places in the hands of every man a weapon against every woman of the vilest kind.

Yours,

Fred. Pennington.

No. CVI.

Mr. WILLIAM FOWLER, M.P. (Cambridge.)

Berkeley Square,

June 17, 1871.

My Dear Sir,—

I am extremely obliged for your note. I am very sensible of the value of your self-denying labours on the Commission. I thank you for them, and I feel that you have more right than almost any one to urge your views on me. I see, too, the great force of your arguments. I have been extremely puzzled throughout as to what would be the right course to adopt. I thought the compromise to which I referred, and to which the Government have assented, would have avoided the difficulty. It still appears to me that it will, because if the Government vote with me, we shall be sure to carry our point, and the Commission will be very anxious to get the division, and so test the opinions of members. But I feel strongly the force of what you say on the other side, and I will carefully consider the matter from your point of view before we meet on Monday.

At this period of the Session, it appears to me a very serious thing to lose my place on Tuesday. You know as well as I how difficult it is to get a day, and I am afraid if I lose this chance I shall not get another this Session, and therefore, if the Report after all is not to our mind, we shall have lost the chance of a division this Session.

Yours faithfully,

W. Fowler.

N

No. CVII.

Mrs. F. PENNINGTON.

The National Association for the Repeal of the
Contagious Diseases Acts.

50, Great Marlborough St.,
London, W.,
June 19, 1871.

Dear Mr. Rylands,—

Mr. Pennington has just announced to our
committee that Mr. Fowler has agreed, after
consultation with several members, to *withdraw* his
motion for Repeal. Is withdraw a mistake for
postpone? No doubt practically, they amount to
the same thing, but won't it look better to the outside
public if it is put in the form of a postponement?
I write this privately, not as from the Committee,
and feel almost sure you or Mr. Fowler will have
thought of this; but I write for the chance of it
having been overlooked.

Yours very truly,
M. Pennington.

No. CVIII.

Mr. ROBERT GASKELL.

Weymouth,
June 26, 1871.

My Dear Sir,—

The debate in reference to the dethronement of the Nawab of Tonk will be renewed on the 30th. Miss Carpenter has asked me to communicate with any members of whom I have any personal knowledge, and to ask the favour of their attendance in the House on that occasion.

I have carefully read a small book entitled " Pilgrimage to the Caaba and Charing Cross ;" the statement of this case therein contained formed the basis of the speeches in the previous debate. I have come to the conclusion that what is asked is a simple act of justice, and the enquiry ought to be granted, unless Sir Stafford Northcote satisfactorily accounts for the dethronement of this native Indian Prince. I hope you will be able to make it convenient to be present when the debate is renewed.

I am quite glad to have this opportunity of conveying to you my admiration of the patriotic position you have taken in the House, and hope that, notwithstanding Dizzy's sneers, you will give them plenty more of your *didactic* drilling. I wish we had such representatives from this benighted place, the folly and knavery of which may have its apt representatives probably in our respective members. We are regularly bought and sold with a price, and

are most admirably nursed, both wet and dry ; and
what is worse, I see no way out of it here.

With kind regards,
I am, Dear Sir,
Yours truly,
ROBERT GASKELL.

No. CIX.

(Central Association for Stopping the Sale of
Intoxicating Liquors on Sunday.)

43, Market Street,
Manchester,
June 26, 1871.

DEAR SIR,—

We have pleasure in sending you the following copy
of a resolution adopted by our Executive Committee
this day :—·

" That the warmest thanks of this committee be
given to Peter Rylands, Esq., M.P., for his able and
praiseworthy efforts made in endeavouring to pass
the ' Sale of Liquors on Sunday Bill.' "

We are, dear Sir,
Yours faithfully,
ROBERT WHITWORTH,
EDWARD WHITWELL,
Hon. Secs.

No. CX.

Rev. T. A. STOWELL.

> Haltwhistle Vicarage,
> Near Carlisle,
> July 6, 1871.

My Dear Sir,—

A statement was made at our committee meeting last Monday, on the authority of Mr. Raper, that you had expressed your unwillingness again to give notice of the introduction of our Bill. Our committee wished me to write and ask you if this was true, and also, if it should be so, whether it would be agreeable to you that we should ask Mr. Birley to give notice to that effect.

I need hardly say how sorry we should be to lose your kind services, though, I am sure, not your sympathy, and how grateful we are for your past co-operation and uniform courtesy.

With kind regards,

> Believe me,
> Yours sincerely,
> T. Alfred Stowell.

No. CXI.

Mr. W. D. CHRISTIE.

32, Dorset Sq.,
July 7, 1871.

My Dear Mr. Rylands,—

I return you Hammond's evidence—or, rather, no-evidence—with thanks. I enclose some questions I suggest.

Pray work out that delusive return of last year to Shaw. As to Hammond's receipt of secret service money, I have been surprised to find by how many persons it is known. It has been known some time to H. Merivale, Under Secretary of Indian Office, and to C. J. Herries, Deputy Chairman of Board of Inland Revenue, among others. It seems, indeed, extensively known. I never heard of it till you told me.

I have not seen your new notice. I should advise you to act as follows :—

Move for a committee to enquire as to whether Foreign Office Secret Service money is or is not applied only to objects recognised as legitimate, and whether it is applied for salaries and pensions where there should and need be no secrecy. State in your speech on your honour as a member of Parliament that you believe secret service money to be appropriated wrongly to salaries of officials and to pensions, naming the cases of which you are sure, but not your authorities, and demand a committee to enquire. With such a statement I do not think they could refuse you.

Excuse me for offering you this advice. Temporising with them is of no use. Evasive official answers will be given as long as possible to simple questions put in the House of Commons, when you have no power of replying or criticising.

You should get the Tories to back you. Drummond Wolff and, I hear, his cousin, F. Walpole, member of the committee, are zealously with you, and I fancy you might rely on the exertions of the Tory whip, for a man understood to be against Hammond. Lowther has lately told me that he simply *hates* Hammond.

Yours very truly,
W. D. Christie.

No. CXII.

Mrs. F. PENNINGTON.

Broome Hall,
Surrey,
July 22, 1871.

Dear Mr. Rylands,—

I am afraid you thought our party very ungrateful on Thursday, and I think some of them are, though, as you know, I am not one of them. Unfortunately, they will persist in expecting all the commissioners on our side to be "apostles." But without being very unreasonable, they are somewhat justified in feeling annoyance at being told by all our opponents, and almost every newspaper, and by Bruce, that "every case of abuse on the part of the police has broken down," and that the statements of opponents of the Acts are mostly "perversions of the truth." *You* know, and *we* know, that this is not the case, but if we attempt to deny it we are floored immediately by being told that it is the unanimous verdict of the commissioners, as all have signed the report, and none have dissented from those parts of it. At the adjourned conference, after the deputation, the feeling was so strong, and the meeting generally so excited, that I asked Mr. Shaw to explain that the particular clauses most resented, and others, were carried by a majority against our friends on the commission. This allayed the tumult to some extent, though many said, " Then why did they sign a report with which they did not agree?" The feeling is still very strong amongst us that something must be done to clear our witnesses and ourselves from the charges brought against us in the report, and money has been subscribed to enable our association to advertise the truth, if it cannot be done any other way. The most effectual way would be for you, and any other commissioners who agree with you, to write a letter to the papers saying that you were beaten on a division ; but this may be contrary to the etiquette of Royal Commissions. If you can't do it, I suppose we may make use of it ; but what reasons are we to give for your having signed that " very inconsequent document," seeing that you differed from it in other points besides those contained in your two Minority Reports? Our committee meets on Monday to decide what is to be done, and I should be glad of a line from you or Mrs. Rylands, addressed to Great Marlborough Street, telling me what can be done. I am very sorry to trouble you when you are away for rest, but it is part of my gratitude to you, for I am reluctant anything should be done in this matter which does not put your share in it in the best light. We shall, of course, publish that the commissioners refused to hear any of the women concerned, and as women are not necessarily liars because they are unchaste, any more than men are, it is difficult to see how they justify the refusal.

Yours very truly,
M. PENNINGTON.

No. CXIII.

Mr. H. LABOUCHERE.

2, Bolton Street,
July 19, 1871.

DEAR MR. RYLANDS,—

Would you be good enough to cast your eye over a letter which I published to-day in the *Daily News* signed "Ensign Jones."

Captain Wellesley, adjutant and lieutenant in the regiment of the Guards (the Captain is only honorary) is the gentleman who is to go to St. Petersburg. He is the son of Lord Cowley. I understand on good authority that Hoyer, the *Times* war correspondent, and, if I remember rightly, one of the officers sent out by the Government to report on the war, and a Colonel who speaks Russian, applied for it. These facts were told me by a Captain who himself is senior in service to Wellesley, who speaks Russian, and who applied.

I need not observe that this is a job, and that it is a mere waste of money to send out a young guardsman to report on the Russian army. Perhaps a question, whether a statement which has appeared in the papers that a young guardsman, who has only done duty as a Lieutenant, is to go as Military Attaché at Petersburg is true, and whether it is also true that gentlemen his seniors who knew Russian, and a well known military officer applied for the place, might elicit something.

The authorities are so cunning that they probably will stave off a compromising reply. I think that, in reality, the appointment is made by the Foreign Office, and not by the Duke of Cambridge.

Yours truly,
H. LABOUCHERE.

No. CXIV.

Mr. HENRY LABOUCHERE.

2, Bolton Street,
Piccadilly,
July 22, 1871.

Dear Mr. Rylands,—

Would you be good enough to let me have the dates of the two questions which you have already put, respecting the application of the secret service money to increase the salaries of officials.

It may be a question whether it will be better to take up the case in the *Daily News* on the Estimates, or on your receiving a reply to your question on Monday.

With respect to the appointment of Lieutenant Wellesley, Enfield will no doubt deny that applications were made to the War Office ; the fact being that officers who wished for the post " sounded " the authorities in the same way as the authorities sounded their eight pets, who thought Russia too cold a climate for their constitutions. Col. Chesney was, I believe, the only man of any mark who refused. I am assured that the Grand Duke Vladimir, or Brunerv, who is very thick with Lord Cowley, really did un-officially convey to the Foreign Office the fact that our friend, the Lieutenant, would be acceptable to the Russian Court.

If you want a fact, in drawing attention to the case on the estimates, to prove the importance of, say, a

good military man at a foreign court, here is one :—
Stoffel, the French military attaché at Berlin, was
given a command during the siege of Paris. The
press protested, and said he had proved himself useless to his Government by not keeping it advised as
to the efficiency of Germany. He, on this, demanded
that his reports should be published. They were
looked up at the Ministry of Foreign Affairs, and
several of them were found to be unopened ; when
published they proved that, had they been read, the
French War Office would have had ample details
respecting the military condition of Germany ; and,
it is to be presumed, would not have rushed into
hostilities.

In one of these reports, Stoffel points out that the
Prussian Government insists upon a certain number
of Staff Officers learning Russian, in order to be used
for missions to Russia.

As the Second-Secretaries in the Diplomatic Service
do not, after perhaps 20 years of service, receive £500
for living and working at St. Petersburg ; it is simply
ridiculous to say that £500 per annum is not a sufficient salary to induce any officer in the army above
the rank of a lieutenant to go there.

Yours truly,

H. Labouchere.

No. CXV.

Mr. HENRY LABOUCHERE.

2, Bolton St.,
Piccadilly,
July 30, 1871.

Dear Mr. Rylands,—

You will see in to-morrow's *Daily News* an article and several letters upon the subject of " Secret Service Money." Pray do not mention my name to anyone in connection with the matter, as, from my having been in the Diplomatic Service, it will be said that I am making use of knowledge which I obtained through having been under the Foreign Office.

With respect to the £10,000 alleged to be spent by Glyn, I, of course, never saw the cheques, but it has always been understood in the Foreign Office, that this amount finds its way to the Treasury for party purposes. Of course, if you inquire of Gladstone or anyone, an attempt will be made to conceal the fact by some sort of official special pleading. What do you think of a question to Glyn himself? He might be asked whether he directly or indirectly receives any portion of the Secret Service money, and whether directly or indirectly any part of it is used for any purposes connected with elections, or with those party functions, which it is understood that he fulfils as Parliamentary Secretary of the Treasury. Perhaps you will be told that it is spent in duties such as are openly notorious, such as printing the whips to members, etc. These, however, cannot cost more than £500 per annum.

Yours truly,
H. LABOUCHERE.

No. CXVI.

Mr. W. D. CHRISTIE.

32, Dorset Square,
August 4, 1871.

My Dear Mr. Rylands,—

I suspect and fear that the *Daily News* has had a hint from the Government not to go on about the Secret Service Money, or at any rate to moderate their tone. Otherwise, I cannot understand their not putting in my last letter signed " A Taxpayer." I do not know if a hint from you, through your channel, whatever it may be, might yet get it put in in time for your discussion. Why should Hammond have more salary than the other permanent Under Secretaries, who all have Secret Service Money to manage? And it is not hinted that any of the others get anything for themselves out of the secret fund. Herman Merivale, Under Secretary to the India Council. formerly Under Secretary of Colonial Office, is at least as "eminent" as His Eminence of the Foreign Office. So is Liddell of the Home Office.

By the way, Odo Russell is doing Hammond's work in his absence. Question to put to Lord Enfield : Is Odo Russell receiving the quota of the £500 a year for secret-service duty ?

Yours very truly,
W. D. CHRISTIE.

No. CXVII.

MR. W. D. CHRISTIE.

32, Dorset Square,
Sept. 23, 1871.

MY DEAR MR. RYLANDS,—

I write you a line to tell you that the Foreign Office have sanctioned a claim from Sir R. Alcock to a pension of £3,200 a year ! ! and sent in their recommendation to the Treasury, where the question now rests. The thing is a monstrosity ; a blunder of our friend Hammond's. The pension has been calculated on the ground of his having 32 years of service, ending with a salary of £6,000, and the calculation is under the Superannuation Act of 1859. But Alcock, for a pension under this Act, cannot, I contend, avail himself of consular service beyond the time when he ceased to be Minister and Consul General in Japan, and then there would be something to be said as to the amount. And perhaps he has the option between a pension under the Superannuation Act up to that date and a pension under clause 15 of the Diplomatic Pensions Act (Hammond's) of 1869. I shall look into it more closely. It is a monstrous pension anyhow, against equity and the spirit of the Pension Acts. If you can do anything by threatening the Foreign Office or Treasury you should do so.

The highest ambassador of longest service gets only £1,700 a year. You may rely on my facts, which I have on the best authority. It will be a precedent for other cases.

Yours very truly,
W. D. Christie.

No. CXVIII.

Right Hon. W. E. BAXTER, M.P.

Kirkcaldrum,
Forfar,
Sept. 27, 1871.

Dear Rylands,—

I have received your favour of 25th, and am astonished to hear of the proposed pension to Sir R.

Alcock. Surely it can't be true. I have written to-day to know.

Ever truly yours,
W. E. BAXTER.

No. CXIX.

MR. W. D. CHRISTIE.

32, Dorset Square,
Oct. 1, 1871.

MY DEAR MR. RYLANDS,—

It seems as if the Editor of the *Daily News* does not mean to attend to you, and enable you to prevent this monstrously anomalous pension for Sir R. Alcock. I suspect that Lord Granville, who is a very insinuating man, has given "a hint" to the Editor, and *Daily News* does not like to go against him.

I hear that Baxter is considered in the Treasury the laziest official that ever was there; and my information is not derived from my son, who (I dare say you know) is a clerk in the Treasury.

Yours very truly,
W. D. CHRISTIE.

No. CXX.

Mr. W. D. CHRISTIE.

32, Dorset Square,
Nov. 2, 1871.

My Dear Mr. Rylands,—

I caused enquiry to be made yesterday about what the Treasury had done in the matter of Sir R. Alcock's pension, and I am glad to find that they have cut down Hammond's £3,200 to £1,300. This is well; it might be a good subject for you next year to question Hammond about. And do you think you could ask Hill to return you that long letter on the Pension Acts, of which I kept no copy, and which might serve as a brief. There is no doubt that the spirit of the Acts was frustrated by the pensions granted to Griffith and Bingham, but then the Treasury was chiefly in fault.

I wish you could take up and lecture on the Civil Service Estimates generally. Here is a matter which I wish you could get some of your economist friends to manage next year.

Soon after Gladstone's Government came in, they made a new salaried appointment of £1,200 a year, 2nd Civil Service Commissioner. Till then the Chief Commissioner, Mr. E. Ryan, was assisted only by unpaid Commissioners. Dr. Dasent (sub-editor of the *Times*) was appointed; Walrond, the Secretary, passed over. Dasent has now become Editor of Fraser's Magazine, £500 a year. Surely Dasent ought to be required to give all his valuable time to his public appointment. There are as fit and fitter men who would take the appointment and give all their good time to it. Dasent, I know, does nothing at the Commission, Walrond is the labouring oar. Dasent writes much, edits the *Times* when Delane is away (very wrong), and now is going to edit a monthly magazine.

My notion of proper economy is that a chief of a laborious and largely responsible office, liberally paid by the public, should give all his business time to it, and that a man who will not give this should not be appointed, if an equally good man, who will give all his time, will take it.

With kind regards,
Yours very truly,
W. D. CHRISTIE.

No. CXXI.

RIGHT HON. SIR G. O. TREVELYAN, M.P.

31, Park Street,
Grosvenor Sq.,
Nov. 20, 1871.

DEAR MR. RYLANDS,—

I am very glad you are going to preside at the Warrington meeting. May the Alliance never have a less useful neutral than yourself! It is what, I suppose, the lawyers call an armed neutrality. I am afraid I cannot come. There is a meeting at Liverpool the next day, and I am not strong enough in mind or body to exceed an average of over a meeting a week, and least of all two on two days running. You and Lawson are made of tougher stuff. If it was a mere question of health and longevity, I should care little, but health, or a certain standard of health, is necessary for usefulness; and really you and Lawson are a battery powerful enough for any single action. We must not waste metal. I regret much not being able to accept your hospitality at Bewsey House, and remain.

Yours very truly,
G. O. Trevelyan.

No. CXXII.

Hon. GEORGE GLYN, M.P.

(Parliamentary Secretary of the Treasury).

Blandford,
Nov. 29, 1871.

My Dear Mr. Rylands,—

I am glad the matter has been arranged at the Admiralty. I quite agree with your P.S., it is clear we shall have trouble upon the Education Question, though I have much faith in the desire of the country to get what good they can out of the Act and not to carp too severely at trifles; still there are many rocks ahead which we must sail over, and if our friends wish it, we can do so without grounding! I think the pressure of other matter will of itself postpone the Irish question, but Fawcett and the Tories make it difficult, or may do so.

I don't at all look forward myself to next session with apprehension, for though the proof of unity of late in the constituencies is not satisfactory, I have more faith than many in our Liberal members sticking to our Leader, and in his power of leading in difficult times.

Yours truly,
G. G. GLYN.

No. CXXIII.

Right Hon. W. E. BAXTER, M.P.

Treasury,
Dec. 11, 1871.

Dear Rylands,—

Did you arrange with Lord Granville not to oppose an addition of £300 to Hammond's salary in place of

what he used to crib from the Secret Service Money ?
I strongly opposed it, but am confronted by the
authority of the member for Warrington.

Ever yours,
W. E. Baxter.

No. CXXIV.

Mr. J. D. LEWIS, M.P.

Westbury House,
Petersfield,
Dec. 20, 1871.

My Dear Rylands,—

The first sentence which met my eye in your address
at Manchester almost took my breath away.

"If we got rid of the traditions of the Foreign
Office, we should find that we could do with a much
less army and *navy.*"

And you expect me to endorse such sentiments as
that I However, on the subject of foreign treaties
generally, I agree with you.   With respect to Belgium,
however, the point always made was not as to the
addition of 40 miles of coast to 929 miles, nor of
4,000,000 of men to 40,000,000, but as to the *Port of
Antwerp.* Napoleon I., if I remember aright, always
spoke of this as a " pistol held to the heart of England."

However, I believe the importance of the port of Antwerp, in this connection, has been much exaggerated, as has been well shown in some letters of Captain ~~Stuard~~ Osborn to the *Times* a year or two ago.

Very truly yours,

J. D. LEWIS.

"But no more about cutting down the Navy, an thou lovest me, Peter!"

No. CXXV.

Mrs. JACOB BRIGHT.

Alderley Edge,
Jan. 4, 1872.

DEAR MR. RYLANDS,—

I write to ask you if you will kindly tell me what day will suit you to take the chair at our Women's Suffrage meeting in Warrington. We should be glad to hold it any time after the 30th of January. We want to form a committee in Warrington. Can you give me a list of names of people likely to help to form one? Miss Becker will then come over and call upon them. We must have Mrs. Rylands' name among them.

If you cannot take the chair after the 30th, what day would suit you? Will you let me have an answer

by return of post, as our committee is making arrangements to hold public meetings in all the Lancashire
and Yorkshire towns, and of course it will greatly
facilitate matters to know what days we have at liberty
for other places. We can get you several good lady
speakers for Warrington. I think Lilias Ashworth
and Mrs. Fawcett will come. They both spoke
beautifully at Birmingham. Miss Becker will speak
if required. Who is the best person to apply to to
get up the meeting?

Please give me the address of that Independent
minister we met at your house, as I want him to speak
for us.

Very truly yours,
Ursula M. Bright.

No. CXXVI.

Mr. C. E. MACQUEEN.

Financial Reform Association,
Lord St., Liverpool,
March 25, 1872.

My Dear Sir,—
Your contribution for next Financial Reformer is
most welcome, anything else which you find time

and inclination to write will always be, and it shall stand No. 1.

I will get the Council on Wednesday to authorise me to write to all our subscribing M.P.'s, and even to the ex-ones, including Mr. Stansfeld, who promised grand things some years ago, when he attended our meeting in the Philharmonic Hall, along with Bright, Pollard, and others, and Mr. Goschen himself, who sent us £5 a year or two ago, with high commendation.

As to expenditure—Royal Parks, Civil List jobbery, Eyre the Butcher, match tax, etc., etc.,—Gladstone seems bent on building up a wall strong enough to break his own head against, and he will undoubtedly succeed in that exploit unless he mends his ways most materially. Anything more sophistical, supercilious, more open to contradiction, or more domineering than that speech of his in answer to Dilke, I never saw. He came in with a blaze, and, at present, nothing seems more likely than that he will go out with a stink.

> " 'Tis true, 'tis pity ; pity 'tis, 'tis true."

Yours truly,
C. F. MACQUEEN.

No. CXXVII.

Mr. EDMOND BEALES.

Osborn House,
Bolton Gardens, South, S.W.,
April 1, 1872.

Dear Mr. Rylands,—

I am glad to see that you intend still to raise the
question in the House of the right of the people to
meet in the parks. I have never had any doubt of
that right, and consider that the Derby Government
acted wholly illegally in closing the park gates against
the Reform League meeting in July, 1866. I could
not afford to incur the expense of an action to try the
question at that time, and there were technical
difficulties also in the way. But I determined to
insist on the right in the following May, 1867, and I
think it is quite clear that if the Government then
felt they could legally oppose the right, or prevent
this meeting, of which I had given notice, they would
have done so, after warning me formally through Mr.
Walpole and Sir Richard Mayne that the meeting was
prohibited; after making large preparations as to both
military and police for forcibly preventing it; after,
also, swearing-in large detachments of special constables, and endeavouring, through various members
of Parliament, to dissuade me from an attempt, which,
it was alleged, might cause much bloodshed and
endanger my own life. It was not till the very
morning of the meeting, and after I had ex-

pressed my determination to persevere at all risks, that they, in accordance with an opinion of their own law officers, which they had had some months in their possession, undid all their preparations, and notified that there would be no attempt to prevent the meeting being held. I considered that a clear admission of the right, for I do not admit that the law, even of trespass, could be applied as intimated in their opinion referred to ; and when Mr. Hardy's Bill was, a few months afterwards, introduced for the purpose of placing the right thus admitted under the control of the Home Secretary, Mr. Mill and others, at my request, successfully opposed that Bill on the ground that the Common Law gave all necessary power for preventing a legal right, like that of public meeting in the parks, being *riotously, or otherwise improperly* exercised. The withdrawal of that Bill was a further admission of the *right* thus insisted on. I cannot understand the attitude of the present Government on this question. I was under the impression that they, equally with me, considered this right to have been admitted and established by what occurred in 1867. I further understood that they actually intended to arrange for convenient places in four parks (including Hyde Park), N., E., S., and W., in the metropolis being allotted for the holding of meetings. Why they should not at once have made known this intention, and their purposes generally, and thus have avoided, instead of inviting, as it were, a storm of unnecessary irritation and unpopularity, I can not conceive.

Of one thing I am certain, that to dispute the right of meeting in the parks is to risk the raising of serious questions as to the title to the parks on the part of the reigning family.

I do not wish, in my present position, to mix myself up unnecessarily with this important question, but I think it only due to you, who are now championing it, to put you in possession thus frankly of my views on the subject, after being formerly so much and so personally interested in it.

Yours faithfully,

EDMOND BEALES.

No. CXXVIII.

MR. DAVID ROBERTSON, M.P. (Berwick Co.)

56, Upper Brook Street,

July 18, 1872.

MY DEAR MR. RYLANDS,—

I have had a most unfortunate sore throat, and have been in bed these three days, where I now am, or I should have had the pleasure of a conversation with you in the House of Commons, and I am persuaded that in five minutes I could convince you of the immense importance and desirableness, in the interests of England, to continue entire the present legation and consulate at Buenos Ayres.

I learn this morning that you also propose not to allow that excellent man Mr. Parish to continue Chairman of the Committee of the Great Southern Railway of Buenos Ayres made entirely by English Capital.

Now it does so happen that I am the Chairman of that Railway, the only company I ever belonged to in my life, and which I am proud to think has done a great deal of good to that country as well as paid its shareholders, from its excellent management, to which Mr. Parish has greatly contributed ; and there is no less amount than £1,200,000 embarked, and it is of immense importance to have a man of Mr. Parish's high integrity at the head of it in Buenos Ayres, which he has been since 1862.

The Consuls in those countries are the worst paid men of all her Majesty's servants abroad, and are the most valuable, especially if you get so able a one as Mr. Parish, in preserving peace between England and the countries to which they are accredited, and in promoting the commercial and other relations of Englishmen. It is also well known that the expenses of living in those countries being so great, the consular pay is quite inadequate to support a man, and it has long been the practice that with the consent of the Foreign Office, Consuls may undertake other duties which will not interfere with their public duties as Consul.

Mr. Parish was appointed, in 1862, the Chairman of our Committee, with the entire approbation of Lord Clarendon, who knew more about these South American countries than any Foreign Minister we have ever had, excepting Lord Palmerston, who took a great interest in Buenos Ayres, and knowing the great value to England of amicable relations and of the increasing interest of England with them, he did everything he could to promote it, and had a high opinion of Mr. Parish, whose father, Sir Woodbine Parish, was the first man sent out by Mr. Canning and negotiated the Treaty, which has led to so much prosperity between Buenos Ayres and England.

I will venture to say amongst the merchants of all England, of whom there are a great many interested in those countries in London, Liverpool, and Manchester, there is not a man who would not concur in stating how invaluable Mr. Parish's services have been to one and all of them, and to all British interests. I will also venture to say that there is not one amongst them who does not highly approve of Mr. Parish continuing Chairman on the Committee of our Railway ; and without the little compensation it gives him he would hardly be able to live at Buenos Ayres and do his duty to them and to all English Interests as he has done.

I believe there is only one man in Great Britain or out of it who would give an opposite opinion, namely Mr. Christie, and that is from pure jealousy and enmity to Mr. Parish. He was unhappily Minister in

Buenos Ayres and in Brazil, and in both countries created such an angry feeling and so completely disturbed our relations with the two Governments, that but for our Government withdrawing him and happily sending that most excellent man, who was beloved by every one at Buenos Ayres and Rio also, Sir Edward Thornton, now our Minister at Washington, who at once did away with the ill-feeling created by Mr. Christie, Heaven only knows what would have happened.

I understand that Mr. Christie has given some evidence before a Committee of the House of Commons about Mr. Parish not being permitted to continue Chairman of our Railway Committee, as interfering with his Consular duties. Now, my dear Mr. Rylands, I pray you to take no notice of the evidence of such a man as Mr. Christie, of whom I say advisedly, and will say publicly in the House of Commons if I am called upon to do so, that he has been the maker of mischief wherever he has been, and rely on it, you will gain no credit in acting upon any opinion of his, which will be held as unworthy of notice by everyone who is acquainted with the subject.

Let me beseech you then as a friend (if you will allow me to call you such) to withdraw the notice which you have put on the Paper on this subject, and take my word for it (which I hope is worth something in the House of Commons and out of it) that you will get no credit by your motion, and find every man in England, who knows anything about the matter,

against you and surprised that you should move in
the matter; and pray

        Believe me,

           My Dear Mr. Rylands,

              Yours most sincerely,

                DAVID ROBERTSON.

No. CXXIX.

MR. DAVID ROBERTSON, M.P.

        56, Upper Brook Street,

           July 20, 1872.

MY DEAR MR. RYLANDS,—

I have the pleasure of receiving your most friendly
letter in reply to mine, and beg to thank you for it.

I am better, thank you, but shall have to go home
on Monday next to Scotland, being quite unfit any
longer for the late hours of the House of Commons,
which are enough to kill us all; and have paired off
with Lord Mahon for the rest of the Session.

However much I admire your disposition to cut
down unnecessary expenses, had you gone on with
your motion about the Argentine Legation I should
most assuredly have spoken in favour of its continuance,—indeed, the absolute necessity of its being
continued, as you can have no conception of the good

it has done and will continue to do. Indeed, I do not know any part of the world where a first-class Legation is so much needed.

The Buenos Ayreans and Argentines are an excellent people and very much attached to England, but like all descendants of the original Spanish race they are a very proud people and easily offended. Quite unconnected with British interests, the continuance of the British Legation, as it is, is necessary, and it would offend the Argentines immensely if it were diminished.

In conclusion, I venture to express a hope that as the time draws near and you obtain further information, you may think proper to withdraw your motion altogether.

I hope that we shall meet another year in the House of Commons and for many years to come, and as we have hitherto been, that we shall always be found in the same lobby. If ever you come to Scotland I shall be charmed to see you at my house, Ladykirk, Berwickshire, on the banks of the Tweed, and pray

Believe me,
My dear Mr. Rylands,
Yours most sincerely,
DAVID ROBERTSON.

No. CXXX.

Mr. T. B. POTTER, M.P.

Pitnacree,
Ballinling,
Perthshire,
Dec. 9, 1872.

My Dear Rylands,—

I have been thinking over the Land Question, and I want to suggest to you that *you should make the question your own.* W. Fowler is a lawyer and will do his part well, but it is not the broad question of justice to the people on the land question, as you would take it up against Massey Lopes, and bringing forward a substantial programme involving the whole question of the burthen of taxation, now very unfairly distributed. The Game Laws, Hypothec, and Leases are fleabites in comparison with the grand effort to bring rogues to justice and make them pay their share of taxes which they have *avoided by humbugging the people* for 200 years.

If *you* take up this great question it will bear you on to high power and to eminence such as Cobden and Bright have attained, and you have all their power and industry. The economical measures lead to no great success in political life, nor even " Foreign Affairs," but the Land question looms larger than all. *You* must take it up. Any little thing I can do, or the Cobden Club can do, will be worked for you, though you and I can go beyond the Cobden Club. Shall the nation be free, or are we to go on as slaveys to the

upper 10,000; the plutocracy *worse* than the aristo-
cracy; the upper 10,000, who want education more
than the dregs, and yet are our rulers.

A son of a noble earl, who fought for us best in the
Corn Law days, asked Bright the other day, at Bass's,
" What were the Corn Laws ? I never heard of them."
This was Mr. M., brother of the present and son of
the late Lord D. This story would require modify-
ing to bear repeating in public, but it is a fact and
would make a good story.

This land question will *begin* a long war, but we
must and shall win, and then how proud you would
be! And how your efforts would be appreciated if
you succeeded in doing what Cobden said would be
such a triumph—obtaining *free trade in land !* Free
trade in Church Miall takes up ; Peter Rylands must
have " free trade in land," and become our leader on
the question. Gladstone will, I think, give us the
Intestacy Bill ; but it is only a starting point, though
the keystone, of primogeniture. The tug of war comes
in the tax question. We shall have to get a real
popular House of Commons to carry this, not a landlords' parliament, which this is, and in which real land
reform is hopeless.

Yours,

T. B. POTTER.

No. CXXXI.

Mr. R. M. CARTER, M.P. (Leeds).

Leeds,

Jan. 9, 1873.

Dear Mr. Rylands,—

Our friends at Leeds have got tired out with the lukewarmness of the Whigs, and have determined to form a Radical Reform Association. They wish to inaugurate their new Society by a Public Meeting to be held about the end of this month, in the Town Hall, Leeds. We are inviting three members of Parliament, Sir C. Dilke, A. Illingworth, and yourself to come to our meeting. Can you do us the honour to come and give us an hour's speech on the necessity of increased activity in political matters, choosing your own subject? Oblige us if you can.

Yours truly,

R. M. Carter.

No. CXXXII.

Sir WILLIAM HARCOURT, M.P.

16, Stratford Place, W.,

Jan. 8, 1873.

My Dear Rylands,

As the time for the meeting of Parliament approaches, you and I must determine what is to be done in *re* Ayrton. We cannot, after what we have done and said, be quiescent. We should be thought to be sneaks if we did, and we must, therefore, give Ayrton " a meeting " and let him have his shot.

If you are likely to be in town I should be glad to talk the matter over with you. My impression is that you should move and I should support. We ought to make the motion such as not to involve the Government as accomplices of Ayrton.

It will not do, I think, to take issue on the Rules when presented. My notion is that we should move a substantive resolution affirming that " The conduct of the First Commissioner in respect of the Park Regulations has been such as to shake the authority of the law," or something to that effect.

I shall be glad to know your views on the subject.

Yours very truly,
W. V. Harcourt.

No. CXXXIII.

Mr. WILLIAM TRANT.

Over Darwen,
Jan. 16, 1873.

Dear Sir,—

I am afraid you will think I am a great trouble to you, but I write this letter at the Co-operative Hall, Over Darwen. The people here are very anxious that you should address them, and as I have arranged a meeting here for Monday, the 27th inst., to advocate the principles of the Financial Reform Association, I should feel it a very great favour if you would be one of the speakers. We have also a meeting at the Town Hall, Blackburn, next Thursday, the 23rd, at which I should also be glad if you would take a part.

I should not be so bold to ask you to do so much hard work for us, were I not convinced that if our principles are to gain ground rapidly, we must have a member of Parliament as a champion. You have done so well in the past, that I dare to ask you to do even more in the future. All great societies are so supported. The Alliance has Sir W. Lawson; the Liberation Society, Mr. Miall ; the Peace Society, Mr. Richard ; the Birmingham League, Mr. Dixon ; and I am convinced that if we are to do well, we must have you.

Yours respectfully,

Wm. Trant.

No. CXXXIV.

Mr. EDMOND BEALES.

Osborn House,
Bolton Gardens, S.W.,
Feb. 10, 1873.

Dear Sir,

After calling with Mrs. Pennington at your residence on Friday, and not finding you at home, I went down to the House in the evening, but, unfortunately, not till just after the House had risen.

As, however, it seems Mr. Bruce is disposed to withdraw the obnoxious Ayrton Rules, and substitute others, it is to be hoped, more agreeable to common sense and public rights, it is of less consequence for me to attempt to render you any assistance in your proposed motion on the subject. But I venture to trouble you thus far.

You and Mr. Harcourt complain of Mr. Ayrton's want of good faith in the House. I have some right to complain of the same conduct to me out of the House. When Mr. Ayrton introduced his Bill last Spring, I wrote to him expressing my astonishment that, after Mr. Gathorne Hardy had been obliged to withdraw, in 1867, his Bill for the restriction of the right or custom of public meeting in Hyde Park, in consequence of the opposition of Mr. Mill and others, supported by the members of the present

Government then in opposition, these same persons should, when in office as a Liberal Government, volunteer a Bill which I understood to be intended to be more prohibitory of this great and most useful constitutional right, the very safeguard of our institutions, than Mr. Hardy's Bill, which Mr. Mill had, in consultation with me on the law of the question, so successfully opposed with the aid of the members of present Government.

Mr. Ayrton wrote in reply, assuring me that his intentions were quite misunderstood, that he intended to " make rules for meetings in an appointed place in each of the parks—North, East, South, and West— so as to accommodate the people—Hyde Park, Regent's Park, Victoria Park, and Battersea Park." I instantly wrote to thank him, stating that I understood his intentions to be to carry out substantially what I had proposed to both Mr. Walpole and Mr. Hardy in 1866 and 1867, namely, that a convenient spot should be selected in Hyde Park for public meetings, so as not in the least to interfere with the ordinary enjoyment of the park by others. How far Mr. Ayrton's rules are in accordance with this letter to me, or for the accommodation of the people, especially as those rules have been interpreted by magistrates and judges, I leave you to determine.

I utterly dispute the doctrines laid down in the Queen's Bench with regard to the rights of the Crown over the park, or that those rights are the same as those of a private gentleman over his property.   If even they were, had any private owners allowed the inhabitants of the district to use a portion of his property for the length of time that Hyde Park has been used by the public of the metropolis, the inhabitants of the district also maintaining this portion at their own expense, he would be presumed in law to have dedicated this land to the public use. The Crown has no power whatever, as Mr. Justice Blackburn intimated, to enclose the park. So long ago as the discussion in 1867 Lord Romilly stated in the Lords that, from investigations he had officially been called upon to make with regard to the Exhibition of 1851, he had ascertained there were immemorial rights of way over the park that no claim of the Crown could override.

In the Act, at the commencement now of every reign, the sovereign for the time being surrenders and transfers his or her life interest in the Crown lands in exchange for the Civil List. By express Acts Hyde Park can neither be alienated nor leased; it is, in fact, national property. It is very doubtful whether the Crown has had any legal estate in Hyde Park since the days of the Commonwealth. It was then sold and conveyed in three lots to three purchasers, and there was, I believe, no reconveyance executed at the time of the Restoration, nor has been at any time since.

I am obliged to throw these views together in haste for your consideration, in case you should think them of any use, supposing you to find it necessary to continue your motion condemnatory of the Ayrton Rules, through Mr. Bruce's proposed substitution not being satisfactory.

Believe me,
Very truly yours,   .
EDMOND BEALES.

No. CXXXV.

COUNT D'ALBECA.

Civil and Military Club, W.,

May 5, 1873.

DEAR SIR,—

I am extremely obliged to you for the kind sending of your speech on the "Right of Parliamentary Control over Foreign Treaties." Really and truly I never saw this question more clearly and in a more sensible way discussed as it is in your "discours." We Continental people take generally your Parliamentary institutions as models in our propaganda of Liberal and progressive measures; and for myself I confess that many times I have been at a loss for a precedent in this matter. It is a serious *lacune* in the English Parliamentary rights. If you succeed in obtaining a serious right of control and discussion of those treaties *beforehand*, I am sure you will save many blunders to your country, and treaties will become something more than an empty scribble.

Yours very truly,

L. D'ALBECA.

No. CXXXVI.

Mr. THOMAS MOONEY.

(Secretary Irish Home Rule Association).

Grafton Hall, Soho,
May 26, 1873.

Sir,—

I have the honour to acquaint you that a Special Resolution of the thanks of the Irish Home Rule Association was passed to the English Members of Parliament who voted on Thursday night, May 15th, against the Irish Coercion Bill. Knowing you to be among the foremost of the friends of Ireland in Parliament, it gives me great pleasure to be the medium of communicating to you the grateful thanks of my countrymen for your honest opposition to the most tyrannical laws that ever emanated from the Parliament of England.

I have the honour to be, Sir, with very great respect,

Your very obedient servant,

Thomas Mooney, Secretary.

No. CXXXVII.

Mr. WILLIAM TRANT.

Financial Reform Association,
Lord St., Liverpool,
July 28, 1873.

My Dear Sir,—

No one can have watched your praiseworthy activity in the House of Commons without fearing that your energy is beyond your strength.   I am not, therefore, surprised, though I am very sorry that you feel physically worse for the good work you have done. I do most sincerely hope that as soon as you can you will take a complete and perfect rest and get strong again as soon as you can, for no one (unless it is yourself) knows better than we do how much hard work there is for you yet to do, and how capable you are of doing it. Perhaps just now you feel worse than you really are, on the principle that you should never ask a man what and how much he will have to luncheon when he has just had his breakfast.   At any rate, I hope such is the case, and that August, September, and a portion of October will make you yourself again, in order that you may do something for us in October and November.   I am sure I need not ask you to say that you will give us the first chance, if you get strong, as I repeat I hope you will. You have no idea how earnest I feel just now, because I think we may win a large portion of our programme if we fight hard this winter.   To do this it is essential that we should have as many members of Parliament speaking for us as possible, and I hope to be successful on this head. When, therefore, I have given you ample time to get well, I shall write to you again, as *your* active countenance, above all others, is very important.

I have written to Mr. Colman and to Mr. Howard with regard to our holding meetings at Norwich and Bedford, but they have not yet replied. I hope, however, they will not give us the cold shoulder. Should you happen to be chatting with either or both of them, will you kindly (without saying you have heard from me) say something to make them do something for us at our meetings. I also intend to try Mr. Dillwyn and Mr. Hoskyns.

I shall be glad if you will get me Mr. Wells' *First* Report, but do not by any means put yourself out of the way about it.

I am, dear sir,

Yours very truly,

Wm. Trant.

No. CXXXVIII.

Mr. F. PENNINGTON.

Broom Hall,

Holmwood,

Oct. 22, 1873.

My Dear Rylands,—

I have been waiting, before answering your letter of the 16th inst., to decide about accepting the invitation of the Stockport Liberals; but before doing so I have to see the Liberals of Christchurch, where I am expecting to go immediately.

I was at Stockport three days last week staying with Mc.Clure, and met at dinner about sixteen of the most influential Liberals. I also went about the town and was introduced to a few of the hardworking men in elections, and otherwise gathered as much information as I could to guide me in coming to a decision. I am to meet Sir E. Watkin after my return from Christchurch, when we shall decide upon our course. I am certainly inclined to go in for Stockport, and think it may be won if properly managed.

I was glad to see by your letter that you disapproved of the women interfering at Taunton, and that you wrote to the Committee to say so. I quite agree with you, it was impolitic for many reasons, and will not aid the cause of Woman Franchise. I enclose a letter from Hopwood, which will inform you who is responsible for the interference.

Yours truly,
FRED PENNINGTON.

No. CXXXIX.

Mr. JAMES WHITE, M.P. (Brighton).

14, Chichester Terrace,
Brighton,
Oct. 9, 1873.

My Dear Rylands,—

Having had so many letters from brother Members, generally approving of my letter replying to the enquiry "*What should the Ministry do?*" a copy of which I sent to you, I confess that I was rather surprised not to get a line from *you* thereanent. I may tell you that that letter was but an amplification of one addressed to our friend John Bright, on the 8th August last, the day I first learned that he had consented to rejoin the Gladstone Cabinet.

After Disraeli's epistle (worthy of the worst scurrilous era of Toryism) it is indeed glad tidings to learn that Hayter won at Bath. Such a success—coincident with John Bright's assuming office, is very encouraging, and I trust indicative of Henry James's return for Taunton. If so, we shall all be in good heart again.

I remain,
Yours truly,
JAMES WHITE.

No. CXL.

Mr. JAMES WHITE, M.P.

14, Chichester Terrace,
Brighton,
Oct. 14, 1873.

MY DEAR RYLANDS,—

I received yours of the 11th instant yesterday, but did not then reply as I wished to know whether my anticipation of the Solicitor General's success was correct or not. I need not tell you how rejoiced I am at the result of the Taunton Election. Our recent successes simultaneously, or rather coincidently, with Bright's assumption of office and Dizzy's letter are indeed encouraging.

Your remarks as to Legacy and Probate Duties are quite right, and I wish I had urged their imposition on the Land Owners, seeing that the Government had consented to relieve them of Local Burdens to the extent of £1,200,000.

Very truly yours,

JAMES WHITE.

No. CXLI.

SIR HENRY JAMES, M.P. (Taunton).

23, Wilton Place,

Oct. 15, 1873.

MY DEAR RYLANDS,—

A thousand thanks. I am dreadfully sorry to leave my old place and friends.

I have had a hard fight. Those women were like tigresses. I am delighted to hear that you have objected to their proceedings. Any man who wishes well for the progress of our country will soon find Women's Suffrage a mistake.

Yours very truly,

HENRY JAMES.

Q

No. CXLII.

Mr. T. B. POTTER, M.P.

Pitnacree,
Ballinling,
Jan. 12, 1874.

My Dear Rylands,—

I am grateful to you for your speech—true, manly, *unanswerable.* However life is precious in the eyes of song, but children are slaughtered wholesale by Typhus, Scarlet Fever, Diphtheria, etc., owing to wretched cottages and neglect of sanitary arrangements. Read the enclosed from the *Scotsman* of the 10th, it is only from their correspondent, I hope there may be truth in in. I have written to Stansfield about *this* district, Strath Tay, where scores of lives are lost annually through wilful and perverse and wicked Landlordism, which is the curse of this country.

"Greed, Tyranny, and Lust" are the attributes of the landlords here about, yet they are all powerful.

Yours sincerely,
T. B. Potter.

No. CXLIII.

Mr. JACOB BRIGHT.

> Alderley Edge,
> Feb. 3, 1874.

My Dear Rylands,—

I was surprised and indignant to hear of your defeat this morning. I had thought better of Warrington. The result of your election makes me anticipate a worse general result than I did before. I feel sure you will not be long without a constituency.

> With deep regret,
> Very truly yours,
> Jacob Bright.

No. CXLIV.

Mr. JAMES WHITE.

> 14, Chichester Terrace,
> Brighton,
> Feb. 15, 1874.

My Dear Rylands,—

By the *Observer* I see that Gladstone intends to make a few peers and baronets before resigning. If Mrs. Rylands would have pleasure in calling you "Sir

Peter " I do think you ought to be one of the new baronets. You have certainly earned that distinction by your plucky attempt to win a county after losing a borough seat so recently.

I may tell *you* that the Tories here did *not* wish to unseat me, and up to the last would have withdrawn their second candidate if Fawcett would have retired, but he would not. Fawcett well knew *he* could not be returned for Brighton months back, but persisted in his candidature and contrived to *coerce* me into a coalition with him, hoping that there was a chance of his riding in on my back as he did in 1868, which this time was fatal to both.

Fawcett has announced that he will never again contest Brighton, so now the Liberals are a united party, and on the next occasion of an election Brighton will prove that it is a truly Liberal Borough.

Some 430 publicans and beershop keepers, besides their respective followers and allies, voted Tory ; also nearly all the Romanists, Ritualists, flymen, chairmen, fishermen, parsons, chimney-sweeps, illiterates, and residuum. Now, knowing this, I am surprised that we did so well, seeing that the total expenses for both the Liberals will not exceed £500, against an expenditure *quite twelve times as much* on the Tory side.

With all good wishes,

I remain, yours truly,

James White.

P.S.—Are we not a noble army of martyrs ?

No. CXLV.

Mr. JAMES WHITE.

14, Chichester Terrace,
Brighton,
Feb. 18, 1874.

My Dear Rylands,—

I have to thank you for your two letters of the 15th and 17th inst., which much interested me. About my late colleague, you and I are of the same opinion.

I do not know, but *hope* we shall soon meet again in the House. I have a strong conviction that we shall soon see a *rapid reaction* Liberal-wards. That is not the opinion of Mr. Bright, judging from a nice, long, and very kind letter I have had from him.

I must conclude this with a characteristic extract from John Bright's letter :—

" This Parliament should be termed in history the ' Publicans' Parliament.' Enormous lying for three years past or more has done much to change the result of the elections, and *State* ministers of the Gospel have gone up to the poll arm-in-arm with the dealers in delirium-tremens ! "

In my reply I have suggested that this Parliament had better be called the *Bung* Parliament, and added that our defeat was mainly attributable to the publicans and republicans.

I trust you will benefit in health by your enforced rest, and with all good wishes,

I remain, yours truly,
James White.

No. CXLVI.

Sir WILLIAM HARCOURT, M P.

14, Stratford Place,
Oxford Street, W.,
Feb. 15, 1874.

Dear Rylands,—

I must write a line to tell you how sincerely sorry I am that you have not succeeded in your two gallant fights. Our benches will be sadly desolate, but we must console ourselves with the recollection of the days that are no more. We had many jolly evenings together and, I hope, may yet again in better times.

I have long seen this smash coming. There has been a great deal too much want of common sense in the conduct of the party. We must learn not to bark when we can't bite.

Yours very truly,
W. V. Harcourt.

No. CXLVII.

Mr. C. E. MACQUEEN.

Financial Reform Association,
Lord Street, Liverpool,
Feb. 23, 1874.

My Dear Sir,—

So the beer bibbing noodles of Warrington have chosen the brewer again in preference to yourself. There is no accounting for tastes, as was said of the old woman who kissed her pig, and the taste displayed by the Warringtonians is very much of that description.

I don't condole with you personally half so much as with our *cause*, on the loss of so zealous and efficient a friend in Parliament.

Earnestly hoping and nothing doubting that some constituency will have the sense and patriotism to send you there again ere long.

I am, my dear Sir,
Yours truly,
C. E. Macqueen.

No. CXLVIII.

Mr. JOHN HOLMS, M.P. (Hackney.)

16, Cornwall Gardens,
Queen's Gate, W.,
March 2, 1874.

My Dear Rylands,—

I have yours of Saturday, and am pleased to think that your old courage does not forsake you ; and that you are now prepared to come back to Parliament, where I am sure you will be welcome to many old friends. As to Hackney, I naturally avoid saying or doing anything about a successor to Sir C. Reed, as it might be taken for dictation on my part. I have no doubt you would be a most eligible candidate, once you were known amongst them. The cost is not so much once one is known, but it is the process of making oneself known that is costly ; it requires meetings, circulars, bills, etc., to an enormous extent with a Borough of 41,000 electors, and I think with great personal work and good management, might be done at £2,000 to £3,000, all dependent too upon the length of the contest. I shall be glad to hear from you if you think you would like your name spoken of.

Yours very faithfully,

John Holms.

No. CXLIX.

SIR WILFRID LAWSON, M.P.

1, Grosvenor Crescent, S.W.,
Feb. 26, 1875.

Dear Mr. Rylands,—

Thank you for sending me the newspaper with the account of your Alliance Meeting at Warrington. It seems to have been a good meeting, and I have read your speech with great interest. But what on earth did you mean by saying that you did not go so far as I go, and then saying that the ratepayers have a right to say *how many* public houses there shall be in a locality?

Why! I only propose to give them power to say *one* thing:—drink shops or no drink shops! If they prefer drink shops, I leave the number to be decided by the Magistrates exactly as at present, or with any amendment of the licensing system as may be passed. But you go for the *very great change* of allowing the ratepayers to select the fanciful number which they may desire. I'm not blaming your Bill, and shall probably support it when you bring it in. Only, at present, I'm not quite such an *extreme* man as you are on this question.

I wish you were back in the House. They are an awfully dull lot, and have very few political ideas among them. The Home Rulers are taking to making orations, but as nobody takes much trouble to reply to them, I hope they will drop the practice by and bye.

Yours very truly,
W. Lawson.

No. CL.

SIR WILFRID LAWSON, M.P.

House of Commons,
March 3, 1875.

Dear Mr. Rylands,—

Thanks to you for answering my little note. As to Permissive Bill, *all I want* is for people to support the *principle* of the Bill on 2nd reading—viz., that irresponsible authorities ought not to be allowed to overrule the wishes of the inhabitants.

When in Committee, I shall be delighted for you clever fellows to devise better plans than mine for carrying out the principle. I must have you back to help me. It will take all we can do to beat these members who have been rolled into the House on Beer Barrels.

Yours very truly,
W. Lawson.

No. CLI.

PHILIP CALLAN, M.P. (Dundalk.)

39, North Great George St.,
Dublin,
Feb. 1, 1876.

My Dear Rylands,—

Yours of yesterday from Warrington, of which I'm sorry you are not the M.P., re-directed from Cooktown here, where I have been residing for the past year, only to hand to-night.

Whilst busily engaged in my own elections, Jan. 1874, I had a "wire" from poor Richard Shaw to interfere in his behalf with the Home Rulers of Burnley. I "wired" then that in the absence of an *avowed* Home Ruler, Shaw deserved well at our hands, and should be supported by the Irish vote. And soon after I was glad to hear from him that the Irish vote had been given to him in his need. Whatever I felt and said about Shaw I feel still more strongly about you, and will be glad to aid you in any way in my power, but I don't know any of the Home Rulers now in Burnley. The local association is not, so far as I can ascertain, in *active* existence, and therefore I really don't know how or in what way to move.

In Jan., 1874, I was actively engaged in organising the Irish vote in England, and in the early part of that month was so engaged in Manchester, Liverpool, Bolton, Bradford, Sheffield, etc., so then was "well up" on the matter; am not so now. Let me know the parties to whom you wish me to write and I'll do so.

Mr. John Barry, of Manchester, whose address you can easily ascertain, is the Hon. Sec. of the Home Rule Confederation of Great Britain. He is an able man, thoroughly honest and dependable, you may rely implicitly on his word. I'll write him to-morrow. Communicate with him, and if you think well you are fully at liberty to show him this letter.

Soon after receiving your letter to-night, I went up to see Mr. Butt. He was hard at work preparing for to-morrow " to open " the great Devonshire fishery case. He requested me to say that he'll write you to-morrow as soon as he delivers himself on the above most important case, and in the meantime authorises me to tell you that he fully agrees with me as to the desirability of your return, and in wishing you every success, and the aid of the Irish vote. You may rely on having, by Friday, if not earlier, a warm letter from him. Mr. Butt purposes crossing over to London on Monday night. I'll probably be in Manchester on Sunday evening.

Wishing you every success,

Believe me to remain,

Yours faithfully,
Philip Callan.

No. CLII.

Mr. T. B. POTTER, M.P.

> Buile Hill,
> Feb. 5, 1876.

My Dear Rylands,—

Enclosed will show you how earnest Gladstone is; the letter is, of course, *private*, but why should you in your speeches not say that *you know Gladstone will come back to lead us when we are worthy of him and his lead ;* or something to that effect. He did not disapprove of our National Reform Union programme, and is dead against stagnation.

Surely, Trevelyan is not abandoning his annual motion : see to-day's *Guardian* report of R. N. Philips's speech, if so, some one else must take it up. Query, P. Rylands?

> Ever yours,
> T. B. Potter.

No. CLIII.

SIR WILFRID LAWSON, M.P.

1, Grosvenor Crescent, S.W.,
Feb. 10, 1876.

DEAR MR. RYLANDS,—

I must just drop you a line to say how anxiously I am hoping for your success at Burnley. Not only are the eyes of England upon you, but the eyes of Lawson—think of that! I do hope that we shall find Burnley better than Blackburn was, but I can't help being a little anxious still, for the epoch of high wages and *heavy drinking* has sunk the people of this country lower than many of us understand. However, I hope for the best.

The House seems to be awfully flat. Even Dizzy's Egyptian conjuring seems to excite them but little. You must come back and stir them up about *Badaihhan*, which is commonly supposed to be a town somewhere in Lancashire.

With heartiest wishes for a great triumph,

I am, yours very truly,

W. LAWSON.

No. CLIV.

Mr. ISAAC BUTT, M.P. (Limerick.)

House of Commons,
Feb. 11, 1876.

My Dear Mr. Rylands,—

I regret greatly that owing to my not coming over for the opening day your letter of the 7th only reached me to-day, having been sent to my address of last year. I think, however, I have done all I could before it reached me.

I have this evening given notice of a motion for a select committee to enquire into the nature, extent, and grounds of the demand made by a large proportion of the Irish people for the restoration to Ireland of an Irish Parliament, with power to ordain Irish affairs. If you are able to say you will vote for this I think you will receive the support of the Irish electors. I do not wish publicly to interfere in any English election, but if you have occasion to see either Captain Norman or the Secretary of the Home Rule Confederation you may show him this letter and say that I would write to both of them, but that I have been detained in the House until just post time.

Wishing you every success,

I remain,

Yours very truly,

Isaac Butt.

No. CLV.

Mr. T. B. POTTER, M.P.

105, Pall Mall, S.W.,

Feb. 15, 1876.

My Dear Rylands,—

I will most gladly attend to your wishes, and shall be proud to be *one* to introduce you. I will speak to Bright, and he will, I am sure, rejoice to be the other. I will see to the certificate; you get it in one of the rooms adjoining the lobby.

We were all ready to cheer you like mad if you had come up. I do hope Jacob will be with you on Monday, though it would be almost too much for Tory nerves to hear the cheers from below the gang-way opposite them.

I do so much want you. A little stern Radicalism will be a Godsend to the House. Mr. Gladstone told me yesterday—"You Lancashire Radicals are an excellent lot; the only fault is there are so few of you." Gladstone was in capital form last night, and full of fighting power.

I rejoice with you and Mrs. Rylands at your success. J. P. C. Starkie, M.P., told me last evening—" Peter Rylands has a seat at Burnley for life."

Ever yours sincerely,

T. B. Potter.

No. CLVI.

Mr. ISAAC BUTT, M.P.

London,
Feb. 17th, 1876.

My Dear Rylands,—

I need not tell you how glad I was to get your telegram. I had written as strongly as I could to the chiefs of the English Confederation, but not having got their replies I was a little uneasy. Everything they could do for you was done, and I believe you have the whole Irish vote.

I hope and believe that the same result will follow in Manchester, but Bright was very obstinate in refusing to say he would vote for my motion. I got to Manchester just in time to prevent an appeal to the Irish not to vote for him. Powell, in the end, anticipated him in his declaration, but I am confident almost all the Home Rulers will vote for Bright.

Up to the very last, your opponents reckoned confidently on the Irish vote. Their disappointment accounts for their rage.

Yours very faithfully,
Isaac Butt.

No. CLVII.

Mr. HENRY LABOUCHERE.

44, Curzon Street,
March 4, 1876.

Dear Rylands,—

I do not know Lange personally. With regard to
Egypt, it seems to me that although both were foolish,
public opinion goes for the purchase of the Canal
shares, but is doubtful about Cave's mission. Cave's
report is favourable, but since making it he has reason
to doubt whether it was not made upon insufficient
data. Cave one night told Barrett, the private secretary of the Khedive, what his report was.

Please do not mention to *anyone* the above facts.

The object of the Reuter telegrams is to force the
English Government to publish Cave's report, for
they are inclined to regard it as a private document,
not being certain whether it can be depended on. I
know what takes place through a person with
Cave, but, of course, I am pledged to absolute
secrecy.

As a party move, would it not be well to ask
whether H.M. Government has authorised Mr. Cave
to give a *résumé* of his report to newspaper corre-
spondents before it has been communicated to
Parliament ? I think that this would be a teaser.
Another teaser would be—" Is there any truth in a
Reuter telegram of Saturday that it became impossible
for the English Government to guarantee the interest

on the entire debt of Egypt, owing to the opposition of foreign Governments ? "

Yours truly,
H. LABOUCHERE.

————

No. CLVIII.

MR. HENRY LABOUCHERE.

44, Curzon Street
Tuesday,
March 29, 1876.

DEAR RYLANDS,—

If you really want to qualify yourself to talk on Egypt, here are a few questions to ask Dizzy.

The key of the position is this : The Khedive is a thief, and is and has been a partner with a gang of usurers to rob Egypt. The gang hold a vast amount of Treasury bills. The chief of the gang is one Soubepan, a natural son of Fould, and the real head of the Société Financière, the Société Agricole, and the Anglo-Egyptian Bank (the latter is Anglo only in name). The credit establishments hold above £10,000,000 of Treasury bills. Naturally they want to get out of them. They will therefore form a syndicate and themselves subscribe to a new loan, the equivalent of what they hold in Treasury bills. The loan will thus nominally be subscribed for, the quotation will be obtained, and by the usual trickery the bonds will, little by little, be shunted on the public.

But even if the public do not take any, the holders of Treasury bills will benefit by the move, for special hypothecations will be given to them, and from unsecured creditors they will become secured creditors. Thus, when the general liquidation takes place they will get as much in the pound as the present secured creditors, *i.e.*, the interest on their loan and on former loans will be equally reduced.

There is no doubt that Pastró is telling every one what Cave's report is to be in order to get up his syndicate before that report is published. If Cave really told him, which is impossible, it is a gross violation of truth. But as, clearly, Cave cannot have advised Pastré's plan, which is a palpable swindle, the Khedive is not acting under Cave's advice; and as Stafford Northcote said that Cave was a sort of John the Baptist to find out whether the Khedive would act under English advice—for H.M. Government, without being sure of this, would not send out accountants—it seems to me clear, that the question being answered in the negative by the acts of the Khedive, according to StaffordNorthcote, accountants should not be sent out. Then why is Rivers Wilson sent ?

Yours truly,
H. Labouchere.

No. CLIX.

Mr. HENRY LABOUCHERE.

Pope's Villa,
Twickenham,
May 9, 1876.

DEAR RYLANDS,—

The House of Commons never seems to have got hold of the real connection between the Egyptian Government and our Government, nor does the question of Sir G. Campbell, notice of which I see in to-day's paper, help to elucidate it.

In England, there are bondholders, in Paris there are Treasury bill holders. All negotiation has been carried on by the latter, and very naturally the former are sacrificed.

Cave said, if certain accounts are correct, Egypt can pay 7 per cent. on about 77 millions. But the existence of the floating debt showed that the accounts which proved a yearly surplus were not correct; the hypothesis, therefore, on which Cave proceeded was overturned by Cave himself. It is consequently absurd to assert that the reorganisation of Egyptian Finance, as decreed, is in accordance with the report of Cave.

But there is no question that the fellahs are grossly ill-treated. Practically everything is taken from them except enough to keep body and soul together. Lately they have had to sell their cattle to pay taxes and forced loans.

If England, therefore, allows Rivers Wilson to be a Commissioner to receive taxes for European creditors which are collected by Egyption task-masters, we encourage investment in Egyptian securities on the plea that they will return 7 per cent., which is impossible, and we encourage the system of oppression which is called in Egypt Government.

Could you not supplement Sir G. Campbell's question by the following? Whether the decrees issued by the Khedive for the re-arrangement of his debts, which place secured creditors in a worse position than unsecured creditors, and which promise a yearly payment of interest considerably in excess of that which, in the opinion of Mr. Cave, Egypt under the most favourable circumstances can pay, have received the approval of Mr. Rivers Wilson, as stated in several telegrams which have been published in the newspapers, and whether H.M. Government will assent to the appointment of an English Commissioner to superintend the payment of interest to Egyptian creditors without some guarantees that the revenue raised in order to meet this interest be proportioned to the means of the fellahs, and be no longer obtained by torture.

Yours truly,

H. LABOUCHERE.

No. CLX.

Mr. HENRY LABOUCHERE.

Pope's Villa,

Twickenham,

Aug. 3, 1876.

Dear Rylands,—

I am sick of the Khedive, he is such a scoundrel. The man has made a treaty with Abyssinia by which he pays to the latter country a heavy war indemnity. This he has, to a great extent, concealed from Europe, and I should be curious to know whether the Foreign Office have heard of it.

Vivian, who has just been made Consul General, is personally a good fellow, but a London dandy. On being sent there before as acting Consul General, he rode the Khedive's horses at a race, arrayed as a jockey. Is it likely that the Foreign Office will receive much useful information from him except what the Khedive chooses to knock into his head ?

You would put Stafford Northcote in a considerable hole (but don't say I told you) if you were to ask him whether he has reason to question the truth of the statements made by the Khedive to Cave, and whether he has since these statements seen Nuba Pacha, and elicited his views respecting them.

Yours truly,

H. Labouchere.

No. CLXI.

Mr. G. T. WALTERS.

Byerden Terrace,
Burnley,
Sept. 10, 1876.

Dear Sir,—

I have read with interest the report in the *Burnley Gazette* (9th inst.) of your speech on " Wesleyanism," delivered at Leyland last Wednesday.

But there is a passage at the close, to which you will, perhaps, permit me to draw your attention. It reads as follows:—"Let us always bear in mind when we see these struggles and controversies that Christianity, which is at the present moment the only religion held by enlightened men, is destined to be hereafter the religion of the world." I should be glad to know if the report is correct, for I cannot otherwise believe that you really gave utterance to the words. Would you not allow that there are enlightened men who hold the Hindoo faith? Among the Brahmans and the Buddhists there are men of great intellect. And you must surely be aware of the fact that foreign missionaries have found that Christianity, as a code of doctrines, can make but little progress abroad. Dr. Rowland Williams told his fellow-Christians that they would never convert the Hindoos to the Trinity, or to our form of Christianity, any more than they could grow our flowers in their soil or climate; they could only

Christianise them by showing that our religion is a higher development of what their religion teaches—justice and self-denial.

At the present day in Japan, the people having rejected their former faith, decline to accept Christianity because, as they say, they might as well have kept their own. Indeed, the popular Christian creed is totally inadequate to fulfil the mission of a universal faith.

I am,

Respectfully yours,

George Thos. Walters.

No. CLXII.

Mr. HUGH MASON.

Groby Hall,

Feb. 20, 1877.

Dear Rylands,—

Surely they are not going to bring in the Prisons' Bill without giving the country time to express an opinion. I think it would be a most improper proceeding. Those who have devoted so much of their time to manage the prisons ought not to be ignored. Take our great Salford Hundred Prison. We do the work and we find the money to a very large extent. **The** Government Prisons, **as** you so ably stated, are altogether inferior. We shall be dragged down **to** their bad level.

Will men like me and others continue to give our time when **we are to** be only treated like servants? You have **a** capital subject, and you have some able coadjutors, and I **hope** you will go forward doing your duty so nobly.

Ever yours sincerely,

HUGH MASON.

No. CLXIII.

RT. HON. W. E. GLADSTONE, M.P.

73, Harley Street,

March 25, 1877.

DEAR MR. RYLANDS,—

Accept my best thanks for your note. If you raise the question of **Sir** H. Elliot's return on Tuesday, I intend to say a very few words, from which I would endeavour to exclude all venom. But I think it due from me to those who are responsible for the proceedings and fortunes **of** the party to express my reluctance **to** advise without knowing what their wishes may be. I do not see any disadvantage in a temperate discussion, but after the events of Friday (in which the Government ended, it seems, with a miserable fiasco) I should be sorry if anything were done which they might think inconvenient.

It pleases me much that you and I are heartily united in this great matter, and I remain,

Faithfully yours,

W. E. GLADSTONE.

———

No. CLXIV.

Mr. W. T. STEAD.

The Editor,
Northern Echo,
Darlington,
April 4, 1877.

DEAR SIR,—

I am much obliged to you for your kindness in sending me the full report of your scathing indictment of Sir Henry Elliot's conduct at Constantinople. There was no attempt made to answer it, either that night or in the last day before the Easter recess. "Vile and calumnious" are simply mud balls, which are a poor weapon of controversy. I express the feelings of multitudes when I say that we are grateful to you for speaking out when speaking out was greatly needed. Mealy-mouthedness has become such a virtue of late that to call a spade a spade will be denounced before long as the vilest calumny.

With regard to the future, we must, it appears to me, at any cost win over the peace party, whose natural, but most unfortunate persistency in deprecating measures of coercion prevents the striking of the grandest stroke for peace that has ever been offered to mankind. The stupendous folly of hesitating to take the decisive step, which would realise the ideal of the poet, the visions of the seer, by establishing really, and not in name, the United States of Europe, with a supreme tribunal, that in ten years would make war impossible, fills me with more sorrow and indignation than even the Turkish leanings of the Ministry. In the *Echo* sent herewith you will find an article developing this. I shall be glad to hear from you as to the best course to be pursued.

I am, yours truly,

WILLIAM T. STEAD.

No. CLXV.

Mr. JAMES HOWARD.

Clapham Park,
Bedfordshire,
April 16, 1877.

My Dear Rylands,—

I have seen your letter upon the Duke of Argyll's pamphlet ; our views entirely coincide. I wrote to Potter to say it was a Paper more fit for *The Quarterly Review* that the Cobden Club Papers. Upon the Land Question and on some others my experience is that the old Whigs are more Tory than the Tories themselves, and far more dangerous, because with a great show of reasoning, fallacious as it is, they appeal to economic principles, forgetting that they as Land-owners are in the enjoyment of a monopoly, and have the advantage of exceptional laws (the law of distraint and hypothec for instance) made by themselves.

The Duke deals with my arguments very unfairly in the first place by misstating them. In another place he disposes of me by saying that my language upon the principle of compensation is often ambiguous. Well, I think after a man had brought in a Bill dealing with all the details of this very question, he ought not to be open to such a charge, based upon previous utterances, particularly as no ambiguous expressions are adduced in support of the charge. Read the few words bracketed in the enclosed. There is no ambiguity here. I believe the argument was

put before the Premier as succinctly as it well could
be.

Yours very truly,

JAMES HOWARD.

No. CLXVI.

MR. HENRY RICHARD, M.P.

22, Bolton Gardens,
S. Kensington,
Dec. 12, 1877.

DEAR MR. RYLANDS,—

I enclose the letters you sent me. I had been
engaged, as you are aware, for several years over the
preparation of Cobden's letters for the press, and had
spent a large amount of time and labour upon them.
Some of them might have been in print long ago, but
for reasons I once explained to you and a deputation
from the Cobden Club. But since Mrs. Cobden's
death the daughters have insisted upon taking the
whole thing out of my hands into their own. I have
offered, in the kindest way I could, to co-operate with
them, seeing that my work was already so far
advanced as to be nearly ready for the press. But
they will hear of nothing but the unconditional
surrender of everything into their hands.

I wished just to give you this explanation in confidence, as I don't know what may be said on the subject.

Yours faithfully,

HENRY RICHARD.

No. CLXVII.

Mr. SPENCER T. HALL.

Burnley,
Dec. 18, 1877.

My DEAR SIR,—

I have been wondering if you would have time or care for glancing through the accompanying "part" of one of my later works. If you should, the chapters on J. S. Buckingham and the late Earl of Carlisle, may recall some of your own experiences of "auld lang syne," and it may interest you to know that John Gratton, sketched in the last chapter, was related on the maternal side to noble John Bright. As Mr. Bright one day put it to me, John Gratton's granddaughter was his (J.B.'s) great grandmother. But this was not told me before the chapter was published, which I regret.

Strange to think how obscure an old writer and lecturer, whose name has been amongst the most popular of his day may live to become amongst those who are themselves comparatively obscure. There are very few of our townspeople here who know that I ever wrote such a book at all; while many think they pay me a sort of compliment by acknowledging me as the author of "Pendle hill and its surroundings," the most trivial thing I ever wrote, however true and genial in its way.

I trust you are well after your last night's most graphic and telling address; and that you. and all you love may thoroughly enjoy Christmas.

Yours, dear Sir, most truly,

SPENCER T. HALL.

No. CLXVIII.

Mr. BENJAMIN CARVER.

7, Lower Mosley Street,
Manchester,
Feb. 21, 1878.

My DEAR SIR,—

Although you would no doubt notice the fate of the Gibraltar Ordinance when, at the beginning of the session, in reply to Mr. Whitwell's question, Mr. Lowther stated that H.M.'s Government had for various reasons decided not to press the measure further. I have been somewhat troubled in mind that I have not addressed a few lines to you to say how deeply grateful the merchants of Gibraltar are for the kind assistance which you and other friends rendered when the battle was being fought.

It was mainly owing to the pressure brought to bear at the Colonial Office that we won the day.

It happened rather curiously that almost at the very time Lord Carnarvon was receiving the deputation on the 26th July, Spain was plotting mischief and raising her already too prohibitory tariff to our special injury.

Believe me to remain,

Very truly yours,
BENJAMIN CARVER.

No. CLXIX.

MR. EDWARD JENKINS, M.P. (Dundee.)

Park House,
Ellenslea Road,
St. Leonards,
March 5, 1878.

MY DEAR RYLANDS,—

You are a man of action and promptitude. If there are not ten righteous men in the House, thank God

S

that there is one Rylands. I have been thinking
about this matter a good deal, and I think we *should*
bring Layard's conduct forward *at once*, and that the
case could be made so strong, with the weight of the
men who would speak to the motion, it would power-
fully affect the country. Why does divine Providence
afford us such opportunities if we wantonly waste
them ? However, what could you do when our best
men are against it ?

Have you read yesterday's *Standard* and its indica-
tion of the drift of Government policy ? This has
again and again been stated. Mytilene, Egypt,
Egean, etc. It appeals to English imagination and
ambition ; it is at the moment a terrible danger. Do
you not see that Garnet Wolseley, who has been
writing urgent letters for some work to do, and
Farrer (Board of Trade) have both been set to try
and convince the English people that we are invul-
nerable and ready for anything ? Once calm English
fears and you may excite English blood. I am
strongly convinced some action ought now to be
taken from our side to force the hand of the Government, and know what they are driving at. The
pretence of any ground for continuing war preparations is taken away. Why not demand of the
Government some explanation of their policy before
they push their preparations any further ?

The weather here is glorious, and I won't come up
even to save my country.

Yours ever and obliged,
EDWARD JENKINS.

CLXX.

Rt. Hon. JOHN BRIGHT, M.P.

Rochdale,

May 5, 1878.

Dear Mr. Rylands,—

I cannot come up to town to-morrow; Tuesday I may be able to leave home, for I have some friends here unexpected, to whom I must pay some attention.

The Government seem utterly careless of constitutional practice and of public opinion so long as they have a subservient majority at their back. I have heard nothing as to the view of Lord Hartington, or of any other of our "front Bench" men on the question of the Indian troops, and I doubt not the "mechanical majority" will support anything the Government dares to do.

I am sorry I cannot be with you to-morrow, but on the first evening after a recess there is not often a full House, or much discussion.

The *Times* has acted in a manner singularly base and cowardly even for it. Its articles are feeble and mean to the last degree. To follow in the wake of the *D.T.* is a degradation they should have avoided.

I am receiving by every post letters of the most ruffianly, and some of a threatening, character, with many others of an opposite character. The Manchester meeting has touched a good many people " on

the raw." Still I think there will not be war, though
facts just now are against me.

Yours very sincerely,

JOHN BRIGHT.

No. CLXXI.

MR. HUGH MASON.

Ashton-under-Lyne,

June 22, 1878.

MY DEAR RYLANDS,—

I am delighted you are attacking that sink of
iniquity—the Bill of Entry. When President of
Chamber of Commerce I did all I could to stop their
plunder. Lowe was Chancellor, and I had a long
interview with him. He was willing; he saw the
nuisance, but said he must wait till the Patent
expired. Do you know M. Daly, of the Customs?
He gave me valuable assistance. No man in England
knows more than Daly on these subjects; he is full
of information, and he takes pleasure in helping
one.

Has Dizzy really sold the vagabond Jingoes, or is
the old villain playing some deep game of his own?
How refreshing to read the *Pall Mall*; it, at all events,
has been sold.

I am delighted to see your useful activities. What has become of Mundella and Rathbone? Has Dizzy tickled their tails?

Sincerely yours,
HUGH MASON.

No. CLXXII.

SIR WILFRID LAWSON, M.P.

19, Wellington Crescent,
Ramsgate,
June 23, 1878.

DEAR MR. RYLANDS,—

I don't think you have ever given us a speech *in* the House on the Permissive Bill. Now's the day and now's the hour! Give us a stave on Wednesday, like a good man, and redeem the credit of Lancashire.

I shan't be up until Tuesday, so shall miss the cattle debate to-morrow night. Isn't it strange to see such efforts made to diminish the supply of *Beef* to the people, while the greatest pains are taken to drench them with *Beer*?

Yours truly,
W. LAWSON.

No. CLXXIII.

Mr. T. B. POTTER, M.P.

> Reform Club,
> July 14, 1878.

My Dear Rylands,—

The Cobden Club Committee put down yesterday *your name* to reply to the toast of the evening, " The Cobden Club."   You will not mince matters, I know, and a short, concise, and plain spoken address, just as no one can deliver better than you, will be useful as a political programme, such a one as Cobden would have laid before the country fearlessly and confidently, if he had been alive now.

> Ever yours,
> T. B. Potter.

No. CLXXIV.

Mr. EDWARD JENKINS, M.P.

75, West Cromwell Road,
South Kensington,
Sept. 27, 1878.

My Dear Rylands,—

I am answering you from my sister's house just before dinner. Ergo, I am hungry and uncongenial. Two hours later I might be in a better humour for writing to a jovial friend. Next week 'tis impossible; the week after not wholly out of the question, were I to return from Dundee, but I am so uncertain I dare not promise. Let me know if your kind, benevolent, hospitable intentions remain in full flower a little longer. Perhaps they have nearly all bloomed away among your charming guests.

You are right. The imposture is now being gradually revealed, and before so very long the impostor will be dismissed without a character, except from his mistress. I hope you are prepared to assist me in forming a ministry. See the *Pall Mall* of to-night for an amusing skit, "The Gladstone Exploitation Company, Limited," in which I have the honour to figure.

Yours sincerely,
Edward Jenkins.

No. CLXXV.

Sir WILFRID LAWSON, M.P.

Brayton,
Carlisle.

My Dear Mr. Rylands,—

> "Even Don Ferdinando,"

we are told,

> "Can't do more than he can do."

So the fact is I have got off any more meetings, except the Manchester annual one on the 22nd inst., during that week. But thank you very much all the same for your kind invitation and programme. I have to go to Ireland in the beginning of November, so I really must not undertake too much.

How about this Afghan war? Are the people of this country mesmerised, or dead drunk, or become heathens, or what *is* the matter with them that they allow such a hideous atrocity to go on? If Government delay hostilities until Parliament meets we ought to stop the supplies until they dissolve Parliament, and get the whole question fairly laid before the country. It is absolutely *infamous*.

Can't you rouse Lancashire?

Ever yours,
W. Lawson.

No. CLXXVI.

Sir WILFRID LAWSON, M.P.

Brayton,
Carlisle,
Oct. 10, 1878.

Dear Mr. Rylands,—

Thanks for your kind note. The fact is that I have engaged myself to stay over the Manchester meeting with friends in Manchester, so I cannot throw them over to avail myself even of a visit to you, which I need not say is really very tempting. However, I shall have a peep at you at the great meeting on the Tuesday night. Don't get drunk and forget the right day, as you did last year!

Afghan looks worse the more it is inquired into. Do you see what Col. Stanley says yesterday?—"So far as he could see we had no reason to complain of the action of our Government at this moment."

So, I suppose, on their own showing it is not Russia which has offended, and these wretched Afghans are to be slaughtered by English Christians because their chief would not receive a morning call from a British officer who went accompanied by 1,000 jingoes. Really, I think we are about the most wicked people going. But Havelock says the war is necessary to promote Baptist missions!

Yours truly,
W. Lawson.

No. CLXXVII.

Mr. HUGH MASON.

Groby Hall,
Ashton-under-Lyne,
March 10, 1879.

My Dear Rylands,—

Our Chamber of Commerce are determined to have an interview with Northcote on Bill of Entry, and will ask Bazley to get us an interview. I should like a good number of Lancashire members to lead us up. Would you believe it, Liverpool Chamber has memorialised Dizzy just now to prolong the Bill of Entry job. I greatly suspect Daly has twisted right round dead against us, and is egging on the Liverpool Chamber. What sop has he had ?

Very sincerely,
Hugh Mason.

No. CLXXVIII.

Mr. MICHAEL DALY.

H.M. Customs,
St. Katharine's Wharf, E.,
March 21, 1879.

My Dear Sir,—

When I had the pleasure of dining with you at your house, I told you that a few years back I had submitted a paper to the Board of Customs with a view to simplicity of arrangements and economy in cost. I now enclose you a copy of that paper, the original being dated the 23rd Oct., 1875.

On the subject ot statistics generally, please refer to paragraphs 20, 21, and 26 to 34; but more especially as bearing on the question of the " Bill of Entry " to 26—34. No mention is made of the " Bill of Entry," but it will be found that those paragraphs contain the starting point for setting aside that establishment. Upon the basis, therein laid down, an arrangement can readily be made by which the " Bill of Entry " concern can easily be dispensed with altogether. This paper is however to be considered as *strictly confidential*. You must not use or refer to it in any way. It is of course intended to be taken as a whole; and if you have the time I would be glad if you would read it all through. You will see the Board's order at the end.

I send you also copy of another paper got up a few years back about me, but which I had to stop as it would probably have done me more harm than good. It is all perfectly true, but people in this country do not care to know the truth about those in their service. It is so very much more agreeable to be humbugged. It is a fact that there is not a man in the whole range of the civil service who can point to anything like the services enumerated in that paper, and yet I dare not use it, and must beg you to keep it private. Still the British public complain of their servants. Well, I owe my masters nothing.

Have you had the Report yet? I understand that when it was presented to the Treasury it was referred down to the Board of Customs, by whom an elaborate Report was made in reply, and in support of the " Bill of Entry." This Report will, I am informed, be given with that prepared by Childers, or his Committee. It will be as well, for then we shall know all that can be said in favour of its continuance. But the time gets on, and the Patent expires in July. Do not forget that. If it is not to be renewed, some other arrangement must be made to meet the public requirements ; and on the plea of "want of time " a new lease may be given to the concern.

Mr. Cartwright is, I perceive, to have his select committee on the wine duties. I am very glad of it, and if well managed a great deal of good may come out of it. The present mode of dealing with wines— I mean fiscally—is troublesome and vexatious to the trade, while it is very costly to the public.

Very faithfully yours,

M. Daly.

No. CLXXIX.

Marquis of HARTINGTON, M.P.

Devonshire House,
April 14, 1879.

Dear Mr. Rylands,—

With reference to your letter of the 6th inst., on the subject of the Motion which you intend to bring forward on the Budget, I am far from saying that there may not be some advantage in a question of this kind being left in the hands of an independent Member. Indeed I think it probable that under any circumstances we should have come to the conclusion that this would be the best course. But I wished, when I saw you, to remind you that at the very time when you gave your notice, without any consultation with Adam or myself, I was in communication with Mr. Gladstone and others as to the course to be taken, and that it was at least possible that some Resolution would be moved in the name of the Party; a course which would be at least rendered more difficult by the action you had taken. I quite admit that independent members cannot, on all occasions, allow their course to be restrained by the opinion of the official leaders of the party; but it appears to me that there is an end of everything in the shape of united action, if we are not even informed or consulted beforehand, on what is proposed to be done on the most important questions which come under the consideration of Parliament.

With regard to the present case, I do not think, as I have already said, that any harm has been done. The wording of the Resolutions might perhaps be somewhat improved, but I think that the advantages of the independent action which has been taken would be lost if I were to make any suggestions which would make me in any way responsible for a Motion in regard to which I am now perfectly independent.

I remain,
Yours sincerely,
HARTINGTON.

———

No. CLXXX.

Mr. EDWARD JENKINS, M.P.

House of Commons,
April 15, 1879.

My Dear Rylands,—

I found your letter at the Club yesterday, and am greatly amused, as well as abused. Our little party is evidently growing in weight and interest! When the *first-rate* members die off or go to glory in " another place," I suppose the second and third rates must come to the front. Meantime, let us wrap ourselves in the *togæ* of our natural modesty.

I have *not* seen the letter to the Newcastle paper, and don't much care about it. You will see a letter of mine on Egypt in to-day's *Times*.   Goldsmid writes and talks much rot—like the rest of us.

While you are idling in the country, I have been getting up Army Discipline, Egypt, Greece, and other questions.   How *can* you expect to be a leader with your indolent habits ?

Ever sincerely yours,
EDWARD JENKINS.

TO MY PETER,—

(Slightly altered from Moore.)

Rylands hath a roving eye
   For jobs and ministerial messes,
Questions, motions, in supply
   But what he aims at no one guesses.

Jollier 'tis to gaze upon
   Samuda's nose, that seldom rises
In its place, but every one
   Its unexpected length surprises !
My serious solemn wise Samuda
Cunning reposes
In many noses
But sense in yours, my dear Samuda !
[Hic nonnulla desunt], etc., etc.

No. CLXXXI.

Mr. HUGH MASON.

Fenton's Hotel,
S.W.
May 1, 1879.

My Dear Rylands,—

Will Mrs. Rylands and you do us the pleasure to dine with us on Saturday at 6.30.   Morning dress you have no objection.

I want to hear all about your grand motion for which the Radicals owe you a great debt of gratitude. If front benchers won't lead, brush them on one side without delay.

Very sincerely,

Hugh Mason.

No. CLXXXII.

Mr. HENRY RICHARD, M.P.

22, Bolton Gardens,
South Kensington,
May 10, 1879.

My Dear Mr. Rylands,—

I am very sorry that anything should have appeared in the *Nonconformist* that is unjust and offensive to you.

But I hardly need tell you that I have no sort of connection with or control over the *Nonconformist*. I am no favourite with the writer of those "sketches," whoever he may be, as his notices of me have often been anything but flattering, though on that particular occasion he took it into his head to pay me a sort of left-handed compliment. But I comfort myself with the reflection, when I see newspaper attacks upon me, that probably they make a deeper impression upon me than upon anyone else. Other people read them and forget them the next day, and the only thing that can give them importance is for the victim to take notice of them.

I think you exaggerate a little, too. I don't think it is "indignity" so much as sheer impertinence, which prompts those comments upon us by men of "our own correspondent" class. I am sure the remarks referred to can do you no harm, though at the moment they are no doubt sufficiently irritating.

I ought to say that I believe Mr. Miall himself is no longer editor of the *Nonconformist*.

Yours very truly,

HENRY RICHARD.

No. CLXXXIII.

Mr. JAMES HOWARD.

Hôtel d'Angleterre,
Cauterêts,
May 22, 1879.

Dear Rylands,—

Your word, " bubbled," seemed to amuse the Press at the time. Taking up a Leipsic edition of *Gulliver's Travels* on the tables at this little place, I found in the dialogue between a Whig and a Tory.

" Tory:—Then all this while I have been bubbled." The word is so expressive, that the country is indebted to you for its revival.

I read *Gulliver* when a boy, but find now much in it worthy of a man's perusal, especially at the present time ; for instance, Swift, in describing to the Yahoo the motives for war, remarks :—

" Sometimes the ambition of Princes, who never think they have land or people enough to govern. Sometimes the corruption of ministers who engage their master in a war, in order to stifle or divert the clamour of the subjects against their evil adminis-tration."

I am,
Yours very truly,
James Howard.

No. CLXXXIV.

Sir WILFRID LAWSON, M.P.

Brayton,
Carlisle,
Oct. 15, 1879.

Dear Mr. Rylands,—

How very kind of you to make out all the trains, etc., for me so nicely. All will suit well and I can stick to your programme. Only I think I must get away on Saturday night at midnight (Hartington won't speak till then, I hope!) as I should like to get home, as I am " on the stump " again in a benighted west Cumberland village on the following Tuesday.

Chamberlain has done well at Glasgow, the best speech of his which I ever read, except one which he once made at an Alliance meeting. Cross is wretched.

> Poor old Cross
> Is at a loss
> To find out what to say ;
> " I'm right—you're wrong,"
> His only song,
> " And who dare say me nay ? "

Ever yours,
WILFRID LAWSON.

No. CLXXXV.

Mr. EDWARD JENKINS, M.P.

20, Southwell Gardens,
South Kensington,
Oct. 11, 1879.

My Dear Rylands,—

By good luck your letter finds me at home. I got back this week from the Continent. Since I saw you I have been twice to Vienna, and have visited Cologne, Frankfort, Nurnberg, Ratisbon, and Paris.

What *is* the *Manchester Demonstration?* I know nothing of it, and am little interested in politics, which is a wild and windy pursuit.

But Massey Hall is attractive; the "houris" so lavishly promised, tickle one's imagination, and awaken lively hopes in a too susceptible heart. The genial face of my Rylands seems waiting to welcome me at the station, with a finger to dig into my ribs, and a cordial arm to draw me to his side. How can I refuse? Yes! I must come. They want me at Bolton. Is that within striking distance of you? Perhaps they *don't* want me at Manchester, I am too sound a politician to go down with your partisans.

To Mistress Rylands my most gracious compliments.

Yours ever sincerely,
Edward Jenkins.

No. CLXXXVI.

EDWARD JENKINS, M.P.

20, Southwell Gardens,
South Kensington,
Oct. 15, 1879.

DEAR RYLANDS,—

At least get me a card for the *Dæmon*stration, if I am to join in the infernal orgies.

I am expecting my wife. Can you give me a bath-room, and let her sleep with the housekeeper if I induce her to come? Or put Lawson in the bath-room, where he will be in his natural element. My conscience pricks me about going among those Lancashire witches (you call them *houris*) without her protection.

I will bring Mrs. Rylands down the 1st Book of *Jobson's Enemies*, which begins to appear in November.

Ever yours,
EDWARD JENKINS.

No. CLXXXVII.

Mr. DUNCAN McLAREN, M.P.

Newington House,
Edinburgh,
Oct. 12, 1879.

My Dear Mr. Rylands,—

A few days since I saw a foolish letter by a man in a passion, written to a Mr. Rylands, who I suppose was your brother. If he was, or if you feel interested in the matter, I beg to give you a bit of information which may be useful to fire off against the passionate man.

The name " Cromwell Road " in London was proposed by the Prince Consort, the husband of the Queen, at a meeting of the Royal Commission, whose land it was ; and the name was agreed to by them on his recommendation. This fact I had from Mr. Bowring, formerly M.P. (Exeter 1868-74) and again a candidate. Mr. Bowring was Secretary to the Commission, and mentioned the fact to me two years ago as within his own personal knowledge.

The public and national affairs are in a sad state.

I am, yours very truly,

D. McLaren.

No. CLXXXVIII.

Mr. A. M. SULLIVAN, M.P. (Louth).

Temple,
London,
Jan. 13, 1880.

My Dear Rylands,—

I read the announcement in the papers; and it struck me as one of the most clever and crafty stratagems the Downing Street electioneers could devise for catching the Irish vote. It is true we Catholic Irishmen have a hearty regard and a high respect for the Duke of Norfolk and his family. Not only is he in social rank "the first Catholic in England" of laymen, but his personal conduct and character are so good and so pure that we all love him and are proud of him as his co-religionists. We Irishmen know him and his family to be quite opposed to us in politics; but, as I said at Sheffield, we do not quarrel with him for that; we leave him to his own convictions on that score, just as he and his family will, we hope, continue to leave us to ours.

I personally shall deeply regret if it be true (as to which it is only fair to reserve judgment) that any member of the Duke's family lends himself to such a transparent artifice in the interest of the Government. Cruel, cruel, I shall call it, nay, indeed, an outrage, to attempt to *exploit* the religious emotions and sympathies of poor Irish Catholics for the party purposes of Lord Beaconsfield. Speaking as an

" Ultramontane " Catholic, I would call it an awful responsibility for any Catholic to put Religion to such a use as this. Until I see it with my own eyes, I shall be slow to credit that Lord Edmond Talbot will do anything of the sort. If the Conservative party wish to return him to Parliament, let them send him in for one of their own constituencies—North Warwickshire, for instance, or Belfast. Or if they run him for Burnley let it be honestly stated that he appeals for support only to those Catholics who belong like himself to the Conservative party. The very men in the Carlton Club who are now joking and rejoicing over this " capital stroke " would be the first to revile and denounce Irish Catholic Home Rulers as " slaves to their priests," if merely because Lord Edmund Talbot is a Catholic they flung political principles to the wind, and voting for him, rejected the honest English Protestant friend who has kept his pledges like a man of honour.

As to all this let me point out that the issue threatened to be raised in Burnley is not new to Irishmen, that Roland Ponsonby Blennerhasset, a Protestant, was elected by the Priests and people of Catholic Kerry in preference to a most estimable Catholic gentleman, Mr. J. A. Dease, whose political principles were unacceptable; that Mr. Mitchell Henry sits for Galway, Mr. Shaw for Cork, Lord Francis Conyngham for Clare, these being about the most Catholic and Celtic countries in Ireland, and that these representatives, all Protestants, were and are enthusiastically supported by the Catholic prelates, priests, and people. From all this I think I am warranted in saying that my fellow-countrymen in Burnley are very unlikely to play a recreant part. I have never had the pleasure of meeting them, but my proud confidence in their intelligence, patriotism, and fidelity is none the less strong and high. The device of the Conservative election managers may put them to a painful trial, but they will come through it with honour and triumph,

Yours very faithfully,

A. M. SULLIVAN.

No. CLXXXIX.

CAPTAIN J. P. NOLAN, M.P. (Galway Co.)

House of Commons,
March 12, 1880.

DEAR MR. RYLANDS,—

I think it my duty, as one of the whips of the Irish party, to state that you have voted with the Irish members in nearly all the principal Irish divisions.

I have found you a most constant friend to Ireland. You have striven always to obtain for us justice and equality, and you have been ready to help us when many others held aloof. I am very sorry to hear that you are likely to have a contest, as I am convinced that if you are not returned to the House of Commons, Ireland will lose one of her very best friends amongst the English members.

> Believe me,
> Faithfully yours,
> J. P. NOLAN.

No. CXC.

MARQUIS OF HARTINGTON.

> Crawshaw Hall,
> Rawtenstall,
> March 30, 1880.

MY DEAR RYLANDS,—

I am sorry that it has not been found possible to hold one of our county meetings in Burnley before your election. It has been thought best to reserve one or two of the next important meetings, including that at Burnley, till the last week. I believe that the present arrangement is that we should visit Burnley on Wednesday, the 7th April, but on this point I must be guided by the advice of my committee, some of the members of which have, I think, been in communication with you upon the subject.

I need not tell you that I take a very strong interest in the Burnley election, and that you have my best wishes for your success, as to which I hope there can be no doubt.

I remain,
Yours sincerely,
HARTINGTON.

———— ——

No. CXCI.

Mr. J. G. McMINNIES, M.P. (Warrington.)

Farington,
April 23, 1880.

My Dear Peter,—

I forgot to ask you if you are going to the banquet to be given to the Liberal members and candidates belonging to the Manchester Reform Club next Wednesday. If you are going and there is any difficulty in getting back to Thelwall, I shall be glad if you and Carrie will stay the night with me at Summer House.

If Lord Hartington's walk to and from Windsor Castle was an intentional slight to him, it was an insult to the whole of the United Kingdom. I hope it was not intentional. The Queen is not a very wise woman, as most of her subjects know, but she is surely not an unmitigated fool. She has never been forgiven down here for refusing to open the Manchester Town Hall, because the Mayor's wife had given a statue of

Cromwell to the city, and if she has snubbed the whole Liberal party in this way she ought never to be forgiven by the nation. Looking at what we have got as a sovereign and at what we may expect, I think we had better go in for a republic and pack the Queen and Lord B. off to Jerusalem.

Ever yours affectionately,

J. G. McMinnies.

No. CXCII.

Mr. T. B. POTTER, M.P.

Cobden Club,
April 19, 1880.

My Dear Rylands,—

I want to speak to you about the annual meeting of the Reform Club on the 6th of May. You know how I have fought, year by year, the jingo element in the club. It is now more rampant than ever, and I am to be turned out of committee on the 6th of May. I have been an active member for nine years or twelve, I forget which, and I hope my friends will support me and not see me kicked out for no other reason than I am a stern political watch dog always at my post.

Ever yours,

Thomas B. Potter.

No. CXCIII.

HUGH C. E. CHILDERS, M.P.

17, Prince's Gardens,
S.W.,
May 4, 1884.

My Dear Rylands,—

You and I have so often fought the same battle that you will believe that I speak with absolute sincerity when I say that I deeply regret your not being in office. I certainly had no idea that you had either time or inclination for it, but when you tell me that this is not so, I can only deplore that Mr. Gladstone was not better informed than myself. If you had given a hint to myself, or to any of those who have taken the same line that you have in opposition, I feel sure that your claims would have been recognised.

Of course, I say this only from myself (for I have shown your note to no one), but you know how much Mr. Gladstone looks to those who have fought the battle of economy through good report and evil report.

I have myself a very hard task before me, not so much this session, for I shall take time to study the grave questions to be solved, but later on, when the difficulties must be boldly grappled with. I may have to task your patience a little, but I hope in the end to shew good results.

Believe me, yours very truly,
Hugh C. E. Childers.

No. CXCIV.

Mr. JOHN PERCY.

House of Commons,

June 3, 1880.

Dear Mr. Rylands,—

If a few members of the House of Commons will listen to what I have to communicate concerning the Science and Art Department, and proceed to act thereon,—provided I advance conclusive evidence, as I can do, of the accuracy of my communication,—a reform will be effected, which, I am sure, will save the nation £20,000 or £30,000 per annum. This money, I shall be prepared to show, is *wasted, actually wasted!* I defy either yourself or any member of the House of Commons, however skilful in interpreting the Estimates, to discover the true state of the case without assistance, such as I can give. Mr. Stansfield has been with me and *has offered* to speak on this matter, and so has Mr. Dillwyn. I have no private object to promote, but I am determined to work on energetically for any time, so long as my health continues, until I see the eyes of financial members, if I may so designate them, of the House of Commons, fully opened.

Mr. Prim informs me that after the questions to-morrow you will give me an interview. I must ask you to be so good as to come to my rooms here, where I have all the documentary evidence duly arranged.

Very truly yours,

John Percy.

No. CXCV.

Rt. Hon. J. CHAMBERLAIN, M.P.

72, Prince's Gate,
June 6, 1880.

My Dear Rylands,—

If Lawson goes on with his Frere motion, or if Parnell, or any one else takes it up, should not you give notice of the previous question as an amendment? It seems to me that this would come best from you, as you could explain with effect, your opinions on the retentions, and at the same time your determination not to embarrass the Government, or to play into the hands of the Tories, and your conviction that the appointment was only temporary, and that, under these circumstances, you are willing to suspend judgment, etc., etc.

If some such amendment is not proposed at once the Tories will probably give notice of one, and they may so word it as to be awkward.

Yours sincerely,
J. Chamberlain.

No. CXCVI.

Sir CHARLES DILKE, M.P.

Foreign Office,
June 30, 1880.

My Dear Rylands,—

Biddulph has written me a tremendous dispatch because I did not contradict the enclosed statement in your Cyprus speech, *Times* report. My impression is that you did not say what you are reported in the *Times* as having said ; but that you confined yourself to quoting Mrs. Scott-Stevenson and Sir S. Baker. What shall I say to Biddulph ? Could you write me a private note which I could confidentially send him?

Yours,

Charles W. Dilke.

[Statement referred to in the above letter—" The Custom House too, at which we had a most important official, was an absolute nuisance."]

No. CXCVII.

Mr. F. W. CHESSON.

172, Lambeth Rd., S.E.,
Sept. 6, 1880.

My Dear Rylands,—

I am very glad to receive your note. I wondered what had become of you, it so rarely happens that you leave town before the close of the session.

Things do not improve in Cyprus, which is now under the Colonial Office. I enclose you some further letters from Rossetto. I hope you will kindly be prepared to take action in the matter next year. You will see that he intends to apply to the High Commissioner for the authorisation necessary to enable him to become a public notary. Dilke informs me confidentially that so long as Biddulph remains in Cyprus, Rossetto has no chance of getting his application acceded to. That, however, is no reason why he should not apply, and send us the correspondence which ensues. I have advised him to do this.

I regret to learn that Dilke is very unwell. After his admirable speech on Saturday evening, he had to go to bed for twenty-four hours.

Believe me,
Very faithfully yours,
F. W. Chesson.

U

No. CXCVIII.

Mr. F. W. CHESSON.

172, Lambeth Rd., S.E.,
Oct. 23, 1880.

My Dear Rylands,—

There is a general feeling among our friends here that the Greek Committee should take some public step at the present moment to show its sympathy with the Greek Government in the existing crisis. As you are aware, the objects of the Committee are limited to the boundary question, but this is of course the very subject upon which action on our part is now called for.

The alternatives open to us seem to me to be the following :—

(1) A public meeting in London or Manchester.
(2) An address of sympathy to be presented through the Greek Minister.
(3) A deputation to Lord Granville, or
(4) A general meeting of the members and supporters of the Committee to consider the line of action to be taken.

I should feel much obliged if you would kindly inform me what view you take of the matter. I incline to the 2nd and 4th.

I remain,
Very faithfully yours,
F. W. Chesson.

No. CXCVIX.

Sir UGHTRED KAY SHUTTLEWORTH.

> 28, Prince's Gardens,
> S.W.,
> Jan. 22, 1881.

Dear Mr. Rylands,—

I have been answering Captain Verney's invitation to me to join " a Committee that has been formed to forward, by all legitimate means, the re-establishment of the independence of the Transvaal." I do not know whether you have joined the Committee, but, as a constituent of yours, I have observed, with some anxiety, the course you have taken since Parliament met on this and on the Irish question. I venture, therefore, to send you a copy of my letter to Captain Verney, feeling that views which I must freely express to others should not be withheld from a representative in Parliament, of whom I have been a hearty supporter. Those views apply with special force to the policy of Her Majesty's Government regarding Ireland. At such a time as this, after the repeated proofs we have had of our leaders' desire to do "justice to Ireland," and after the great unwillingness they have displayed to resort to exceptionally severe measures for maintaining order, and preserving life and property, I feel that every man who has professed confidence in Mr. Gladstone and Lord Hartington, should stand by them and assist by vote (if not by voice) in strengthening their hands, so long, at least, as they

have neither said, proposed, nor done anything to
forfeit our confidence.

Believe me,

Dear Mr. Rylands,

Yours sincerely,

UGHTRED KAY SHUTTLEWORTH.

No. CC.

CAPTAIN E. H. VERNEY.

2, Great Stanhope Street,

Park Lane, W.,

Jan. 24, 1881.

DEAR SIR,—

The Transvaal Independence Committee was formed
as a focus to gather in the names and sympathies of
all those who believe that the ultimate independence
of the Transvaal in due time is the object to be worked
for.   This object we keep steadily in view ; we do not
presume to dictate to the Government when or how it
is to be brought about ; some of us are for active and
energetic agitation ; others are for waiting ; as indi-
viduals we differ widely ; as a committee we are
determined to take no line that may embarrass the
Government or encourage revolt.   We believe the
public don't know the merits of the case.   We propose

to disseminate accurate information. We believe the Government would welcome any pressure of public opinion that would enable them to wash their hands of the Transvaal altogether.

As a committee we adopt and adhere to a tone of studied moderation, and are careful to offend none who desire the ultimate independence of the Transvaal. The withdrawal of your name will be a discouragement to us. Your admirable exposition of our case in the House of Commons gladdened our hearts.

I have not the pleasure of knowing you personally, so must earnestly beg you to accept my excuses if I ask you, at least for the present, not to withdraw your name. I will gladly wait on you, if you desire it, at any time and place, to inform you more fully of our proceedings and intentions.

Faithfully yours,
EDMUND H. VERNEY.

No. CCI.

CAPTAIN VERNEY.

Travellers' Club,
Pall Mall, S.W.,
Jan. 25, 1881.

Dear Sir,—

I am obliged for your note, and will have your name removed from the list of the committee. To-morrow I am going to Birmingham for the annual meeting of the National Liberal Federation. On my return I will take advantage of your kind invitation to call upon you at the House. No doubt you know my father ; I will ask him to bring me into the lobby one day.

Faithfully yours,
Edmund H. Verney.

———

No. CCII.

CAPTAIN VERNEY.

Transvaal Independence Committee,
Draper's Gardens, E.C.
Feb. 1, 1881.

My Dear Sir,—

I quite agree with you that there is nothing to be done immediately ; this committee is not influential enough from any point of view to have weight with Lord Kimberley, even if he would consent to receive a deputation, which I doubt. Until the constituencies begin to make their voices heard I expect we shall see no signs of a better mind among those in power. The work of arousing the constituencies on this subject, and informing them, and enlightening them, on the oppressive injustice and iniquity of the war being waged against the Boers, is the work to which this Committee is now addressing itself.

> Very faithfully yours,
>
> EDMUND H. VERNEY.

No. CCIII.

Mr. JOSHUA RAWLINSON.

> 16, Nicholas Street,
> Burnley,
> Jan. 31, 1881.

DEAR SIR,—

I have had it in my mind to write you ever since you omitted to vote for the address, but for various reasons I have deferred doing so till now. I can scarcely express to you the feeling of disappointment, if not consternation, that prevailed amongst the great bulk of our friends, when they found that your name was not in the Division list supporting the Government.

It is quite true that your abstention pleased a few of the more noisy and rampageous liberals, but as far as my own experience and judgment are concerned, I have no hesitation in saying that ten were displeased where one was pleased. I know you will vote in each case as your own conscience dictates, irrespective of what this or that person may think of it, and I, personally, am in favour of leaving the hands of members as much unfettered as possible. But when we consider that the great issue on which the election was fought was confidence in Mr. Gladstone, I think that you will not wonder at the surprise and anxiety expressed by your friends at the course you, no doubt, felt compelled to take.

As to the Bill for the protection of life and property in Ireland, I do hope you will be able to give Mr. Gladstone your hearty and unfaltering support in each stage of the measure. Liberals here are not pleased that the Government should be dependent on the opposition to carry their measures, and they feel that any measures of repression recommended by Mr. Gladstone and Mr. Bright, ought to receive the earnest support of all sections of the party. As to the Irish members, intense disgust at their conduct is the universal feeling, even amongst those opposed to coercion, and they feel that the only course open is to give the Government a loyal and hearty support.

Trusting you will excuse this trouble I am giving,

I remain,

Yours faithfully,

JOSHUA RAWLINSON.

No. CCIV.

Mr. BLANCHARD JERROLD.

27, Victoria St., S.W.,
March 23, 1881.

Dear Mr. Rylands,—

Have you remarked in the *World* of yesterday and in the *Standard* of to-day authoritative statements to the effect that the French Government has in the Foreign Office archives the admissions of a leading statesman lately in office, acknowledging the claims of France to supremacy in Tunis and her right to exercise a Protectorate over the Bey; and further that this admission was made immediately after the annexation of Cyprus.

The hostile action of the French authorities towards the Bey, and the sending of war ships to Tunis, is regarded as a beginning of the assumption of this Protectorate. Could we persuade you, in the interests of freedom and independence guaranteed to the weak, by the treaties of the strong, to put a question to the Government on this subject?

I send you the *East*, in which you will find much material on the general question.

Faithfully yours,
BLANCHARD JERROLD.

No. CCV.

Mr. F. KIMBER.

22, Queen's St.,
London, E.C.,
April 9, 1881.

Dear Mr. Rylands,—

I am glad you are going to bring the subject of " corrupt solicitors " before the House. It is high time they were struck off the rolls. Their evil example and influence is most baneful. Other people say " if they bribe why should not we ?" All my life I have been fighting against this curse to the profession. Read the two enclosed addresses I have just sent out. They may open your eyes. This Hughes is the Conservative agent for the city, but knows very little law.

Yours faithfully,
F. KIMBER.

P.S.—I think my friend Mr. Firth will help you in the House if necessary.

No. CCVI.

Mr. JOSEPH WRIGHT.

> Summer Hill,
> Macclesfield,
> April 16, 1881.

Dear Sir,—

Some of our friends are anxious to have an interview with you to ascertain your views respecting the present unhappy state of affairs in our Borough, and I intended to have called upon you in town last week, but had to leave sooner than expected. At a meeting held at my office this morning, I was requested to communicate with you, and to ask if it would be convenient for you to receive a friend and myself in Manchester or elsewhere, during the ensuing week. If this would be acceptable to you, it would be much valued by the leaders of the Liberal party here.

> I am,
> Yours faithfully,
> Joseph Wright.

No. CCVII.

Mr. JOSEPH WRIGHT.

Macclesfield,
April 21, 1881.

My Dear Sir,—

Mr. Alderman Bullock and myself met a few of our Liberal friends this morning and told them of your kind reception and generous and friendly offer of assistance, and I was desired to write and thank you on behalf of the meeting. I send you by this post a printed copy of the Commissioners' report, and whenever we receive a blue book of the evidence we shall be glad to call your attention to it in detail.

The four Conservative magistrates received on Tuesday a letter from the Lord Chancellor asking them to resign.

I have the honour to be, Dear Sir,

Yours faithfully,

Jos. Wright.

Both parties here ask why was not Mr. Eaton scheduled? His treasurer, Mr. Godwin, to whom he paid the money, has lost his J.P.

No. CCVIII.

LIEUT.-COL. OUVREY.

Lymington,
Hants,
May 15, 1881.

Dear Sir,—

As you have always shown yourself ready to redress, as far as possible, public grievances, I take this occasion to bring to your notice, now that the question of opening Lincoln's Inn Fields is being mooted, that not only Lincoln's Inn Fields but many other London squares *were once open to the public.* If you will take an opportunity of consulting " Stowe's London," which you will find in the British Museum Library, if you have not a copy in the House of Commons, there you will see plates of Bloomsbury, Hanover, and other squares with paths through them, and open to the public.

I believe that 150 years ago all squares were open ; and if this should prove to be the case I think that they could only have become so by the authority of Parliament, and the same authority which was wrongfully asserted to rob the public of these open spaces can, I should think, be now employed to restore them to their legitimate uses.

Yours faithfully,
H. A. Ouvrey.

No. CCIX.

SIR GEORGE BALFOUR, M.P.

6, Cleveland Gardens,
Hyde Park,
May 13, 1881.

My Dear Mr. Rylands,—

I see by a notice in the *Daily News* that there was a meeting of a few members to advocate the exclusion of military officers from the House of Commons, and that you sent an apology for not being able to attend.

I appeal to you not to set the example of advocating the exclusion of any class. Surely we have had sufficient experience of the evils of class legislation. I appeal to you to support the claim that Sir A. Gordon, Sir H. Havelock, and Major Nolan may justly make of having been true by their votes to the Liberal interest. I may also ask to have a single vote given by myself challenged as opposed to the Liberal cause. Speaking now from more than fifty years' observation, I do assert that one of the great mistakes made by the Liberal party has been the neglect of the interests of the army. If officers of the Liberal party had been encouraged, I have no hesitation in stating that the cost of the army at the present day would have been four millions less than it now is. Look at the officers in power at present, nearly every one of the Conservative party, every office of trust being held by this class. But, I ask, why should officers be excluded ?   There are many drawing money from the public funds.

There are also others who have held contracts, and whose relatives expect contracts.   Again, why should lawyers remain when they draw money from the public.   Take the Attorney-General, who received nearly £12,000 besides his pay in the year before last, and the Solicitor-General nearly £5,000 for fees.   Also the Advocate and Solicitor-General for Scotland received extra fees.   There are also men receiving pensions; for instance, Walpole, Villiers, Wilmot.

Yours very sincerely,

G. BALFOUR.

No. CCX.

SIR GEORGE BALFOUR, M.P.

Caterham Valley,
Surrey,
May 18, 1881.

MY DEAR MR. RYLANDS,—

I agree with all your views, even to the extent of Full Pay Officers.   And as regards this class, I only urge that they are few in number and will be fewer hereafter.   I only know of three in the present Parliament, viz. :—Lt.-Col. Horne, Major Nolan, and Lt.

Fort ; there may be a few more, only I have not taken notice.

Now it is a great point not to allow objections to be raised by the Executive Government as to those who stand for Parliament. Every one qualified or fit to represent the People should be free to come forward.

Last year Nolan consulted me about the intended objection to his getting leave of absence from his Battery, and which the General Officer in command had indicated his intention to refuse when Parliament became *non est*. I advised him to appeal at once to Col. Stanley, who promptly decided to tell the Commander-in-Chief that no interference must take place with Major Nolan's freedom to stand. Major Nolan was very attentive to his duties. I took the pains to enquire of him. He joined his Battery immediately on Parliament rising, and served constantly during the recess.

Lt.-Col. Horne is very attentive. I have known him after a division, between 12 and 1, go off, this year, to join the men who were kept out from an alarm about the Barracks, and he goes up and down to Windsor with great regularity.

Lt. Fort is praised by his Commanding Officer for his marked attention to his regimental duties, the Regiment being at Hounslow. I merely mention these details to shew that I have been watching these results.

On Havelock consulting me about taking the command, I at once asked about Parliament, and he replied that the condition was to give up the House ;

now that is very proper. If Nolan were offered a staff appointment, then the authorities might rightly require him to retire from Parliament on condition.

Lt.-Col. Horne has lately obtained his Lt.-Colonelcy in the Blues, and it *might* have been right to make his promotion depend on his giving up his seat. But in fact, at the present day the abuse is slight compared with the evil which power in the hands of the Commander-in-Chief might create by meddling with members, and with men standing for election.

As regards Nolan, I may add that the authorities could have removed him from his Battery, now at Rangoon, if they had desired. There are many Artillery Majors anxious to go out to India. As it is the Battery has now a Captain and three Subalterns to 80 gunners. When I was a boy, under 17, I commanded a company stronger than this, and I was told did it very well.

Yours very sincerely,
G. Balfour

No. CCXI.

Mr. JOHN PERCY.

House of Commons,

June 15, 1881.

My Dear Mr. Rylands,—

I have pleasure in presenting you with my last published volume on Metallurgy, the fifth, on silver and gold. I have indicated certain places to which I beg to direct your special attention.

If I live I shall complete the series. I have nearly ready a new edition of my " Iron and Steel." I have spent nearly 40 years of my life in the study of metallurgy, and the writing of the volumes I have published has cost me 20 years. I did the latter solely with the object of promoting the School of Mines which I laboured hard to establish, or assist in establishing. I have made no profit whatever from these volumes, but I am *amply repaid* for my labour by the fact that they have been well, more than well, received in France, Germany, Austria, Italy, Spain, the United States, South America, and the Australian Colonies.

My collection, which it has cost me forty years to form, can never be got again.   Not all the money in the Treasury could purchase many of the specimens, because they are unique. I intended to have bequeathed it to the nation, but now, thanks to the action of Mundella's immediate predecessors, it shall go to America, anywhere, even to the bottom of the sea, sooner than that department at South Kensington shall have it.

Very truly yours,
JOHN PERCY.

No. CCXII.

MRS. H. P. COBB.

Wealdstone House,
Harrow Weald,
Stanmore,
Nov. 4, 1881.

MY DEAR MR. RYLANDS,—

Ever since I have seen you I have so often thought of your views of the Coercion Act, and how you wished that all prisoners had been let free on the passing of the Land Act, and I have so much wished I could know what you thought of the arrest of Mr. Parnell and his chief colleagues, that I thought I might write to ask you. At first I felt dreadfully sorry about it, but so soon after it really seemed as if order were at last coming out of chaos, and the people going to use the new Land Courts in a fair spirit, that I could not help believing it was right to have silenced the man who so tried to keep up the chaos. Do you think so now? A letter Mr. Goldwin Smith wrote in the *Pall Mall Gazette*, of Oct. 14, influenced me very much. I wonder if you saw it. I always do agree with him. He says " It is not in my line to condemn any man for wanting to overturn a Government if he thinks it is bad, and that he can put a better in its place," but he still thinks the Union ought to be maintained, and the Government has been right unless it meant to forfeit all authority.

It really does seem hopeful, does it not, that the people are trying to give the Land Act a fair trial, and the way the priests speak in favour of order is satisfactory too. I am so very fearful, finding myself through all times of history sympathising with the revolutionary side, that I now am false to my principles in not being heart and soul with *these* insurgents, and I should like to know very much what you with your Radical principles think. Please do not write to me if it is a trouble, and forgive me for troubling you.

I hope that Mrs. Rylands is well.

Believe me,

Sincerely yours,
ELIZABETH COBB.

My husband is not at this moment at home, or he would send some message.

No. CCXIII.

Rt. Hon. J. STANSFELD, M.P.

Hyde Park Gate,
London, S.W.,
Nov. 9, 1881.

Dear Rylands,—

I have *determined* to take the opinion of the House next session on Contagious Diseases question, and not to be longer delayed and shunted, and put off. The question is ripe, though the Committee has not reported; for, at least, in my opinion, the hygienic case for the Acts has broken down. I am quite determined to begin the real fight, and that it shall be *real*. Under these circumstances I confidently rely on your active and friendly aid and co-operation, both in the House and out of it.

Out of the House the request I have to make is that you will accede to the request which will be made to you, to speak at Bradford on our subject. I intend to speak at Halifax. In the House you will help me in the Debate, I feel sure. You will not refuse me, I feel sure, either on public or on private grounds.

Truly yours,
J. Stansfeld.

No. CCXIV.

RT. HON. J. CHAMBERLAIN.

72, Prince's Gate, S.W.,
March 13, 1882.

MY DEAR RYLANDS,—

Many thanks for your friendly note. I made up my mind not to do anything rashly, or to give the enemy a chance; but I don't intend to let those d—d snobs have it all their own way. It is monstrous that it should actually be a disqualification for membership of a Liberal Club to have been in any way distinguished as a Liberal. But I agree with you that indignation would play into the hands of fellows we want to beat, and must not be thought of while anything else remains.

I find the good people at Birmingham are furious. They will come up and storm the club, if something is not done. We can do a good deal, however, to prevent such cowardly spite in future, and about this I will talk to you when I see you.

Meanwhile again thanks for your letter.

Yours very truly,
J. CHAMBERLAIN.

No. CCXV.

Mr. E. G. SALISBURY.

13A, Gt. George Street,
Westminster,
May 2, 1882.

My Dear Rylands,—

I saw Firth on Sunday evening, and read over to him my draft petition, and we afterwards decided that it was only due to Sir Henry James that he should be warned not to commit himself to any statement about Chester in answer to anything Mr. Charles Lewis may say, until he had seen me. Of course I am very angry that those whose duty it was to serve me, by stating the true facts to the Lord Chancellor, and, indeed to the Commissioners, should have acted otherwise, but that is no good reason why I should let Sir Henry James fall into a trap, and I accordingly agreed that Firth should see him. I understand that he has done so, and will tell me what passed between them, on his return from Leeds, where he has gone for a couple of days. The Draft Petition is now settled, but as I am soft enough to hesitate about printing it, and silly enough to hope that, after all, I may be saved from doing so, I have not got it engrossed. The proper thing and just must be for the Lord Chancellor to "hear" me formally, as is provided for by law, but I am too proud to go to him cap in hand, when I know that he has unwittingly done me a great wrong, although I am told by those who know him well that he would only be too glad, as dear old Lush was, to be set right.

I shall be here all to-morrow if you have occasion to write me.

I am, my dear Rylands,
Yours very truly,
E. G. SALISBURY.

———

CCXVI.

MR. E. G. SALISBURY.

Glan Aber,
Chester,
May 20, 1882.

MY DEAR RYLANDS,—

Tired to death, almost, I managed to slip away from town yesterday, and am now quietly reposing in my old corner at home, trying to find out what our local Tories have to say about Mr. Lewis, and his proposed Chester motions in Parliament. He is supposed to be nursing some spite against Mr. Dodson, but why or wherefore I cannot find out. I am satisfied, however, that he knows nothing of the *true nature* of the suppressed paragraph in my letter to Lord Richard Grosvenor, but supposes it to have reference only to something relating to the Duke of Westminster !

This arises, I suspect, from a letter of mine to Mr. Dodson (in which the Duke is referred to), and which he so unfairly and needlessly handed over to the Commissioners, and which they so spitefully printed in the evidence ; but, as I told you, the Duke is in no way alluded to in my letter to Lord Richard, and we may rest content, therefore, as to that particular, unless some of the Commissioners have let the cat out of the bag.

I have not, of course, proceeded further with my petition since we met, but it is ready for engrossment. My unwillingness to drag Mr. Gladstone's and Lord Richard's names before Parliament remains as strong as ever, and I am still hoping, even against hope, that the Law Officers of the Crown will hit upon some method of relieving me from the false, unjust, and (I think) illegal position in which the Commissioners left me. Had there been any pretext for their action I should have remained passive, but as there is none, and seeing also that I had acted in thorough good faith and in compliance only with Lord Richard Grosvenor's and Mr. Dodson's wishes, and upon the assurance of counsel that I was legally entitled to act as I did, I feel very strongly that the Government are bound in honour to stand by me. Herbert Gladstone asked me to see the Attorney-General, but I cannot do that uninvited ; but I suppose no progress will be made with the Bill until after the holidays. This will give me time not only to confer

with my friends here as to the course I should adopt
in the last resource, but will give him time to consider what he can do for me.

Meanwhile, if you hear anything more I should be
glad if you would write to me here, where I propose
remaining for a fortnight.

I am, my dear Rylands,

Yours very truly,

E. G. SALISBURY.

No. CCXVII.

MR. E. G. SALISBURY.

Glan Aber,
Chester,
May 28, 1882.

MY DEAR RYLANDS,—

AMEN! I wish on many accounts your prayer
were answered quickly, for we true Reformers are
being led a very ugly and painful dance, and in the
very nature of things we must suffer. But low down
in the depths I find a sort of clinging affection for the
"Grand Old Man," though my reason and my experience of him would fain lay violent hands upon
"Grand," and say the "Old Man," is on the wane.
If Providence did but provide the way for escape I

think Lord Hartington, with very many short-comings, would be a safer and a better leader in these degenerate times. I daily lift up my voice in praise that Forster has gone to his own, and after seeing the stuff Lord Granville is made of I can have no manner of doubt that Lord Hartington is *the man* for our money. I am very glad he took in good part the "snub" of Thursday week; it was not meant for *him*, for we renegades felt and do feel that it was a downright shame to deceive him. We very soon learnt that the race was ours, and if we had to fight it over again we should add a hundred to our number. I do not know Lord Hartington, but they say he was far too busy in that business, and in reward for his good service against "the Party," as they put it, he will, I am told, have to fight a Liberal at Haverford-west next election. Bad as I am, I've not got that far yet, and I am a sufficiently good Liberal and Welshman to object to that little game; but if our Treasury people are such fools as to go on annoying their own supporters and patting the Tories on the back, I cannot say that I will stand to my Welsh guns much longer.

Lewis, I hear, has gone to America. Good luck to him! for however much I should like to see Master Ingrate Dodson trounced, I suspect Mr. Lewis would have done us no good service. I thank you very much for giving Mr. S. G. a poke. The pot is boiling, and I can see the froth rising, and, in view of a possible storm, I have told Lord Richard that if I put in my petition I must have him examined. Should it come to that pass, both he and others will fare badly, I am sorry to say, but they will have brought all upon themselves, because they have not believed the dictum of Lord Justice Knight Bruce that "dishonesty was the worst possible policy *in the end."*   May your rest be sweet, and till we meet in the wicked upper room at Pall Mall, where *native Peers* do most congregate on Saturdays,

Believe me to remain, as ever,

Yours very truly,
E. G. SALISBURY.

———

No. CCXVIII.

MR. E. G. SALISBURY.

Glan Aber,
Chester,
June 6, 1882.

MY DEAR RYLANDS,—

The enclosed will be pleasant reading for you, if you can only manage to wade through it.   The first letters gave me a fair opportunity of writing and printing my own, and I hear that it is looked upon in certain quarters as the warning of a coming storm, but that is far more due to the following *fact*, than to the letter itself.

Lord R. G. had professed to be working away like a nigger with the Lord Chancellor on my behalf, and on the 18th of August last he wrote to me, " I am sure every one feels for you, and I can only regret as I do, that my efforts with the Lord Chancellor produced no good result." Of course, I believed him, but in October last a friend told me he knew he had done nothing, and Mary like, I nursed the statement in my heart until I could fairly challenge the noble lord to say *ditto* to the above or to assert the contrary. The opportunity came last week, and I wrote to ask, if he had ever seen the Chancellor, or written to him on my behalf ; the reply was (in my opinion) a shuffler, and I accordingly required a distinct *yes* or *no* to my question, and the other day I got this letter. " I thought that I had made it clear, for the reasons I gave you in my letter of Thursday that I did *not* approach the Lord Chancellor in your behalf !" Whereupon, I sent him a copy of what he had said in Aug., 1881, and if that leaven does not work the whole lump, there is more in store that will put others of the co-fraternity in just the same sort of hole. If these people are resolved to act so unjustly to myself, and other good friends who have helped them ; well, they must be prepared to bear the burden of their own sins, for if they refuse to be warned by barkings, the bites will play old Harry with them. My patience is all but exhausted, and sorely as it will sorrow me to pay them back in their own coin, it will have to be done I fear. I am remaining here as long as I can do so, but am coming up the moment my clerk wires for me. A Tory friend has been wanting me to tell him, *in confidence*, what the " suppressed paragraph " contains, but I laughed at him, and told him they had better ask Mr. Lewis, who pretended to know all about it. " Ah !" said he, " it is about the Duke of course," and I laughed again, for he rubbed his hands with glee, because he *thought* he had me. Keep it dark, for although I owe our own friends nothing, it would be fine fun to see these fellows dropped into a hole of their own making.

I am, my dear Rylands,
Yours very truly,
E. G. SALISBURY.

No. CCXIX.

MR. E. G. SALISBURY.

Glan Aber,
Chester,
June 30, 1882.

MY DEAR RYLANDS,—

I have had to run home for a mouthful of fresh air, and shall remain here until my clerk says I am wanted in Committees. I have a letter this morning from a friend who says there is no chance of the Disfranchisement Bill proceeding, for he says, " the Government has more to do than it can accomplish, and I am not at all sure that the ministers are not glad enough of an excuse to get out of the foolish bill." I am told Bright will not remain in the Cabinet if troops are landed in Egypt, and I hope the statement is true, for after the words he used to us on Saturday last, it is manifest he is no " Jingo." But I am afraid the diplomatists will persuade the Porte to let us occupy the country, and so get over "the act of war " which Bright spoke of.

I sincerely hope we have sufficient non-interventionists in Parliament to protest against an act of aggression which has the elements of danger in it, and that they will be honest enough to do so, whether "the grand old man " likes it or not. I even hope that *he* is not so far lost to every sense of honour as to become a party to the policy which he has so often condemned. But my faith in him has been falling away so rapidly of late that I can only just *hope*, and nothing more.

I have got Mr. William Brown to put the 1865 story into writing for me, so that if anything should happen to him, he having been the chief mover in it, and my principal informant, I may have at hand a document which will prove that Lord Richard's " not true," is no better founded than the statement he himself made to me in 1881 in writing, and then flatly contradicted in June, 1882, under his own hand.

I am, my dear Rylands,

Yours very truly,

E. G. SALISBURY.

No. CCXX.

Mr. E. G. SALISBURY.

Glan Aber,
Chester,
Nov. 7, 1882.

My Dear Rylands,—

You know what a heaven-forsaken people we are
in this doomed city, politically speaking, but there
are some good Liberals here who have not bowed
down and worshipped the great Idol, and who think
with Bright that the moral law has some force left,
though it be not binding upon the nation unless it has
been blessed by Gladstone. The rank and file of the
party, however, swear by him and none else, and if
he bade them crucify the Saviour afresh they would
do so with the greatest pleasure. But just now the
evil and the good politicians are wanting a Liberal
meeting, and as I happen to be "chief boss" at
present, it falls to my lot to determine what sort of a
meeting it is to be, and to bring down to it a swell
who can speak. We propose to have the meeting
early in December, and this is to be the order of it,
as fixed in my own mind :—

1st.   A few wise words from the chairman.

2nd.   A formal resolution, proposed and seconded
by local men, approving of the three hundred selected
for the " caucus " devildom.

3rd.   A resolution calling upon the Government to
pass home measures of a Liberal character, and to

reduce the public expenditure and taxation. That to be proposed and seconded formally by local men, and supported by a swell M.P. who can speak to it with power.

Will you come and play "the part" in this great performance?   I have asked no other friend, nor shall I do so if you will come.   I am, as you know, anti-Coercion, anti-Egypt, anti-Clôture, but I do not propose to air my fancies now, nor do I expect you to do so, although I suppose we are all but one in faith, but if you wish to do so, you are welcome, and no one shall say you nay.   All I ask is that the "Grand Old Man " may be allowed to enjoy his eminence in peace, for greater far are the objects we have at heart than is the eminence of the chief—at least, it is so with me, for I do not care very much for the brightness of the outside of the platter, when I have a very strong, though unwilling, anxiety that the inside is but so-so, at best. It has taken line upon line to bring my lagging heart to the point, but the " moral law" business settled me, and I stand at " attention."

Let me have a quick reply and an affirmative one, for upon this rock, Peter, I place my trust.

I am, my dear Rylands,
Yours very truly,
E. G. SALISBURY.

Y

No. CCXXI.

Mr. JAMES HOWARD, M.P. (Bedfordshire.)

Clapham Park,
Bedfordshire,
Dec. 16, 1882.

My Dear Rylands,—

The *Warrington Guardian* enclosed was sent to me, I assume, by Mr. Thomas Robinson. On looking at the first leader I was surprised to find it a reproduction from the landlords' Tory paper, the *Chamber of Agriculture Journal*, often styled "Pell's Gazette," Albert being the chief wire-puller. What can Robinson be thinking about in disseminating Tory sentiments on the Land Question? I enclose you a copy of my last speech, the one referred to, as it shows the lines upon which advanced men think the tenant right question should be based. I also send you a copy of my evidence; just glance at Bonamy Price's cross-examination.

With kind regards to Mrs. Rylands,

I am, yours very truly,
James Howard.

No. CCXXII.

Mr. T. B. POTTER, M.P.

105, Pall Mall, S.W.,
March 31, 1883.

My Dear Rylands,—

I was yesterday talking to Mr. Samuel Whitbread, M.P,, about the advisability of republishing our little volume, the correspondence relative to the " Budgets of Foreign Countries," with a view to the enlightenment of Members of Parliament and others on the subject of forming some sort of *Estimates Committee* for our own country. He thinks well of the idea, and is to give me further advice.

You should read up the little volume which was edited by Probyn, and of which we distributed 3000 copies. Of course, now, extensive additions could be made, and Whitbread might give good counsel in the matter. This question should form part of your speech on Friday next.

Without some sort of Estimates Committee to control prospective expenditure, *before* the money is spent, all the efforts of men like you and Joe Hume will be comparatively fruitless.

Ever yours,
T. B. Potter.

CCXXIII.

Mr. JOHN GADSBY.

12, Cambridge Road,
Brighton,
April 9, 1883.

Dear Sir,—

I venture to think that my name will be familiar to you as that of an old Manchester man ; I was the printer and publisher of the Anti-Corn-Law League.

Referring to your Bill on the National Expenditure, I will give you a *fact* or two. I knew a young man some years ago who was a clerk in the Admiralty ; I called upon him several times at Somerset House; on one occasion I said to him, " you don't appear to be killed with work here." " Killed," he replied, " there are three of us in this room with £300 a year each, and I could do double the work of all three, but it is not for me to say so." I knew another case. There was a change in the Government, and some consequent changes were made. I was taking supper with a gentleman, not more than 45 years of age, when he said, jocularly, he was out of work. " Here," he said, " I am in the prime of life, and have been made into a pauper by Mr.————" (the new Prime Minister,) "he has superannuated me on full pay, £800 a year." Now these are facts ; this is the way our money goes.

I heard of a third case, my informant assuring me he knew the parties. A warm supporter of the then Government applied for a berth for his nephew.

" Oh yes," said the Premier, " he shall have £300 a year." Months passed away, but nothing was heard of the berth, therefore the uncle told the Premier he had forgotten his promise. " No," replied the Premier, " I have not ; if he will go to Somerset House, he will find his quarter's salary waiting for him." I wonder if he had to enquire where Somerset House was.

Yours truly,
JOHN GADSBY.

No. CCXXIV.

SIR WILLIAM WEDDERBURN.

14, St. James's Square, S.W.,
July 1, 1883.

DEAR MR. RYLANDS,—

With reference to our conversation, in which you expressed a wish to become more familiar with Indian affairs, I take the liberty to enclose copies of the prospectus of a Magazine, which we have lately started, intended to bring Indian questions more before the English public; I am sorry to say that, hitherto, we have not been successfu. in getting it a circulation in England ; in part, I think, because retired Indians are, for the most part, at present

strongly against Lord Ripon's measures, approved by
the native Press, and, therefore, we do not get support
from those naturally interested in India. What we
specially desire is to get the Magazine into the
reading rooms of popular Libraries, Institutes, etc.,
so that it might be generally read, and I thought that
perhaps you could kindly help us in this respect as
regards Lancashire, which has a direct interest in
Indian prosperity. In India we have a circulation
of over 500, but (alas!) in England, where a circulation
is really important, we have only some 50 subscribers.
In a separate packet I forward a copy of the last
number issued.

Believe me,
Yours sincerely,
W. WEDDERBURN.

———

No. CCXXV.

Sir WILLIAM WEDDERBURN.

14, St. James' Sq.,
London, S.W.,
Sept. 7, 1883.

My Dear Mr. Rylands,—
I am sure that you will be glad to hear that I had a
friendly and sympathetic reception from the Chamber

of Commerce, and they have asked me to give a public lecture on the subject of Agricultural Banks ; this I hope to do about the beginning of next month. One of those who took the most interest was the Mayor of Salford, and I was in great hopes that his name would turn out to be Young in order to fulfil the prophecy of the spirits, but unfortunately his name is Husband. However, I think the young ladies will be glad to hear that the spirit was partly correct.

My interview with Sir A. Colvin was a brief one, but I was glad to find that he holds " sound " views regarding the Indian *raigat*. I also, to-day, saw Sir Louis Mallet and had some talk with him on the topic we discussed. He seemed to think that Lord Hartington was inclined to a reform of the Indian Office, and I have no doubt Sir Louis himself would give effectual help when out of harness. He seemed to think that the first step would be to get a Parliamentary Enquiry.

With kindest regards to Mrs. Rylands and yourself, and thanks for my very pleasant visit,

Believe me,

Yours sincerely,

W. WEDDERBURN.

No. CCXXVI.

Mr. J. E. JOHNSON-FERGUSON.

Kenyon,

Dec. 2, 1883.

Dear Mr. Rylands,—

I am duly in receipt of your letter of the 1st inst. I am both astonished and disappointed on receiving last evening from Mr. Blackly the programme of the meeting.   I instructed him to reverse the order of the resolutions, which places you fourth in order of speakers, and if you wish you can move in place of supporting the resolution.   No doubt they placed your name to a resolution dealing with the franchise rather than to one expressing unabated confidence in the future administration of national affairs by the Government, as you have so often opposed the Government that they felt doubtful whether it would be agreeable to you.   But it would be better, in my opinion, *if agreeable to you*, for you to move or second, and Mr. Russell to second or support the first resolution of confidence in the Government; and let the second resolution on the Franchise be dealt with solely by local men.

It will be a great disappointment for our people not to see you, and no inconvenience to arrange the resolutions as you may wish.   I, therefore, hope we may see you.

Yours truly,

J. E. Johnson-Ferguson.

No. CCXXVII.

Sir WILLIAM WEDDERBURN.

48, Welbeck St.,
London, W.,
December 19, 1883.

Dear Mr. Rylands,—

Since I last saw you I have been working at the scheme for a small and informal committee of independent members for the management of Indian Affairs in the House of Commons. I now enclose a printed memo giving a sketch of the scheme. This I have shown to Mr. John Bright, who is, I think, willing to take the lead in the matter. Mr. Slagg, who is now in London, is taking much interest in the proposal. We think that Colonel Osborn would make an excellent secretary, as he is well informed on all Indian subjects, sound in his views, and very accurate. He is willing to give us his services.

I should have much liked to see you again to talk over the matter, but unfortunately I have to leave for India next week (Monday, 24th). I have the pleasure to enclose copy of a lecture I have just been giving about the Indian raigat.

Please remember me very kindly to Mrs. Rylands and the young ladies,

And believe me,
Yours sincerely,
W. WEDDERBURN.

No. CCXXVIII.

Mr. M. DALY.

> Bostall House,
> Abbey Wood,
> Kent,
> Feb. 1, 1884.

My Dear Mr. Rylands,—

It is a very long time since I have had this pleasure, although I have often wished to write you, but not liking to bother you I always put the idea aside.

Lately I have thought a good deal about your last speech on the public expenditure of this country, a subject which has not received or met with that attention in Parliament which it deserves. The enormous burdens of taxation in this country are frightful, the worst feature of which is the rapidity with which they are increasing without any effectual check upon them. And this is general in every department of the State. In the two great Revenue Departments, the Customs and Inland Revenue Departments, notwithstanding the abolishing of so many duties and the simplification of others, the total cost has been making steady advance year by year. In some cases the increased cost can only be properly described as a scandalous misappropriation of the public money. The whole thing is perfectly astounding, and it seems altogether inconceivable that such a state of things should be allowed to exist.

I do not know if it is your intention to take any action in the matter next session. My hope and wish is that you may. I do not think, however, if you will permit me to say so, that a mere Resolution will have any good result. A select committee, with an open enquiry, would be far more useful. Should you decide upon any action, I need scarcely say that I shall be delighted to assist you in every way I can, and give evidence, if a Committee is appointed.

Believe me,

Very faithfully yours,
M. DALY.

No. CCXXIX.

Mr. G. G. ADAMS.

126, Sloane Street,
Feb. 14, 1884.

DEAR MR. RYLANDS,—

Having noticed that there is to be a new equestrian statue of the late Duke of Wellington, I prepared a group for the competition promised by Mr. Shaw-Lefevre in the House of Commons, and reported in the *Times* of Aug. 10, 1883. I was appointed to cast the features after death of the great Duke, and after producing a bust, received a commission from her

Majesty to execute one in marble for Buckingham
Palace.   I have execnted many for H. G., the
present Duke, and also many for others of the nobility;
one has been placed in the Church at Waterloo,
Belgium ; in competition I obtained the commission
for the bronze statue of the great Duke, erected in the
city of Norwich ; this has given me opportunities of
portraying the exact lineaments of the hero, which
should, I think, obtain for me the greater consideration
for the commission.   I executed, amongst other
statues, the colossal bronze statue of General Sir
C. J. Napier, Trafalgar Sq., London.   I forgot to
mention that the present Duke, the family, and all
who knew him best, have pronounced mine as the
authentic head of Wellington.

And believe me, I am,
Yours very truly,
Geo. G. Adams.

No. CCXXX.

Rt. Hon. G. SHAW-LEFEVRE, M.P. (Reading.)

House of Commons,
March 5, 1884.

Dear Rylands,—

I am quite ashamed to have to ask you to put off
your question again about the statue; I expect,

however, to receive the report from the Prince of Wales Committee, on the subject, in two or three days' time, and till then, I shall not be in a position to answer. Cavendish Bentinck has put off a question on the same subject till Thursday in next week, and if you will do the same I will answer both at the same time.

Yours very truly,
G. SHAW-LEFEVRE.

No. CCXXXI.

MR. G. G. ADAMS.

126, Sloane Street,
April 7, 1884.

DEAR MY. RYLANDS,—

This is to thank you for all you did in the House of Commons on Thursday last, with regard to the Wellington equestrian group. I hope to see you soon and to thank you personally. I find you are commended on all sides for your good endeavours.

And believe me, I am,
Yours very obligedly,
G. G. ADAMS.

No. CCXXXII.

Rt. Hon. G. A. F. CAVENDISH BENTINCK.

3, Grafton Street,
Bond Street, W.,
April 19, 1884.

My Dear Rylands,—

If we don't look sharp Shaw-Lefevre will jockey us. He has never presented the report of the Wellington Statue Committee, without which the question manifestly cannot be properly discussed, and if he brings the vote on next Monday he will distinctly violate the promise he gave to me. I have sent to the House to-day, when I was informed that the report had not yet been presented to Parliament. I have written to Shaw-Lefevre on the subject, but like all Radical ministers he is sure to repudiate.

Considering that the Government handed over the decision of the question to the committee, I do not see how we can decide the question without the committee's decision and the grounds of it.

Yours faithfully,
G. C. Bentinck.

No. CCXXXIII.

Mr. G. G. ADAMS.

126, Sloane St.,
April 28, 1884.

Dear Mr. Rylands,—

Thanks for your kind letter, and thought I must acquaint you with a fact which I have just heard, that I am chosen to produce an equestrian group in preference to Mr. Boehm, and by, I am told, comparison of work; it will be colossal. It appeared to me Mr. Shaw-Lefevre's wishing to postpone your motion was to take advantage, as a kind of doubling upon you, forming a new committee and giving the commission to Mr. Boehm.

I shall hope to see you in a day or two, and I shall be most interested in watching matters with regard to the Board of Works, etc. Mr. Cowan was sorry to have been absent, but will be present on the next occasion.

In haste, I am,
Yours very faithfully,
Geo. G. Adams.

No. CCXXXIV.

Mr. C. B. LAWES (Sculptor).

16, Michael's Grove,
                        S.W.
                    May 3, 1884.

Wellington Statue.

Sir,—

I see by the report of your speech that you are already well informed on this subject; and I write to ask you (if it is not too late) if you would bring forward a motion to the effect that "It would be more just, and give greater satisfaction to the country. if Messrs. Birch and Brock were asked to send in sketches as well as Mr. Boehm," Messrs. Birch and Brock being the two artists who by common consent have most distinguished themselves in the production of equestrian groups (besides Mr. Boehm).

I may add that the two artists who shall be not selected should be paid for their time and trouble.

I put myself at your service in any way you may desire for supplying information, etc.

I remain,

Yours truly,

C. B. Lawes.

No. CCXXXV.

Mr. DUNCAN McLAREN.

Newington House,
Edinburgh,
Dec. 29, 1884.

My Dear Mr. Rylands,—

In nearly all you say I agree, but still I think there are blots in the Bill, and that the Tories have got great concessions. My published letters were of course written before I had seen the Distribution Bill, but I have good reason to believe that from copies of my published letters and private letters sent to Mr. Gladstone and others an important protective safeguard was inserted (sub-section 3 of clause 8) which struck at the root, preventing rich men having more than one vote in large towns. My fear is that " faggot votes " will be largely increased in counties. There is nothing to prevent a man having qualifications and voting in each of the 23 divisions of Lancashire, for example, by purchasing forty shilling freeholds, whilst the poor man, who formerly voted for *two* members, can only vote for one, owing to the single member system. But the admission of all householders will cover a multitude of defects. In Scotland, the class now admitted will be nearly all Liberals, and very few Tories can by any chance be returned to Parliament.

I am always pleased to see your name in the debates, holding up the Radical flag as of old, and I trust there will be many helpers returned to assist you in the

z

battle.   In a fortnight I shall have completed my 85th year, and I feel very well in health but very deaf.

Believe me,

Yours very sincerely,

D. McLaren.

———

No. CCXXXVI.

Mr. W. MELLOR.

23, Samuel Street,
Crewe,
Jan. 24, 1885.

Dear Sir,—

I thank you for your letter, which I received yesterday, though, I assure you, we at Crewe are not at all likely to forget the claims of Mr. Latham.   The association of which I am president will support that gentleman's candidature, and I have good reason to think we shall carry him at the meeting of the District election Committee, which is to be held at Crewe on this day month.   His only rival, I think, will be Tomkinson, whose friends have been very busy during the last few weeks.   Hence the rather audacious proceedings of the Nantwich people—or, rather, of a few of them who have promised to act for the rest. In Crewe, however, I only know of one man of any influence whatever who is in favour of Tomkinson as against Latham. We are nearly half of the Division, and shall have 122 votes on the Election Committee, the whole number of members of that committee being between 250 and 260. I am aiming to secure perfect unanimity among our Crewe men, and having secured that, the rest will be easy. How the rural populations will go I cannot tell, as they are new to us and we to them, for the most part; but we shall be all right if we can only secure a few of them. I respect Tomkinson, but he will compare badly with Latham as a politician, and, moreover, his place seems to me in his own locality. The people in his own Division want him, and I should be glad if he will comply with their request.

Truly yours,
W. MELLOR.

In March, 1885, the following Letter of Thanks was sent from England to those colonies which had offered troops for the campaign in Egypt:—

"We, the undersigned subjects of the Queen resident in the Old Country, desire to express our gratitude to our countrymen and kindred beyond the sea for the generous offer they have made to send troops for active service. We have always believed that our ties of blood and common love of freedom would keep the Empire one and indivisible. We thank you for this proof that our faith is founded on truth."

Among the signatures to this letter was that of Mr. Peter Rylands, which called forth from Sir Wilfrid Lawson the following ironical note :—

No. CCXXXVII.

Letter of Thanks to the Colonies.

This is what it *ought* to have been :—

"We, the undersigned Dukes, Lord Mayors, Goschenites, Forsterites, jingoes, philosophers, poets, Marquises, and recreant Radicals, resident in this crazy old country, desire to express our gratitude to our countrymen and kindred at the antipodes for the idiotic step which they have taken in sending their fellow-citizens to be slaughtered in the Soudan.

We have always believed that our common love for bloodshed, rapine, and plunder, and hatred of all right and justice would keep us thoroughly united when we could discover any weaker nation whom we could rob with impunity.

We thank you for this proof that you are as blood-thirsty humbugs as we are ourselves, and remain,

Your fellow bandits,

Peter Rylands, etc., etc.

No. CCXXXVIII.

Mrs. JOSEPH KAY.

18, Hyde Park Gardens, W.,
May 14, 1885.

Dear Mr. Rylands,—

I promised to write to you again when all the arrangements were made for the cheap edition of my husband's book, " Free Trade in Land." I took the proofs of the Title Page, etc., back to Messrs. Kegan, Paul, Trench & Co. the day before yesterday, and in a short time I hope the book will be out, as the publishers are anxious it should be ready as soon as possible.

I told you that I wished the " Note " about Lord Cairns' Act, etc., should be written by " a Chancery Barrister of high reputation and Liberal views," and I have succeeded, beyond my hopes, as Mr. Osborn, Morgan's " Review of recent changes in the Land Laws of England," which he has most kindly and generously written *for me*, and *this cheap edition* of " Free Trade in Land " is very interesting, and will add to the interest and value of the Letters. The Review will take the place of the Appendix, which, as you know, is omitted in the present edition.

The copies which the Cobden Club have arranged to take will, I believe, be ready before the dinner (of the Club) takes place.

Believe me, Dear Mr. Rylands,

Yours sincerely,

Mary E. Kay.

No. CCXXXIX.

Mr. E. G. SALISBURY.

Glan Aber,
Chester,
Aug. 25, 1885.

My Dear Rylands,—

You will, no doubt, have seen that Morgan Lloyd has been acting upon my suggestion, when we last saw him together at the Club, and he is, in my opinion, carrying all before him. Pope* addressed a very "Pope-" like letter to him, calling him over the coals, etc., and threatening all sorts of pains and penalties if he persevered in his wicked ways, and—as I think—very foolishly, and unfairly, published it, before Lloyd could have a chance of answering it. I have cut out Morgan's reply and send it to you, as you may not have seen it.

I have another *brew* on hand now, and expect to play old gooseberry with another of the blood and thunder Gladstonians, but it will take some little time to bring it to pass. The Chester fiasco is being worked out, and so far it looks healthy.

I am, my dear Rylands,
Yours very truly,
E. G. Salisbury.

*Gladstone.

No. CCXL.

Mr. MORGAN LLOYD.

Aberdovey,
Sept. 27, 1885.

Dear Rylands,—

Here I am, fighting two, as you are probably aware, and my Liberal Opponent* is unscrupulous, and scattering his money right and left. I propose having a demonstration at Blænau Festiniog, the only really populous place, here I am very strong, and I want some help. Can you come and help me? You will be received by the electors like a Prince. Salisbury has been with me, and I hope he will come to Blænau Festiniog. You would do me a great service if you could come. Would Saturday next suit you, or would some other day suit you better? Say the following Saturday.

Yours sincerely,
Morgan Lloyd.

---

* Mr. Robertson, of Pale, who was elected.

No. CCXLI.

Mr. F. SCHNADHORST.

National Liberal Federation,
Birmingham,
September 9, 1885.

Dear Sir,—

Although writing under the above heading, I am not writing on a political matter, but to ask you if you care to assist some humble friends of mine. To-day, a Mr. Church, whom I have known some years as a secretary of a trade society, called upon and told me that he and a few other workmen had started a co-operative society for the manufacture of vegetable ivory buttons, and to ask me if I would write to you and beg you to get your firm to give them a chance of showing what they can do. I know the men to be honest and steady, and if you can give them a chance at the beginning of this undertaking, I shall be much obliged.

Pray excuse my troubling you upon a matter of this kind.

I am,
Yours faithfully,
F. Schnadhorst.

No. CCXLII.

Sir WILFRID LAWSON.

Brayton,
Carlisle,
Nov 2, 1885.

Dear Mr. Rylands,—

Thanks for yours. These stupid people keep writing me stupid letters, and I am obliged to send them stupid answers of some kind or other.

I don't in the least doubt that you will go as of yore *against* the publican and for the public. Are not things going on grandly?

> The Bishops, the Beershops, and all of that lot,
> Like lightning, I tell you, they're going to pot;
> Though Goschen and Hartington put on the brake,
> It all is in vain, for the folks are awake.
> The horses are good, and Joe Chamberlain steers
> Smack bang over publicans, prelates, and peers,
> While Rylands and Lawson, as pleased as can be,
> Stand up in the dickey both yelling with glee.

Ever yours,
Wilfrid Lawson.

No. CCXLIII.

Mr. JOHN RAMSAY.

Western Club,
Glasgow,
Nov. 28, 1885.

Dear Mr. Rylands,—

I congratulate you on your return as Representative of Burnley to your seat in the House of Commons. The poll in my case does not take place till Friday, the 4th prox., and I have been thinking this evening that if convenient and you are not engaged, you might possibly be willing to come North and address a meeting to promote Liberal unity among the electors, and secure the seat against the Tory who is opposed to me. For my success against that person himself I should have required no aid, but as two carpet baggers have entered the field you will easily understand that the votes of the Liberal electors may be divided and the Tory may gain the seat.

Of Mr. Mason, the Tory candidate, I know nothing, but he is said at one time to have been the General Manager of the North British Railway, and to have been requested to resign. Some of those who know him say that he would not well maintain the position of a Scottish representative. Mr. Mason, as I have said, would not have had a chance of success, indeed I think he would not have come forward, were it not that a Mr. Weir, from Hampstead, who, it seems, is a nominee of the London Land Restoration League, and a German Jew from Manchester, a lad of 22 years of age, have both become candidates, claiming to be regarded as extremely advanced Radicals, further advanced I presume than even Chamberlain. None of the three are known here, but the two Radicals would doubtless each receive votes, and this would so divide the electors as to give the seat to the Tory.

Several respectable men have been privately asked to take my place, and I would gladly have withdrawn, but no one would come forward, and my friends are anxious I should go to the poll. I have agreed to do so. In these circumstances I think if you could make a speech at Hamilton on the evening of Thursday, the 3rd prox, you might aid the Liberal cause, do me a personal service, and gain the seat. Consider this, and if you possibly can come *wire* to let me know.

You will excuse me for making such a request, in any case.

I am ever,

Yours very truly,
JOHN RAMSAY.

No. CCXLIV.

Sɪʀ UGHTRED KAY-SHUTTLEWORTH.

Gawthorpe Hall,
Padiham,
Nov. 28, 1885.

Dᴇᴀʀ Mʀ. Rʏʟᴀɴᴅs,—

We heartily rejoice that Burnley is true to you and the Liberal cause, and that you are again our M.P. It is most satisfactory that the combination of two unscrupulous parties against you and the Liberal party has failed, and that your majority is within 60 of that you gained in 1880. If another election occurs within the next year or so, as seems not unlikely now, your seat will be held by a larger majority than ever.

I get letters daily from Liberal politicians of various degrees of Radicalism, attributing their difficulties or disasters to our friend Chamberlain and his programme, and the spirit in which he has thrust it forward. There is an able article in to-day's "Economist," supporting this view. We have all to take to heart the fact that the truest Liberals and Radicals should be, and should show that they are, Conservative in the true sense of the word, and show that they are not Jacobins.

How utterly the *Times* fails to realise the situation, and the danger of Toryism, especially Randolphian Toryism, in office by favour of Parnell, and at the mercy of him and his henchmen ! It is conveniently ignored that there will be more Liberals than Conservatives in the Parliament, when Wales and Scotland have spoken, and that the Conservatives will really be in a helpless minority.

Lord G. Hamilton is vulgarly offensive at Shaw-Lefevre's expense.

I hope a week hence I may claim to be your colleague.

Yours very truly,
U. K. SHUTTLEWORTH.

No. CCXLV.

MR. JESSE COLLINGS, M.P. (IPSWICH.)

Edgbaston,
Birmingham,
Dec. 31, 1885.

MY DEAR RYLANDS,—

Many thanks for your letter. So far as we know or can guess in any way there is not the least grounds for a petition. No one could be more careful than we were, or could take more precautions than we did. The Tories were quite sure of winning, and had my effigy and a coffin ready to bury me, on the declaration of the poll. Their rage against me knows no bounds, and was expressed over and over again while I was at work in the County, before I got to the Borough. When they lost not only the Borough, but every division of the County (where no Liberal had ever been before), they declared they would "get me out by hook or by crook."

The money is supplied by the Carlton Club and others outside, not a penny by the Tories in the Borough. Unfortunately they do not claim the seat, for we have many clear cases against them, which, we cannot, in consequence, deal with. Indeed, their corrupt action is notorious.

There is no charge brought against me personally, but against *agents*, and it depends what agency is. If I am made responsible for every act of everyone whom I do not know, and over whom I have no control, and after I have (which is the case) used every endeavour, these elections will be very difficult. However, they won't care what happens if I can be got out. In any case they can give me much trouble and create great expense. The position is rather a comical one. I am credited, generally, with having redeemed the Borough from corruption, so far as the Liberal party is concerned. Three elections have been fought since 1880, absolutely pure, and though the Tories have used their old practices, they have in each case lost, and now they are charging with corruption the very people who have opposed and destroyed corrupt practices.

Believe me with all good wishes for you and yours for the coming season.

Very truly yours,
JESSE COLLINGS.

No. CCLXVI.

Mr. J. HENWOOD THOMAS.

H.M. Customs,
London, E.C.,
Dec. 5, 1885.

My Dear Mr. Rylands,—

Now that the fight is over and you have had time to take breath, will you allow me to congratulate you on your victory at Burnley? I felt very anxious about your contest, because I did not know whether there might be a large contingent of Irish electors who, voting with mechanical obedience to the Nationalist wire-pullers, would turn the scale against you. I was much delighted when I saw the telegram announcing your success. My satisfaction was, of course, largely due to personal regard, but it was increased by the hope that you will insist on the appointment of your Committee on Public Expenditure. As editor of the *Civilian*, I have encouraged the service to believe that the result of the enquiry which you have in contemplation must be beneficial to the "working bees," while getting rid of the "drones," as your committee would ascertain the why and the wherefore of all the main items of expenditure

At present the two departments of Customs and Inland Revenue are in a most deplorable condition. The administrative policy pursued in both has created, and is deepening, a feeling of positive disgust in the official ranks. Men who are thus treated and disheartened are those upon whose zealous and voluntary activity the security of the revenue depends, and I am not surprised to hear, consequently, that smuggling is largely on the increase at numerous ports, while illicit distillation seems to be simply rampant. It really amuses me to see statesmen and journalists speculating on the causes of a declining revenue, when I feel certain that much is due to the " penny wise, pound foolish " policy that is dignified with the name of administration. The constant violation of implied contracts is not conducive to zealous service. It may be both wise and equitable (I don't think so) to reduce the salary of one official from £180 to £80, and at the same time to increase the salary of another from £900 to £1,000; also to take away sixpence a day (given by Treasury order on account of long and good service) from a number of men whose day pay is but 3s. 6d., and give a lump sum of £400 as a gratuity to a man whose maximum salary is £1,000; also to deprive men, whose pay is hardly sufficient to enable them to keep body and soul together, of sixpence a day allowed for travelling expenses when employed at the distant docks, and to give £100 as " removal expenses " to a man who is promoted to an office with a salary of £1,400. The policy which such cases represent may be wise, but I know that it creates disgust, and I believe that instead of being economical it is really wasteful, because it destroys the zeal upon which the safety of the revenue depends.

It is high time for your committee to enquire into the work and expense of administration.

Yours very sincerely,

J. HENWOOD THOMAS.

———

No. CCXLVII.

MR. W. COLLINGE.

St. James' Street,
Burnley,
March 24, 1886.

MY DEAR MR. RYLANDS,—

I read your message anent the political situation at our last meeting of the Executive Committee. I presumed you would have no objection to this, seeing that your name has been frequently mentioned in connection with the subject in the papers. Personally, so far as Mr. Gladstone has declared himself, I am strongly in sympathy with the position you have taken up, and so are many others. Still, as you know, there are many in Burnley who swear by Mr. Gladstone, and if there is any probability of an election soon, no doubt you would poll best here by adopting a waiting policy before declaring yourself strongly against his plan. This is a very awkward question, and without the Irish vote we cannot afford to alienate any large

AA

section of the party. However, you know best what course to adopt.

Excuse this hint. With kind regards,

I am, yours sincerely,

W. COLLINGE.

CCXLVIII.

MR. JOHN BARON.

Burnley,
April 13, 1886.

DEAR MR. RYLANDS,—

I hope you will excuse me writing a line to you in the present crisis in political matters, but I feel I cannot refrain from doing so. It is announced that you are to speak at a meeting in London to-morrow night, along with Lord Hartington, Lord Salisbury, and others, against Gladstone's Bill for the future government of Ireland. I can assure you the feeling in Burnley is very strong against the action you are taking in this matter. Many think it will seriously prejudice you with the electors, that you will split up your own supporters, further alienate the Irish in the town, and, on a contest, the Tories would, to a man, go against you.

It is thought that although you cannot see your way at present to support Gladstone's Bill, it would be very much better for you to pursue a waiting policy for a little while, at any rate until you see further development of the scheme. You will, however, take the course which your judgment guides you.

I trust you will forgive me troubling you at all on this subject.

Accept regards.

Yours truly,
Jno. Baron.

No. CCXLIX.

Mr. JESSE COLLINGS.

Edgbaston,
Birmingham,
April 13, 1886.

My Dear Rylands,—

I wrote you a letter the other day about the Ipswich election, pointing out what was a fact, and a fact which the Judges dwelt on, that the Liberal managers of the petition had put everybody required, and indeed *everybody* who was named, into the witness-box, and had shown the most ardent desire to conceal nothing. I would not, of course, consent to any course of which this was not the basis, and I was glad to hear the Judges at Norwich fully admitting this fact, and comparing it favourably with the reticence which was being shown by the parties in that borough.

I write now, however, to refer to the few words I addressed to you in the Lobby of the House of Commons on this subject, which I feel were wanting in moderation and were very hasty, and I fear, might be taken by you to be a little offensive. I want, therefore, to withdraw them. The worries of the past month or two have made me nervous and irritable, but I should be doubly sorry to say anything to annoy such a good old friend as yourself, and one whose invariable goodness and kindness to me have been so valuable.

Excuse my writing. but this little incident has been on my mind.

Believe me,
Sincerely yours,
JESSE COLLINGS.

P.S.—I am glad to notice that you are taking part in opposition to the Grand Old Man's impracticable proposals. Time will vindicate your position; infallibility in politics is as bad as infallibility in religion.

No. CCL.

THE O'DONOGHUE.

Ballinahown Court,
Athlone,
April 12, 1886.

Dear Mr. Rylands,—

As we sat for so many years on the Liberal side, and voted so invariably in the same lobby, I am sure you will not object to my saying that I felt revived when I saw that you had, with your usual thoroughness, declared against Mr. Gladstone's most ruinous and most insidious proposals. Their effect would be to diminish, seriously, the strength and prosperity and glory of England, and absolutely to rend the Irish social system.

When the rumour reached me that Mr. Gladstone was about yielding to the pressure of the Parnellites I could not bring myself to believe it, and told everyone there was not a particle of truth in the report. It appeared to me inconceivable that the very man who had just proved the readiness and capacity of the Imperial Parliament to do full justice to Ireland, should be the man to set about impairing or destroying the authority of that Parliament. No one points to a single Irish grievance with which the Imperial Parliament refuses to deal.

All recent movements have had for their object the redress of some specific grievance or grievances. O'Connell's agitation for the repeal of the Union, the agitations for the repeal of the Corn Laws, for the Disestablishment and Disendowment of the Irish Protestant Church, all derived vitality and force from charges of injustice successfully brought against the action of the Imperial Parliament. Now, no such charges are brought, or can be brought, and the present movement is purely and simply a " veiled " revolt against the authority of the Imperial Parliament for reasons that cannot be maintained without shocking the conscience of mankind.

Mr. Gladstone has constantly pointed with legitimate pride to all that has been done for Ireland, and I fully expected that he would have taken his stand upon the broad and solid ground that the Imperial Parliament was able and willing to meet all the requirements of the Irish people, but that to an abridgment or surrender of its authority he could never consent. You well know that when Mr. Pitt carried the Union, it was not with the view of interfering in the local affairs of Ireland. For years and years after the Union our local laws were different from those of England and Scotland. What Mr. Pitt wanted to do was once and forever to preclude the possibility of having seated at Dublin a hostile legislature, which, in moments of difficulty and danger might hamper and thwart the action of Great Britain, and probably lead to grave disasters. It is ridiculous to pretend that the danger which Mr. Pitt sought to avert is a thing of the past. It is, in truth, greatly intensified by many circumstances peculiar to our time, and by the notorious character of the body

which Mr. Gladstone proposes to invest with legislative authority.

O'Connell was a near relative of mine, and the
object of my devoted attachment and veneration. I
am well versed in his history and that of his family.
He was loyal to the Crown, to the connexion, to the
greatness and glory of old England, and I am convinced that he would recoil with horror at the idea of
placing the Government of Ireland in the hands of
what is now known as the Irish Parliamentary Party.

With best wishes for the success of your patriotic
efforts,

I am, yours truly,
O'Donoghue.

No. CCLI.

Mr. MORGAN LLOYD.

53, Cornwall Gardens, S.W.,
June 7, 1886.

My Dear Rylands,—

Referring to our conversation on Saturday I need
not repeat the views on the present crisis which I
have more than once expressed to you, but I may say
that I shall be prepared to do my part in Wales
should a dissolution take place. I would suggest that

you could not do better, so far as Wales is concerned, than to get Mr. Thomas Gee, of Denbigh, the proprietor of the *Banner* newspaper, to publish some of the " Leaflets " in Welsh. Mr. Gee is opposed to the Irish Bills, but he is a Radical, and agrees with Chamberlain. He knows the Welsh people's way of thinking, and could therefore give the " Leaflets " a form which may be acceptable to them. What may take in England would not necessarily promote the cause amongst the Welsh people. We shall probably see our way more clearly after the Division.

Yours sincerely,
MORGAN LLOYD.

* * *

CCLII.

RT. HON. JOHN BRIGHT, M.P.

One Ash,
Rochdale,
June 24, 1886.

MY DEAR RYLANDS,—

I see some of your old friends are at war with you, and am sorry to see it.

They make no allowance for what they deem an error, even when viewed in connexion with many years of honest service, and when the future may show that, what to them is error, may turn out to have been patriotism and wisdom.

It is grievous to see with what bitterness Liberals can treat Liberals. whose fault is that they have consistently supported principles which all Liberals accepted less than a year ago.

Honesty and capacity in a member are, with some, of small value, in comparison with the suppleness which permits or enables him to " turn his own back upon himself," when a great political leader changes his mind and his course.

I am surprised that any real Liberal should be induced to oppose you ; he cannot excel you in a faithful discharge of public duty, and I think he should rather admire, than blame, your steadfast adherence to the policy on which you believe you were elected in November last.

If I have a place in the new Parliament, I hope I may find you in your seat, which is very near the one I often occupy.

Believe me, sincerely yours,
JOHN BRIGHT.

No. CCLIII.

Mr. JOSEPH COWEN.

Blaydon-on-Tyne,
July 4, 1886.

My Dear Rylands,—

Although you " have gone wrong," I must cordially congratulate you on your re-election. I was sincerely delighted at it.

You will now have an opportunity of expounding the " wrong " way in a way that your critics and censors won't like.

I hope you are well and hearty.

Believe me, my dear Rylands,
Yours truly,
Jos. Cowen.

———

No. CCLIV.

Right Hon. Sir G. O. TREVELYAN.

8, Grosvenor Crescent,
July 15, 1886.

Dear Rylands,—

In answer to your very kind letter I can only say I had rather I was out than you, so you may imagine that the joy of battle and of victory is not the

sentiment that is uppermost in my mind. The last
returns, showing a genuine rally in Scotland and so
largely increasing the Liberal Unionist contingent, are
very gratifying. You have been the worst used of
anybody, so that your return has been our greatest
success of this great campaign.

Ever yours sincerely,

G. O. TREVELYAN.

No. CCLV.

MR. G. W. LATHAM.

Bradwall Hall,
Sandbach,
July 22, 1886.

MY DEAR RYLANDS,

I have not written to you since your election;
partly because I have been out of heart and spirits,
and partly because politically I did not feel sure that
I could honestly congratulate you. But though
perhaps I might in one sense have rejoiced if the poll
had gone the other way, yet I can rejoice for your
sake that you have not after years of service been
turned adrift; and I am so sure that, when this
temporary difference has passed away, we shall all be
at one again, that I count you as good a Liberal as
ever. I rejoice that the Government has not

challenged a vote of non-confidence before resignation. A division on that would have accentuated our differences and made the breach irreparable. As it is we shall soon unite on the common ground of opposition to Conservative maladministration.

I want to tell you about myself and why I have given up all my dreams of Parliament. The old symptoms which came on last Autumn, and were the prelude to my breakdown, reappeared, and I went to one Christopher Heath, who is said to be the surgeon who knows most on these special troubles. He told me that I could not live through a contested election; that, even were the seat uncontested, I should very likely not be able to take my seat in November, and that speaking broadly, I had the seeds of mortal disease in me, and must preserve by rest and quiet every particle of vitality which I had. I should have been well content to have worked on, and if it need have been to have died in harness; but my own family and my constituency had to be considered, and I resigned all after a hard struggle. I was wise, for I am going pretty fast down the hill already, though I am certainly better than I was in the middle of last week.

How solitary I should have been. Our benches below the gangway have suffered more than any part of the House. About half of the occupiers are turned out. Cheshire too has almost reverted to Conservatism.

All kind regards.

Yours sincerely,
G. W. LATHAM.

No. CCLVI.

Mr. D. W. MACFARLANE.

> Oriental Club,
> Hanover Square, W.,
> July 23, 1886.

My Dear Rylands,—

Many thanks for your note of yesterday. I am not very deeply grieved at the result of my election, for I shall take advantage of it to spend the winter yachting in the Mediterranean, and thus escape the jaws of an English climate. If I had voted as you did I should have been returned unopposed, but I would give the same vote again and take the same consequences. " The wicked flourish like a green bay tree," but it is only for a time. I have no doubt, and I never had, that the old man was driving faster than public opinion justified, and he has come to grief for a time, but Home Rule is as sure as to-morrow's sunrise, and you will vote for it before long. I was beaten by panic, terrorism, abstentions and undue influence, but they might be hard to prove, and I am not going to worry myself with a petition.

I daresay I shall miss the smoking room at first, but I shall not think of it in time.

Kindest regards to your circle.

> And believe me, yours sincerely,
> D. W. Macfarlane.

No. CCLVII.

LORD RANDOLPH CHURCHILL, M.P.

Treasury Chambers,
Whitehall, S.W.,
Aug. 27, 1886.

My Dear Rylands,—

The Government intend to appoint a Royal Commission to examine and report upon our public departments, their management, and the expenditure involved by them. May I inform the First Lord of the Treasury that he has your authority to submit your name to Her Majesty as one of the Royal Commissioners?

The Government are anxious that the enquiry should be assisted by your long experience and knowledge of the public expenditure.

Believe me to be,
Yours sincerely,
Randolph S. Churchill.

No. CCLVIII.

Mr. A. B. FORWOOD, M.P.

House of Commons,
Sept. 9, 1886.

My Dear Sir,—

The First Lord of the Admiralty and myself are anxious to have a thorough investigation conducted by independent business men into the system of obtaining and receiving supplies, and contracting for work by the Admiralty.

We think such an enquiry may lead to suggestions of alterations that will be of benefit to the service. Knowing the great interest you have ever taken in public expenditure, and appreciating your large business experience, we feel that if we could have you on the Committee of Enquiry, we should obtain the services of a most valuable auxiliary. May I therefore ask if it would be agreeable to you to be a member of the Committee, which will be composed of myself as Chairman, Sir James Corry, M.P., The Accountant-General to the Admiralty, and possibly one more? It would sit some time in November, and I think need not be of long duration.

Very faithfully yours,
A. B. Forwood.

No. CCLIX.

Mr. W. S. CAINE, M.P.

House of Commons Library,
Sept. 10, 1886.

Dear Rylands,—

I am very sorry indeed to hear you have been so il!. I had no idea you were so bad.   I hope you will soon be your old self again.

There is nothing either to bring you up, or to pair you for.   Parnell's Bill is the only thing, and we don't intend to bring our men up for it.   Chamberlain couldn't vote for it, and Hartington probably will, so we let everybody do as he likes, as the Government are quite safe without us.

I am off to the Tyrol and Austria on Monday, and don't want to hear the word " Ireland " for six weeks.

My kindest regards to all your circle.

Yours very truly,
W. S. Caine.

CCLX.

LORD JOHN MANNERS, M.P.

Belvoir Castle,
Grantham,
Oct. 20, 1886.

DEAR MR. RYLANDS,—

I have, with pleasure, given instructions for Mr. N. P. Gray and Mr. Joshua Rawlinson to be placed in the Commission ot the Peace for the Borough of Burnley on your recommendation, and in recognition of their services in connection with the Royal Hospital.

May I add that it affords me much satisfaction to be able to comply with a request made by you ?

Believe me,
Yours very fathfully,
JOHN MANNERS.